MW00611718

RAINBRINGER

ADAM BERG

CARPE VITAM
PRESS LLC

For Kathy,
Thank you for teaching me about myself.

DAY 1

Yara's Journal

Time to starve to death.

So stupid.

I wish I could say the island was hit by some ungodly typhoon that killed every edible thing on it. Or that I was so sick I couldn't swallow. Or that I was caught in a landslide, trapped under a rock, severely injured and couldn't move. Nope.

I'm sitting in a room, by myself, staring at a plate of fruit.

And I'm gonna die of hunger.

At least I'm not hungry yet. A year of fattening up, followed by a lavish feast, saw to that. I'd guess it's only been six hours since my last meal. So, I won't be hungry tonight or maybe even in the morning. But from then on...

For now, I've inspected the hut. Everything is in place, including my secrets. The rainbringer hut is one giant room made of bamboo stalks and a frond roof. Only one section of it is blocked off by a sliding wooden door. That's the waste room.

My sleeping mat is sitting against the far wall under a hanging net for mosquitoes—which are fortunately far less problematic when it's raining. There are also two tables (one on the eastward side, the other on the westward), one plate of fruit, and a pile of clothes. Yes, I've already taken off the obnoxious rainbringer dress. All five layers of it. That's right, five. And we live on a tropical island. Tradition is no friend of comfort.

But I'm alone now, so it's naked time.

And journal time.

I'm not entirely sure who you are, other than the person who found my journal. More likely than not, you are a future rainbringer. Maybe the one who takes my place next year, maybe one from many years from now. I may never find out. I definitely won't if I actually starve to death in this stupid hut. Hopefully I succeed in my ambition, in which case, you are me – years from now. Old and fat and happy.

Right now, I'm young and fat and not so happy. Sixteen is a terribly young age to be sentenced to death. And like I said, I am wonderfully round. It's a relatively new shape for me. I was quite average until last year when I was appointed the rainbringer and given a year of queenly living. I ate everything. Not because it was good – although it was good – but because I needed be fat. The fat ones always last longer. I did the best I could at getting large, with the village's help.

Ugh, the village—nothing more than a group of 600 traditionalists who line up every year to punch the same person in the face. Not literally, of course. The reality is far worse—starving.

I'd take a punch to the face right now just to break up the nothingness of being in here alone. I'm not saying that because I don't know what it's like to get knuckles thrown at you. I'm well aware. It's happened many times. The first time by my friend, Nika, when we were both eight. She was feeling moody and my yapping mouth needed to be silenced one way or another. This was the first of many punches, probably because it did shut me up. As usual, I was being rather loud-mouthed and annoying about something. In this case, how to construct crab traps. Then pow. Right in the eye. It was black and purple and yellowish for a week. I thought it looked really cool. I pestered Nika a year later so she would give me another black eye. It took some work too. She's usually fairly tame. (But it's fun when she's not.)

Once she saw the first black eye, she turned into a frazzled ball of guilt. For weeks. Not just the type of guilt that kept her apologizing over and over again. That's annoying. It was the kind of guilt that got her to do my chores and bring me gifts. That's the opposite of annoying.

Metaphorically speaking, I've been punched in the face by everyone on this dumb island. And they've all had the same guilt Nika did, bringing me food to make themselves feel better. This was the queenly living I was talking about. As if cooked boar would somehow make up for the fact that I was going to die for them.

But what they don't know is that I wanted this black eye. I want to be here, in this hut, staring at that dumb plate of fruit, ready to face my end. Through the power of my own genius and guile, I am the rainbringer.

So here I am, Yara the rainbringer, sitting alone in my hut as rain drips from the sky—ready to save this whole island by myself.

You're welcome, idiots.

Nika

The doors to the rainbringer hut closed for the first time in nearly a year, locking Yara inside and sealing her fate. The moment the door latched shut, a raindrop landed on Nika's cheek. She stood on the beach, facing the hut, ignoring both the pit in her stomach and the villagers around her.

More rain dripped from the sky, leaving dots on the sand.

She walked to the stairs leading up to the hut and put her hand on the banister. The closed doors loomed above, sending chills down her back. Closing her eyes, she tried to picture Yara on the inside, sitting alone. *What are you up to? How are you doing?*

Despite a year of prodding Yara to talk about her feelings of being chosen as rainbringer, Nika never managed to get her to open up. The conversation never sat right. It was the only time Yara ever held her tongue—an occurrence so rare she would normally call it a miracle. But something was wrong. Yara was plotting and Nika could tell.

The shamans lined up in order of succession, the eldest at the front. Heads bowed, they started their march back to the hallowed shrine where the next rainbringer would be chosen.

As if in unison, the villagers turned their backs on Yara—now physically as well as figuratively. They trudged behind the shamans, heads hanging low, bracing for news of who would be locked inside the hut in a year's time.

Nika squeezed the railing. Her hand trembled under the wave of anger welling up in her chest. The village never liked Yara. She was loud, hard-headed, and brutish if you asked the boys that were clearly threatened by her domineering attitude. 'Juvenile' was the word Nika's parents' used when they thought she wasn't listening. But they were wrong. Looking around, Nika found herself alone, once again the only person on Yara's side. She was the one who could see Yara for what she truly was—alive.

The irony stung. The most alive person on the island was the one sentenced to death.

Nika calmed with a deep breath, pulled herself away, and chased down the village procession. She eyed the crowd for any sight of Yara's parents, but didn't see them. Had they not been so cold to Nika over the last year, she would have insisted on being together. Nika didn't blame them though. This year's rainbringer was going to be a 16-year-old girl and this island only had two—her and Yara. So if Nika had been chosen, Yara would have been spared.

But it wasn't Nika's fault, not only because she wasn't the one doing the choosing, but because she had been deathly ill during the choosing ceremony and was therefore disqualified. Yara was the only option. The memory of her sickness clenched her throat. Even through the endless vomiting and dehydration, knowing Yara's fate was the worst part of the ordeal.

The crowd of islanders reached a giant canopy—the one space in the village that could house everyone. Nika stood on a stool at the edge of the crowd, giving her enough height to see the shamans working in the middle.

The eldest retrieved a box and lifted a handful of flat stones from it. His assistant held a large, thin bowl out in front of him.

"*Ma'ha'lenti*, great rain spirit, lead us to a suitable offering. Protect this great island of Asa'hali." The eldest shaman's hands trembled as he lifted the flat stones.

"In all things, a sacrifice," said the people in unison.

The flat stones fell into the bowl. Before Nika could crane her head to take a look, the old shaman bent over the bowl to read the stones.

Nika scanned the room, only to see downturned lips and sunken faces. She clenched her teeth. The looks weren't for Yara, the young girl currently saving their lives. They were for themselves, the mark of dread over the possibility of taking Yara's place this time next year. Only one of them, whoever was next, deserved to look so sullen. Whoever that was, Nika knew she'd spend the next year at their side —aiding them, comforting them, preparing them for their end. Serving every future rainbringer was how she could honor Yara's sacrifice—and, admittedly, face her guilt.

"*Ma'ha'lenti* blesses us." The shaman lifted his head from the bowl. "The seventy-ninth rainbringer shall be a woman, seventeen years of age."

Gasps broke out from every corner of the audience. Heads turned to Nika, staring at her with furrowed brows. With Yara gone, Nika was the only seventeen-year-old woman left. Another death sentence.

A warm anger swelled inside Nika, keeping the cold chill of fear from creeping in. Yara once mentioned there was something wrong with the rainbringer tradition. This all but proved it. The stones could have landed in millions of different ways. Yet, two years in a row, they specifically targeted the same two girls—as if the purpose of their tradition was to kill her and Yara, instead of save the island.

"Come here, Nika." A shaman lifted his chin, tilting his circular hat up to reveal an aged frown. The baggy sleeve of his robes slid down his arm as he extended a hand to her.

She took it and followed the shaman to the center of the room. Kneeling on a pillow, she bowed her head as the eldest dripped rainwater from a cup over Nika's head.

"May *Ma'ha'lenti* watch over you." With the cup now empty, he handed it to Nika. "Now go. Climb to the highest peak. Commune with the great rain spirit until the cup is filled. And drink. Then you may return to us, worthy of our reverence."

Nika stood. Cup in hand, she left without giving anyone so much as a glance. Had her parents joined her at the choosing, she'd have considered a respectful bow. But they stayed behind to tend their flocks. The thought of telling them she had been chosen made her shrink. Their tender hearts broke at Yara's choosing. This news would destroy them, but it wasn't hers to give. Tradition demanded she depart for the mountain peak immediately. The shamans would inform her family.

The hike to the tallest peak took at least two days and must be made alone. That gave her four to five days before anyone expected to see her again. Or rather, four to five days to throw tradition out the window and find a way to communicate with the one person who might be of some help—Yara.

DAY 2

Yara's Journal

I'm pretty sure a group of boys came to the hut last night, which they are not supposed to do. As I was dozing off, I heard one of them whisper about trying to see me.

Perverts.

As a sixteen-year-old girl, naked, alone, and defenseless (sort of), this did not sit well. I yelled at them through the only window in the place, but didn't see anyone. I also couldn't see any tracks in the darkness.

I guess maybe they wouldn't have known I was naked though. So maybe not perverts. Morbid spectators, sure. But not perverts.

Bye-bye naked time. I won't be loafing about in that horrid rain-bringer dress though. Looks like it'll be a chest wrap and underskirt from now on. Ugh.

I slept terribly, which made getting up at dawn and slithering back into the rainbringer dress even more miserable. I won't have much interaction with the shamans while I'm in here, but I'm supposed to be dressed and kneeling when they bring in more food.

Not long after daybreak, one of the village shamans brought another plate and placed it on the eastward table – exactly opposite the fruit on the westward table. Now the room looks symmetrical, which I suppose is pleasing. Both tables have plates with one mango, one passion fruit, and one dragon fruit.

Ugh. I love passion fruit. It's sour and slimy and makes my tongue feel alive. I can taste it if I just close my eyes. I can feel the seeds crunching between my teeth. I'm fine to not eat it now – my last meal was rather extravagant. Chicken. Boar. Crab. Passion fruit, of course. Spiced rice. No vegetables—why bother? And many other things, I assume, but don't remember. But I'll admit that a bit of hunger is sneaking up on me.

I can ignore the passion fruit. For now.

I have somewhere between forty-five and sixty-five days before my body gives up on me. Since I'm young and pudgy, I should last longer than most. Two years ago, the rainbringer died on day forty-seven. He was older, fifty or so, I think. Last year, the rainbringer died on day sixty-two. It was very impressive for a person to last that long. The woman, in her thirties, reeked horribly when we took her body. Much worse than usual.

I'm a mortician's assistant, by the way. I know it's weird, but I like death. Not that I want to die, or enjoy when people die, or anything like that. I just find it fascinating. One day you're here and the next you're nothing but a stiff, empty shell. But is that shell you? Who's to say?

Whoops. Tangent. Anyway....

No rainbringer has failed in the seventy-seven years of rain-bringers. One died on day fifteen. That was before I was born, but still holds the record. The old man starved to death, so everything remained in order. Hmmm. I'm not sure how much you know.

Almost eighty years ago, spirits from the ocean depths clawed their way onshore. They are monstrous creatures—twice as tall as a man and many times broader. They have huge muscles, translucent skin, fish-like features, and eyes that look like red gems. The rain-water keeps them at bay. They resurface every year, but as long as the storm protects us, they do nothing more than saunter about. Although there are stories of the spirits stalking people for weeks, but I've never seen it. They just want to eat people. With their jagged teeth and gaping, lipless mouths, it wouldn't take much effort on their part. (Thanks, rain.)

Back when they first appeared, the chief shaman begged the rain spirits to protect my ancestors. Most of the spirits ignored him. One did not. The compassionate rain spirit, *Ma'ha'lenti*, conjured a storm and washed the spirits back into the waters. But the spirit of a storm lives only as long as the rain is falling. So it gave its power to the shaman, the first rainbringer, and instructed him on how to conjure the storm.

The tradition was born. The island is protected so long as the appointed suffers both starvation and temptation.

Naturally, the first rainbringer died. But the power is transferred before the body is interred. And the chain continues to today, to me.

I've been the rainbringer for a year. The island (metaphorically) punched me in the eye and now my time has come to actually starve. And it would be so much easier if I didn't have two passion fruits calling my name. But that's the temptation part.

Sure, I could eat them. I could eat any of the food they will continually bring in every day. And it will get more tempting. The hungrier I get, the more food there is. But if I do eat, the storm stops. The rainbringer power will vanish with the storm. The seabed spirits will tear into everyone on this island, including myself. They'd do to me what I want to do to that passion fruit. There's really not much choice in the matter.

For now, it rains.

I was actually relieved when the rain started. Yes! Rain! My designation as the rainbringer was not a fluke. The power successfully transferred to me and was working. And it was that moment, when the chief shaman closed the door to the rainbringer hut, that my fate was sealed. I would die of starvation, surrounded by food.

I'm getting a headache.

And I suppose I owe you an apology, whoever you are. This diary is not supposed to exist. Nor is it supposed to be finished. I am the seventy-eighth rainbringer. If my story ends the same way as the others', then there will be no ending. You could turn the pages of this book until the writing stops and see what words will be my last. But it won't tell you my ending. There is no way to record my own death, and my tale will be forever left unfinished.

But that's dumb. I'm going to walk out of this hut one day and punch Nika in the face, just because I can. She owes me anyway.

Enough rambling. Time to write down the pertinent things of the day.

There's something I know that no one else does. Two years ago, while embalming the rainbringer's body, I found something. A note. Well, a word—stomach. The fifty-year old man cut the word 'stomach' into his belly. At first, I was shocked. How? Why?

The man's nails had grown long, but he had somehow sharpened the nail of his right pointer finger. I assume that's what he used to cut the word 'stomach' onto his skin. Why? Well, when you're starving and alone, you probably go a little insane. But that's not it.

I'll confess. I cut him open. I wasn't supposed to, seeing as how he had fulfilled his sacred duty and was to be respected or whatever. I don't care about that. I cut open his stomach and found something. Food. Some partially digested meat and bones.

The word 'stomach' was a message. He must have wanted me to find the food. He wanted me to know he ate something, which should have resulted in everyone dying, but no one did (other than him). There's something else going on here. And I do mean here specifically, in this room.

And I'm going to find out what it is. Because I believe that there is something inside these walls and that something is killing the rainbringers. It's waiting until they're weak and starving and then it takes their life. But I'm going to put an end to that. I'm going to kill it first, just as soon as I figure out what it is.

I know this hut better than anyone. I've been cleaning it for years.

Just as soon as something is out of place, I'll know. I'll figure out what shouldn't be here.

So far, I've found nothing.

I've scoured every inch of the wooden floorboards, the tables, the bamboo walls, the sliding door to the waste room and the room itself – twice. Nothing looked like it had been tampered with, at least any more than the tampering I secretly did over the past year.

Yes. I tampered with the hut. It's sacred, I know. But I'll either be a hero for doing so or dead. Either way, I don't care if anyone is offended.

The tampering wasn't easy either. I had to work at night, which meant being quiet and losing sleep, which I could only dismiss as a bad night. No one knows. Not my parents. Not Nika. And especially not the shamans. But I managed to create several hiding spots for small objects – some of which are this diary, ink, and plume. So if you've found this, you already know of one of the hidden compartments. Good luck finding the rest. (There are five.)

My hand is cramping.

I guess I'll blow out my candle, toss myself onto the lush bed, and call it a night. Besides, I'm hungry now. I wish I had someone to punch.

Nika

"Ow." Nika pulled herself through her bedroom window, hitting her head on the wall. Rubbing her forehead, she sat up.

Hours had passed since the sun set. She'd spent the day waiting for her parents to leave their house, but they never did. With any luck, they were sound asleep in their bedroom—but Nika doubted either of them would get a wink after the news of Nika's calling as the future rainbringer.

Their house was nothing extravagant, unless one were to compare it to the rainbringer hut. Two bedrooms fed into a hallway before opening up into an entrance where they ate meals and entertained guests. The space was still small enough to carry almost every sound, a feature Nika often found bothersome—especially now as she tried to sneak into her own home.

She crawled to a box in the corner of the room. Lifting the hatch, she squinted as if she'd suddenly be able to see in complete darkness. As carefully as she could, she dipped her hand into the box. A sharpness pricked her. "Agh." Poking her finger into her mouth, a warm metallic taste covered her tongue—blood, but not much.

Nika tilted the box to get a better look inside, but its contents spilled onto the floor. A jar of dried fruit rolled into her leg. Two plumes and a bottle of ink dropped out with a thud. A soft clang sounded as her machete hit the floor. The noises froze her. Biting her lip, she paused to see if anyone in the house stirred.

Nothing. Silence.

She reached for the machete and swung it in the air, remembering how comfortable it felt in her grip.

A door creaked down the hall. Footsteps drew near.

Nika dropped the machete out the window and pressed herself against the wall.

The door swung open, covering Nika behind it. Her heart thumped through her ears. If her parents found her, they'd know she wasn't climbing up to the highest mountain like she should be. They'd know she wasn't following tradition like she always had. They could see through any lie she'd tell and figure out she had no intention of becoming a rainbringer. Her hopes of getting to Yara would die.

"Hm." The deep voice of her dad mumbled in the darkness. He shuffled about.

A faint light crept through the open window.

She clenched her jaw and tightened her sweating fists.

A hollow thump sounded—the jar of dried fruit.

Nika peeked out from behind the door.

"Oh, Nika." The light from the window revealed her father picking up the objects on the floor and depositing them in the box. He brushed the back side of his hand across his cheek.

An emptiness sank into her gut. Her face fell. Her fears vanished. A wave of sadness washed over her, bringing guilt and pity in its wake. The sight of her father mourning his daughter drowned out everything else.

She leaned back against the wall, hiding behind the door.

More footsteps shuffled. Her father sniffed. The door closed.

Nika put her hand on the door, wishing she could hold onto her father on the other side. She turned to the window. These feelings didn't need to last. She'd take the machete, cut down bamboo, fashion a ladder, and work with Yara to make sure neither of them died. This nebulous hope might be nothing more than a dream, but at least it was better than reality.

Yara

Yara rolled on to her side, silently cursing her insomnia. She took in a deep breath through her nose, held it in her lungs, then pushed it out her mouth. Rolling onto her back, she took in another breath.

The sound of exhaling met her ears, but she was still holding back the air in her chest.

Yara froze. Her shoulders tightened. She exhaled.

Silence.

She took in another breath.

A labored wheeze travelled across the room.

Yara turned her head. Her eyes wandered, seeing nothing but the same boring room she'd stared at all day. She breathed in.

Another wheeze.

Throwing herself out of bed, she lit a candle with a tinderbox.

Her hand trembled as she held up the light, much to her own annoyance. "Hello?" Yara swallowed hard as if forcing down a rock. She took in a breath.

A withered snore echoed back—like the strained gasps of a dying beast.

"Who's there?" Yara spun around, casting faint candlelight through the room. She held her breath.

Silence.

She exhaled with as much force as she could push out her lungs, but no harsh voice mimicked her. Whatever made that noise was either gone or silent.

Yara sat against the wall, the candle at her side. This was her first clue—a voice. Whatever it was—or whoever it was—would reveal the true nature of the rainbringer hut. She wrapped her arms around herself, repeating in her mind that this discovery was a good thing. But a chill ran over her skin.

Her eyelids fluttered as she fought back sleep. Her only solace was knowing none of the previous rainbringers died on day two.

DAY 3

Yara's Journal

I t's hit me. The hunger. I hate it and everyone and everything, and I would eat my own hair if I could. At least I'm not thirsty. I can drink rainwater because it's sacred or whatever. All these dumb rules are driving me crazy.

I should stop complaining, otherwise I will use up every blank space in my journal to tell you how hungry I am. You get it. It's day three without food. At least the meat hasn't started coming. Just more fruit. More passion fruit. I'm gonna chew on my hair to see if that helps.

Nope. It's gross.

At least I don't want to eat my hair anymore.

I wanted to ask the shamans who the new rainbringer will be next year, but we're not supposed to talk. The odds of it actually being someone I care about is pretty small. Especially right now when I don't care about anyone unless they're a passion fruit. And I already saved Nika once – last year. I convinced (threatened) a younger shaman to throw the choosing stones a day early just for me. That's when I knew it would be either me or Nika. So I poisoned her. Granted, I may have gone a little too heavy on the poison because she was insanely sick. Like violently sick. But she was fine and it guaranteed that I got here. This is where I wanted to be. And as it turns out, the younger shaman sissy-man was right. His stones came up with the same result as the old man's. So the poisoning was worth it.

But I wonder what those shamans would do if I did talk to them. Panic? Cry? Explode? That would be satisfying. Maybe then they'd stop bringing me more food every day. I'm sure their blinding sense of tradition would take over though and the food would keep coming. That's how they're 'helping' in this nonsense.

Maybe I should throw the fruit out the window. Nah. I'm honestly a bit afraid to touch it because then I'd know it was real. Then what little control I have over myself would be gone and I'd lose my chance to finish my experiment. That and doom my people.

I can do this. I just need to keep telling myself that every time I'm hungry. So about eight hundred times a day. But hey, nothing else to —I hear something.

Not words. A little bit of wheezing again. It's breathing. I think. It's faint. But it's definitely inside. I think it's by the food.

Nope. It's gone. I can't hear it any—it's back. By my bed.

Nope. I checked there too. Nothing. Which makes me think it's moving. So that's what I know. It's alive. It's breathing. It's moving. I was right. There's something in here with me. I just can't see it. I wonder if I could eat it.

Nika

The last trace of sunlight vanished beyond the ocean horizon. Thunderclouds kept the world dim, hiding the stars and masking the moon. Raindrops tapped against the rainbringer hut.

Nika jogged along the beach and ducked under the hut, weaving between the bamboo stalks that held up Yara's prison. She knelt down and plunged her hands into the sand. They grasped at nothing, moving around until bumping into another bamboo stalk. "Ah." She took hold of the bamboo and pulled it up, lifting the makeshift ladder she'd constructed the night prior. Hunched over, she dragged it out into the rain and propped it up against the hut's only window.

Strands of wet hair clung to her face.

"*What* are you doing?!" Yara peeked out the window.

A jolt of fear shot through Nika, rattling her. "Agh. You scared me."

"*I* scared *you?*"

Nika reached the top rung. "We need to talk."

"Kind of a bad time, don't you think, Nika?"

"Just let me in." Nika gripped the window sill.

Yara pushed against Nika's shoulders. "You can't come in. You shouldn't even be here. I don't want any extra attention on me right now."

"Which is why you should let me in." Nika slipped an arm into the window and pushed against Yara to get inside. "You don't want a ladder and the bottom half of next year's rainbringer to be flailing around outside your window."

Yara stepped back.

Nika flung herself inside, landing on her hands and rolling on the floor.

"You're next year's rainbringer?" Yara stood still, her eyes wide.

Rising to her feet, Nika turned to the window and tipped over the ladder. "There. Now we can talk without a ladder drawing anyone's attention, hopefully."

"How are you gonna get down?"

"I'll jump." Nika tilted her head and squeezed water out of her hair.

"It's a long way down. And there are rocks."

"Not *that* many rocks."

"It only takes one to break your foot." Yara shrugged. "And it's dark, so you can't see them."

"When did *you* become the cautious one?" Nika threw her hands up.

Yara scowled.

"Just listen to me for a second. I am the next rainbringer. Do you know what that means?" Nika tied her hair into a bun.

Yara nodded. "You're doomed." Her face softened. "The choosing stones. Hm. It seems the universe wants you dead."

"It's too much of a coincidence that the both of us would be randomly chosen as rainbringers." Nika peeled off a layer of wet clothes and walked over to the rainbringer dress on the floor.

Yara plopped onto her bed. "But it is possible. It could just be a coincidence that the stones chose our age and genders two years in a row."

"We're the only two people in that category though. It's arguably the least likely pairing of age and sex with the fewest number of people to fill that role. And it could have been me twice, had you not been here." Nika wrapped part of the dress around her and sat on the floor. "It makes much more sense that these aren't random selections. Someone—or *someones*—want me dead." Nika swirled her finger on the floor, her head aching as she thought through the number of explanations floating in her mind.

"Or they want both of us dead." Yara crossed her legs. "It could have just as easily been you in here this year and me next year."

Nika nodded. "It's either the shamans or *Ma'ha'lenti*."

"Huh?" Yara tilted her head. "*Ma'ha'lenti*? The one spirit protecting us?"

"I'm not saying it's likely. In fact, I'm confident our death sentences are from the shamans. But if there's a miniscule possibility that this is all a coincidence, then there is also a miniscule possibility of *Ma'ha'lenti* being the one behind the decision." Nika pulled her knees to her chest and held them close. "You're going to starve to death all because I got sick at the worst possible time last year."

"Well, no." Yara crawled off the bed and sat in front of Nika. "First of all, I am not going to starve to death. I have a plan. But also, I poisoned you last year so you couldn't be chosen." Yara scrunched her face into a fake smile.

Nika's jaw dropped. Her mind blanked. She threw her fist into Yara's arm.

"Ow!"

"I can't believe you! How could you do that to me?"

"You mean, save you?" Yara pressed her palm against her aching arm. "You were only sick for a few days."

"Yes. And it was horrible." Nika tightened her fists and pulled them back, ready to swing on a whim. "But I don't care about that. I thought it was my fault you were going to die and miss out on a long life. I've spent a year terrified of the thought that I'd spend the next seventy years knowing I killed my best friend."

Yara shrugged. "Well, good news then. You'll be dead in a year."

Nika swung at Yara's face, but stopped her fist an inch from Yara's brow. "Not funny." She poked Yara between the eyes.

"Sorry." Yara rubbed her brow. "I needed to be here. There's something seriously wrong with the rainbringer tradition."

Nika groaned. "Yes. You mentioned that. And it's only become more and more apparent."

Yara bit her lip. "But why kill us? It's not like we've ever done anything."

Nika shook her head.

A brief silence sat between them before the faint sound of breathing interrupted.

Nika turned her head toward Yara's bed. "What is that?"

"The breathing? So you can hear it too. I wondered if I was just going crazy. That's relieving, even with the creepy voice that travels the room." Yara scratched her head. "Whatever it is, it started breathing last night. I think it's alive."

"Uhhh..." Nika leaned forward. "Well, you're not totally crazy. You *are* weirdly calm about it."

"It was here last night, but nothing happened. I'm not sure it's actually something to be scared of." Yara reached into the waistband of her sarong and pulled out a thin wooden case.

"What is that?"

She grasped both sides and pulled the case apart, unsheathing a short dagger. The light of the candles flickered on its surface. "Something I might need in case that voice is... well, something to be scared of."

A mix of relief and worry fought inside Nika. "*You* are something to be scared of."

"Thanks." Yara returned the dagger and hid it away in her clothes.

"Well, I should be going." Nika stood. "I've got to go pretend I climbed a mountain."

"The hike!" Yara scrambled to her feet. "It's only been three days. They'll know you didn't go to the shrine."

"What shrine?"

"The shrine. The rainbringer shrine. You have to go there after being chosen." Yara covered her mouth.

"I thought they just give you that cup and you go up there alone to commune with *Ma'ha'lenti*. By yourself. No one's going to know."

"No, Nika! That's what they tell you, but there's a shaman stationed at the shrine. It takes two and a half days to climb up there. He knows you're late. He'll know something's wrong."

Words flew around in Nika's head, but failed to form a coherent thought. She stared at the floor.

"You have to go there. Now!" Yara took Nika's arm and pulled her to the window. The rainbringer dress slunk off her.

"But I'll be three days late."

"Figure something out." Yara picked up Nika's wet clothes and threw them out the window. "Nika, look at me."

Nika's eyes met Yara's.

"Run. Go now. Get to the shrine as fast as possible. The shamans can't know we aren't following tradition. They'll step in and watch our every move. We won't be able to find the truth about the rain-bringers. We'll both die."

Nika lifted a leg and sat on the windowsill. "I'll fix this. I'll figure something out." She whipped her other leg outside and dropped.

Yara poked her head out the window. "And hide the ladder!"

DAY 4

Yara's Journal

I ... hate... everything.
I got no sleep last night. I've been sick to my stomach not just because it is completely empty and consuming itself and shooting stomach acid up my throat, but ALSO, and this is fun, Nika is the next rainbringer. And she is completely ruining my plan. If by some miracle she gets to the shrine three days late and somehow wards off all suspicion that she's not following protocol (and that I am not following protocol—nor have any intention to, since following the rules means I DIE! And then Nika dies. And then who cares about the islanders?), then maybe, just MAYBE, the shamans won't close in on us and we can keep going.

There is also a new window in the hut. It's in the waste room and is roughly the size of my foot. It's created a nice draft. I'm gonna go ahead and blame its existence on Nika and the fact that I spent all day boxed up in that little room.

I'm too hungry to be near the food. And drinking more water just makes me feel sick. So I've been lightly sipping, at best. I did lick the backs of my sweaty hands a couple times today. Mostly to get rid of the bile taste in my mouth. I'm so glad sweat is salty. And also that it apparently doesn't count as food as far as these dumb rules go. It didn't occur to me until after I licked my hands that sweat might count as food and therefore doom us all if I ingested it. So, glad that worked out. I assume it's because the rainbringer trial is both temptation *and* starvation and sweat really isn't tempting in terms of filling the void in my gut.

Or is it?

Ugh.

The only other thing that happened today was my becoming an artist. I hid myself a nice sharp dagger (although it is probably less sharp now). I've been carrying it because, you know, ghost monster breathing or whatever. And since I have NOTHING to do but think about killing everyone I've ever met for a piece of fruit, I decided to scratch some drawings into the walls of the waste room.

They're lovely. One is of me strangling Nika with my bare hands. One is of all the shamans in a circle with their heads exploding like volcanoes. One started as a passion fruit, because I had a short lapse of sanity. I turned it into a monkey bending over and slapping its butt. That one is my favorite.

I'm gonna go fling myself onto my bed.

Nika

The trail to the rainbringer shrine had already muddied by the time Nika started her trek. The rain seeped into her shoes, caking them with a leafy sludge. All traces of sweat washed away by the growing storm. She ran for as long as she could, but the uphill climb took her breath, forcing a steadier pace.

Nika turned a corner in the trail. She broke through the trees into an open grove, exposing her to a cool wind. She pressed on, straying from the path to walk on the wild grass where her feet wouldn't stick to the ground.

Despite racking her brain for an excuse as to how late she'd be, she still had no solution. And Yara had been no help at all. She had only gotten angry for something Nika didn't even know about. No one had ever mentioned a rainbringer shrine. She had witnessed the choosing ceremony every year of her life and not once did a shaman speak a word of it. They were only instructed to go to the highest peak. But why?

Something was there. And someone – a shaman. But she knew all the shamans and each of them were present at the choosing—or so she thought. It's not like she did a head count. But now there was another one? Did he live at the shrine? Was he being isolated? Punished? Or perhaps honored in some secret fashion? Trusted to keep such a holy place? Or was he there to guard something? That felt right. There was something at the shrine meant to be hidden. If Nika was going to spend at least five whole days on this trip – when every day neared Yara's last – then she knew she had to make it worth it. She had to uncover whatever secret was up there.

A long tree branch in the grass caught her eye. She walked over to it and picked it up. It stood about as tall as Nika and was thick enough to support some of her weight. "Finally, a decent walking stick." She returned to the path, pushing the stick against the ground with every other step. "I shall call you... Meepers." Nika laughed at the meaninglessness of the random sound that came out of her mouth.

She wondered if Yara would find it equally entertaining. Or if she would just get annoyed about something dumb like Nika jumping out of the window and breaking her foot on some hypothetical rock. Nika looked down at her feet then up at Meepers. This was the solution to her tardiness problem.

She steadied herself with a couple short breaths. Clenching her teeth, she turned her right foot inward and stepped onto it. The ankle rolled, just as planned, sending her falling. Her hands tried to brace herself with the walking stick, but lost their grip before catching the grass. "Agh!" She groaned and rolled onto her back.

It didn't take long for her foot to start throbbing. She hoped the damage she'd done wouldn't be too severe. But if it didn't swell or bruise at all, this excuse wouldn't be convincing. She was still at least a day away from the shrine. That would give her ankle plenty of time to fall apart.

Nika stood. She tested her ankle with a slow step. It hurt, but not too bad to walk– for now. With Meepers in hand, she started back on her trek. "Ow." Step. "Ow." Step. "Owwww." The pain grew. "Well, this is going to be awful." She sighed. "Let's go, Meepers."

DAY 5

Yara's Journal

B liss. Absolute bliss. I can't believe it. It's gone – the hunger. I AM NOT HUNGRY! I don't know how it happened. Or what happened. Or who worked some mystical whatnot on my body to make it go away and send me into a state of peaceful euphoria. I want to kiss that person on the mouth until we both run out of air and have to gasp for breath. And then more kissing. Bless you, whoever you are!

I feel amazing. Powerful. I can think! My head is finally clear and I understand how all those rainbringers before me lasted longer than three minutes in this awful hut. The air is fresh. The future bright. The sun... isn't shining because it's day five and the rain has been picking up, but the rain smells good. And not like a dreary reminder of my accursed state.

Again, who can I kiss right now? I'll take anyone. Give me some hermit, covered in mud, with no teeth, one eye, and a scraggly beard you could use to scrape scales off a fish. Someone needs to be thanked for this and it may as well be that hermit.

I suppose I should be thanking *Ma'ha'lenti*, the great rain spirit. But I don't know how I feel about him right now. Give me the hermit instead.

All I know of this mysterious thing inside the hut is that it moves and breathes. I have almost no information and even fewer tools, but I think I can track it. I've decided to place candles at various points in the room. I can't cover every part, but with any luck, the thing's breath will flicker the candle and help me know where it is. It's a long shot, I know. And I only have five candles. But they're supplied by the shamans, so if they go out, they'll just give me more. I hope.

So I've placed one on each table, one by the bed, one at the door to the waste room, and the last next to me and this diary. So here I sit, waiting. Listening. Smiling. Dagger in hand.

Whatever's in here, I'm ready for you.

Nika

"You're late." A shadowy figure appeared uphill. A wide-brimmed hat circled his head, keeping the rain from soaking his robes. "How are you still so far away from the shrine?"

Nika scrunched her nose. Leaning on her walking stick, she cleared her throat. "I rolled my ankle three days ago." Her stomach sank from the lie.

The man lifted his robes at the knees and carefully stepped down the rocky pass. "You rolled your ankle on the second day of the storm? The land you were crossing shouldn't have been very steep— nor slick."

"Well..." Nika leaned on her stick and hobbled up the trail. "It wasn't. But no matter how friendly the terrain, my clumsiness always wins out."

The two came face to face. The man tilted his hat upward, revealing a soft expression. His unblemished skin put him at about twenty years of age, but his hair had already grayed. Had she not been so nervous, she might have appreciated his blue eyes and curly hair. A scar divided his left eyebrow, which to her own annoyance, charmed her. "Are you in pain?"

Nika nodded.

"Let me take a look." He gestured to some steps on the trail and led her to them.

"Thank you." She took his hand and sat.

The man bent down and lifted her swollen ankle to his face. Tilting it from side to side, he scowled. He pinched down on her foot with little pressure, but enough for Nika to wince. "You really shouldn't be walking on this."

"Hence my tardiness."

"Get on my back." The man placed Nika's foot on the ground.

"You want to carry me?"

He nodded.

"I'm drenched." Nika waved a hand in front of herself. "And you're somehow dry."

"We're about a half day out from the shrine and at your pace you'll put me days behind my work." He spun around and patted his shoulder. "So come on."

Nika leaned her walking stick against a tree and threw her arms around the man's neck. After a bit of shuffling, they started up the trail.

"Strange." The man sniffed.

"What is?" Nika ducked under his hat and rested on his warm shoulder.

"You are."

"Me?" Nika shot up, knocking the hat to the ground. "Ah. Sorry."

Bending over, the man's knees wobbled. He swiped the ground, retrieving the hat and threw it on Nika's head. "Yes. You."

Adjusting the hat on her head, she leaned over to cover them both. "How am I the strange one here? You're a shaman I've never seen and I've lived on this island my whole life."

"Only the shamans and the future rainbringers see me." He readjusted his grip on her legs that were wrapped around his waist. "You are strange, though."

Nika rolled her eyes. "Again, how?"

"You're lying."

Time stopped. Nika clenched her teeth. Breath escaped her. The world held perfectly still while chaos erupted in her mind. What did he know? Had she been caught? What would he do if he knew Nika hadn't been following the elder shaman's instructions?

"Lying?" Something nudged the word out of her mouth. "What would I be lying about?"

The man hummed for a second. "Your ankle."

Not a single thought came to mind.

Nodding his head, the man hummed again. "Yes. The ankle. But now I wonder which part of your story was the lie."

"Uh..." Nika bit her lip.

"Oh, I don't expect you to answer. Lies beget lies and I am entirely uninterested in them. But truth will stand the test of time. The truth will reveal itself. But for now, I will record the lie. Because the lie has become part of this truth's story."

Nika held her tongue. *And I'm the strange one.*

"My name is Heren, the record keeper. It is a pleasure to meet you." He bowed his head.

"Nika." She swallowed hard. Heren was going to be a problem. But for now, she rested on him, happy to be off her ankle.

Yara

Yara's five candles sat undisturbed at their various locations in the room. The patter of rain sounded melodic in her head, lulling her mind to sleep. The sun set hours ago, but how many, she couldn't guess. She rubbed her eyes, trying to keep them from feeling heavy.

A breath sounded from across the room, jolting her awake.

Her shoulders tensed. She squeezed the dagger in her hand.

The *thing* continued pulling in air, pausing, and releasing it. Her eyes darted from candle to candle, but none of them flickered. Clasping the dagger, she rose to her feet.

The breathing ceased.

Silence.

Yara's eyes watered—a feeling she'd only ever had as a child when the seabed spirits lurked about. She cleared her throat.

The breathing reappeared in another dark corner of the room, but only for a single breath. Again, it moved to one of the few dark spaces of the hut, seemingly avoiding the light.

Yara bit her tongue. She curled her toes, fighting a numbness in her feet. "I can hear you." She peered into the darkness. A dryness stung her eyes, reminding her to blink.

"I can see you," whispered a ragged voice.

A pit in her stomach opened up.

The candle at her feet puffed out. Yara swiped the dagger through the air, hitting nothing. She ran to the nearest table for light. "What do you want?"

Silence.

The faintest of taps came from where she was just standing. A light scratching permeated the room, somehow more audible than the rain on the roof.

"What do you want?" She picked up the candle and held it in

front of her. Her hand shook despite her strangling grip. With each step forward, the light inched towards the blown-out candle.

The scratching continued.

The candlelight caught a flicker of movement. Yara stood back, squinting. Her journal sat open on the floor. The plume danced across its surface then fell lifeless.

Yara stepped back, her knees like jelly. "What do you want?"

A puff of air blew behind her, extinguishing a candle. Another puff blew, killing a light. Yara spun, trying to watch her surroundings but only seeing more and more darkness. Another candle flickered away, leaving only the one in her hand to keep her safe. She marched toward the journal and held the light over it. Her eyes widened, reading a crudely scribbled message.

sLeeP WeLL yArA

DAY 6

Yara

The light of the morning sun turned the darkness to a soothing gray. Yara clenched her dagger. Her candle neared the end of its wick, but lasted through the night. Whoever spoke to her had not even tried to enter the waste room where she'd kept fort. Her head felt heavy, somehow even heavier than her eyes.

The clinks of an unlatching door reached her ears. The shamans had arrived to deliver more food. A surge of panic shot through her chest. The journal was still sprawled open on the floor. They would take it.

She dropped the dagger and threw open the waste room door. Her footsteps beat against the bamboo planks as she marched full speed into the room.

Two shamans carried plates of food – freshly cooked meat by the smell of it. The sight of Yara drew their attention but they averted their gaze in unison.

"Yara, dear, some decency."

Only a bandeau bra covered her chest and a sarong wrapped around her waist—which, as far as Yara was concerned, should have been the traditional rainbringer garb. "Sorry."

"You can't talk in here." A shaman stomped his foot, but kept his eyes off her.

Yara scooped up the diary and plume and stuffed them in her bedding. She slipped on each layer of the rainbringer dress and kneeled between the tables.

Neither shaman dared look at her. Each fidgeted more and more as their patience waned.

Yara cleared her throat.

One shaman turned his head and gave her an annoyed look. "Be ready tomorrow. On time."

They placed the meat next to the fruit already on the table. After five days of sitting out, the fruit still looked fresh – a detail of this experience Yara had yet to make sense of. Every year the tribe celebrated the end of the rainbringer storm by feasting on the food in the hut – food that should have spoiled over the weeks of the storm. Something always kept it from rotting. Something unnatural.

One of the shamans walked outside and turned around to wait for his companion. The other approached Yara, looking her over. "You look terrible."

"I didn't sleep."

The shaman threw his hand over Yara's mouth, pinching her cheeks between his thumb and fingers.

Yara froze. She had been warned once already that tradition forbade her from speaking to them.

"No talking." The shaman released his grip and wiped his hand on his robes. "We'll bring you a washing basin tomorrow. Clean yourself up." He waved a hand in the air over Yara's head. "May *Ma'ha'lenti* watch over you." He stomped out of the hut and closed the door.

Clinking sounded as the door latched outside. The beating of footsteps faded as they descended the stairs.

Yara threw off the dress and ran to the bed. She pulled out the diary and flipped its pages to the latest entry. Nothing new. A strange sense of relief came over her. She took a deep breath. After a night of frantic worrying, she had convinced herself that there would be more writings from an unseen hand. But no.

With the shamans gone and the sun out, she could finally rest. The ghostly being had never revealed itself during the day. She couldn't stay awake forever. Now seemed like the safest time to close her eyes.

Yara returned to the waste room to fetch her only weapon. The stub of a candle smoked, filling her nose with its fumes. She looked to the floor. No dagger. Her eyes darted to the corners of the room, scanning every inch.

Nothing.

Her heart thumped. The floor was clear.

She turned her attention to the main room, thinking – hoping – that she had kicked the blade out of the waste room in her haste to hide the diary. Every corner looked empty.

Had she knocked the blade toward the shamans and one of them picked it up without saying anything? She hit her head with the butt of her palm. That made no sense.

She rushed to every part of the room, looking it over and over for any sign of the dagger, but it was nowhere to be seen.

A chill ran up her spine. She turned to look into the waste room. The smoke from the candle had vanished and with it, the flame—but she had never snuffed it out. The dagger was taken.

Nika

The end of the trail arrived. Heren, the record keeper, walked up the last steps of the mountain pass and entered a small clearing. Jungle surrounded the area on every side, save where the mountain peak towered above. A stone hut protruded out of the trees, an unusual sight for a people living in bamboo homes.

"At long last." Heren trudged over to the hut and lowered Nika to the ground.

"You're stronger than you look." Nika leaned against the stone wall, keeping off her swollen foot. "I don't think any of the boys I know could have carried me up a mountain."

Heren wobbled his head from side to side. "I'm sure they could if duty called upon them to do so." He opened the door and waved Nika inside.

Bracing herself along the wall, Nika hobbled into the hut. She planted herself in the only chair and took in the room. A wall of books covered the far side, spilling pages onto a simple table. Most of the floor sat buried under piles of dried wood.

Heren took to starting a fire in the hearth. "This should warm us. And dry us." The fire ignited. "It gets much colder up here than it does down below, especially as the wind gets blowing."

"Thank you." Nika smiled and nodded. They hadn't made much conversation since their initial meeting—partly due to Heren's labored breathing and partly due to Nika not wanting to incriminate herself. She still hadn't figured out how to ward off Heren's suspicions – right as they may be – that she lied to him about her ankle. A sudden thought popped in her head. "No bed?" She looked around. "Where do you sleep?"

Heren pointed to a latch in the floor. "Downstairs."

"Downstairs? Why do you sleep in the ground?" She wanted to laugh at the idea, but held back for the sake of politeness.

"Because that is where my bed is." Heren bent down and took hold of Nika's calf.

She flinched, surprised by his bold touch.

He lifted it and rested her heel on the table. "Keep it elevated. That will help."

Nika nodded.

"How about some tea?" He nodded back, seemingly satisfied with himself.

"Please." The thought of a hot drink already warmed her.

"Then tomorrow you start your prayers to *Ma'ha'lenti*." Heren wandered over to a shelf next to the hearth. "Where is the cup the elder gave you?"

Nika's eyes widened. "I... don't know." Her thoughts swirled. Losing the cup could only make her look more suspicious, but she truly did not remember the last time she had it.

Heren shrugged. "No matter. It's just a cup."

"It is?"

He bit his lip and jutted out his chin. "Strange how you didn't know and you lost it all the same." He produced two cups and placed them on the table. "I look forward to spending a couple days with you, Nika. It seems that nothing about you is orthodox and I hope to find out why."

"Well," Nika licked her lips. "Don't expect too much. I'm sure I'll bore you."

"Nonsense. Nothing about your journey here reeks of boredom." Heren peered into her eyes – pausing as if searching for her secrets. He blinked. "Tea?"

———

Yara's Journal

Hello Yara.

How disappointed I was to see that you did not make an entry tonight. I seem to have scared you off. Apologies. I suspect it is because I took your dagger.

I know you are cooped up in the small room again, behind a closed door, just like last night. But you must surely see this from my perspective. It is unfriendly to threaten me with a weapon when I have done you no harm.

I am not your enemy. I did not take your dagger to show
you what it's like to fear it. As you can see – or could
see, if you were with me – I am not wielding it. I simply
took it to keep myself from harm—to protect me. I'm
sure that was your intention with it—protection.
You understand. Truth be told, I am not certain it could
hurt me anyway.
But now I am writing to make a request. Eat the passion
fruit. Eat the charred boar. Fill your gut to your
stomach's delight. It will satisfy you beyond your
comprehension.
This is a meal sent from the great spirits. Unspoiled.
Unrotting. Unblemished. True perfection unknown to
man. That is, unknown to any man not chosen as the
rainbringer. What the shamans don't tell you – what
they don't know – is that your taste has been exalted.
What little delicacies you enjoyed in life pale to the
savor of this divine offering. Eat it and know what none
living know.
Glorify yourself, Yara. Eat.

DAY 7

Yara

"Wake up Yara," whispered a hissing voice.

Yara's eyes shot open. Nothing. Only darkness. She gasped for breath. Pulling her blanket tightly around her, she sat up.

An orange light snapped into existence, lighting a candle on the floor.

Yara clenched her jaw. "What do you want?"

A brass candelabrum scraped across the floor as it moved toward the bed—seemingly on its own. The light flickered, sputtering from the movement.

Yara tucked her feet under the blanket as if it would do something to protect both them and her. "I don't understand." Whatever game this creature was playing was still unclear. Her only solace was the fact that it hadn't attacked her – at least not yet.

"Read." The voice exhaled a pained breath.

"Read?" Yara frowned. She adjusted on the bed. Something bumped her leg. The journal. She pulled it and her plume out from underneath her. The bottle of ink fell to the floor with a clunk. "Can't we just talk?"

"No... read."

Flipping through the first pages, she landed at an entry she'd never seen. The handwriting struck her as something crude and jagged, like a child's. Her body clenched. This journal was no longer her own.

Her nerves sent tears to her eyes, watering them as if her inner fear was also a rainstorm. She scanned the latest message under her last entry, somehow written after she closed the book just hours ago.

The unseen creature claimed to be a friend, or at least not an enemy. Its assertion about her heightened sense of taste sat oddly in her mind. Something about it didn't ring true – whether because it wasn't true and something inside her knew it, or it was true and she didn't want to believe it. "Who are you?"

The bottle of ink tipped upright. "Write."

Yara uncorked the bottle and dipped her plume.

Who are you?

She placed the journal on the floor, laying the plume atop its pages. The journal slid away. The plume animated, scratching a message. With a few flicks, the plume fell lifeless and the journal scooted back to Yara.

I don't know. Who do you think I am?

Yara hadn't anticipated a conversation, especially one with the myste-rious entity she suspected might be the cause of the rainbringers' mysterious deaths. A smile crept onto her face. Not only did the conversation break up her isolation, but it was an invitation to be cunning. It was an opportunity to outsmart a creature she didn't understand. But at least it didn't understand her either.

Yara's Journal

I do not know who you are, but I could venture a guess. Temptation incarnate. My trial as the rainbringer is divided into hunger and temptation. As my hunger grows, so too must my temptation. I thought bringing in more and more food would suffice, but I suppose that isn't the case. The spirits have something else in mind—you.

> *An interesting theory. I can't say how true it is – I don't*
> *know myself. But it would explain my development.*
> *I remember nothing before this hut. Life started out in*
> *darkness. A faint noise interrupted the nothingness,*
> *followed by blurred images of what turned out to*
> *be you.*
> *As time goes by, I crave for one thing. I too am starving. But*
> *I do not wish to feed myself. No. I hunger through you.*
> *I need you to eat. Partake of the rainbringer feast. Feed*
> *us both.*
> *I have known nothing but starvation. It pains me. End both*
> *our misery, Yara. I beg you.*

I can't. If you've read the earlier parts of this journal, you should already know this. My people will perish at the hands of the seabed spirits who wish to devour us. You said the food here would taste better than any meal I've ever had. You spoke of the shamans and what they know, but you say your life has just begun. You talk about

being new to this world while also talking about things that came
before your supposed "birth". Explain.

> *I watch the shamans enter every morning and lay down*
> *the food. They glow, faintly. If I look outside the world*
> *is dim.*
> *But you, Yara, are bright. It can be blinding at times. And*
> *the food, when it enters, has no glow. But the longer it*
> *sits on the tables, the brighter it becomes until it too*
> *shines like you do.*
> *There is power here, power that does not exist on the*
> *outside. I can see it. I can feel it. Can't you?*

I know of the power you speak of, but my eyes do not see it. Tell
me, what is your name?

> *I do not have one, nor do I know any other than the ones*
> *put here on these pages. Yara. Nika. Ma'ha'lenti.*
> *I would like a name, if you could indulge me.*

Are you male or female?

> *Male, I suppose.*

What do you look like?

> *I don't know.*

Is there anything you'd like to be named after?

> *You.*

I have never named someone before. You have also not given me
much to work with. But here is a name for you, if you like. Rajani.

What does it mean?

The unseen hand.

It pleases me.

Then you can keep it.

Thank you. But our conversation must come to an end. I will now rest. The sun is rising. The shamans will be here soon. Let us write again tomorrow.

You know where to find me.

Yara

The journal flipped closed without her touching it. Yara corked the bottle of ink and slid the forbidden objects into her bed. She leaned down and blew out the candle.

The blackness of night had already dissipated into a dull gray. She didn't know how long she and Rajani had talked. It took a long time for him to etch his messages into the journal. But for the first time since entering the hut, Yara felt in control. Nothing Rajani wrote could be trusted. But there was much in his writings to decode. The more he wrote, the more information she had. She just didn't know what information, if any, was true.

Yara walked to the window and leaned against the sill. An inkling in the back of her mind told her that something Rajani wrote was a lie – some word, some message, some subtle meaning meant to deceive her. If he was the thing in the hut that meant to kill her, surely he would try to coax her into his trap. He already tried to get her to eat—a thought ever-present in her head. The rainbringer two years ago ate, which showed the flaws of the tradition, but he still died. Even if she had decided to risk it, she'd have to wait until there was enough food on the tables for her to sneak some unnoticed. Some of the evidence suggested she could eat and still live. But if she were wrong, eating anything would lead to the violent death of every person living on Asa'hali.

For now, she'd have to test Rajani's information, prove it true or false. Anything she could learn from the night scribbling messages to each other would only give her the upper hand. But it was the idea of falsehoods that nagged at her. That was where the most valuable information hid. That would reveal Rajani's weaknesses.

She huffed. All this plotting against Rajani only made sense if Rajani actually was the thing that ended the life of the rainbringers. As much as she didn't want to entertain the idea, it was still possible that Rajani—whatever he was—was not the thing she hunted. There could be something else, something still in the shadows. In which case, Rajani could be an ally.

Yara craned her neck, cracking several bones. She scratched her hair and pulled it out of her face. A glimmer of red glinted from the beach. A knot in her stomach tightened, this time not from hunger.

Another speck of red glinted from the water. They were back— the seabed spirits. The legends say it takes seven days for them to trek from the ocean floor to the shores of the island. Yara swallowed hard. Today was the seventh day. The rain would keep them from rampaging through the village, but it didn't stop them from loafing around and reminding everyone of their titanic bodies and jagged teeth.

Their translucent-skinned heads poked through the water. The light of their gleaming red eyes could be seen from far away and through the heaviest of storms. It would be another day before they set foot on land. But from now until her death, their ghastly, beastly forms would do nothing but roam the shores.

Enemies, Yara thought, *everywhere.*

Nika

"This is the wall of guardians." Heren waved a hand in front of the stone wall behind him. A list of names had been etched onto it, with plenty of room for the list to continue.

Nika's eyes scanned the names, stopping at the last one – Yara Ondur. Her thoughts jumped to the rainbringer hut. She bowed her head, hoping Yara wasn't suffering a shred more than necessary.

"Here you will pray until the cup is full of holy rain water." Heren motioned to the ground. "Would you like me to bring you a chair, considering your ankle and all?" His tone changed, abandoning the tone of mindless recitation.

"No." She shook her head. "But thank you." In truth, a chair would agitate her ankle much less, but now was the time to keep up appearances and that meant being orthodox.

Nodding, Heren continued. "Once this cup is full, you will drink it and your designation will be complete. You will be able to return to the village and live a most celebratory year." He withdrew a face-down cup from his robe and presented it to Nika.

She took it and turned it face-up.

"And now your prayers begin." Heren stepped away, but paused. His light blue eyes met hers. "I will be running an errand and will be back shortly."

"Where are you going?"

"Just mind your prayers." Heren turned away and walked. "I won't be long."

Nika eased herself onto the ground, keeping as much weight off her ankle as possible. The swelling died down in the night, but it was still sore. She stared at the wall and the names etched on it. Her mind should have been praising the great rain spirit, but she had no intention to follow protocol. No one would know she wasn't praying anyway.

The boredom of staring at a wall struck within seconds. If she weren't praying, she was doing nothing but sitting in the rain, waiting for a cup to fill. At least Heren was right, it shouldn't take long. Most rainbringers would have started their prayers on the third day of the storm, before the showers fell in full force. Even now, on the seventh day, the storm was still considered calm, but noticeably heavier than the third day. So the cup should fill faster than normal.

Nika grunted, unhappy with waiting. She wanted to go back to Yara, to the village, to figuring out what was truly going on. Time was precious and shouldn't be wasted staring at a list of martyrs.

The books!

She rose to her feet. With Heren gone on an errand, she didn't have to sit idle after all. There was a wall of books that she could familiarize herself with. Heren hadn't said how long he'd be, but everything was far from this hut, so she would undoubtedly have at least some time to abandon her post. She placed the cup on the ground, propping it up with rocks to resist the breeze, and made for the hut.

After gently closing the door behind her, she peeked out the window for any sign of Heren's return. Nothing. No sight. No sound. She grabbed a rag and dried her hands. Every book on the wall looked identical, so she grabbed a stack and dropped them on the table. The first was titled *Herbology*. The second taught mathematics. The third and fourth and fifth were all genealogy. The sixth was blank. Nothing.

Nika returned to the window. No signs of Heren. She hobbled back to the bookcase and returned the ones she pulled. Her heart pounded. Worried that she'd find nothing valuable and get caught all the same froze her in place. *No.* She shook her head. She needed to keep going for Yara, for herself, for everyone.

She pulled out another book and flipped it open. *Astronomy.* Its neighbor was a book about illnesses. The rest of the books on the shelf were blank – newer books Heren had yet to fill. With what, she didn't know.

The sounds of footsteps breaking through the jungle interrupted her frantic search. She paused. More footsteps. Shoving the books back into place, she tapped them all, hoping they looked undisturbed. Ignoring her ankle pain, she walked to the door and went outside, unsure of what to say. "Heren, I was just...." She walked around to the side of the hut.

Standing on its hind legs stood a monstrous creature, bulging with muscles under clouded skin. Its red eyes gleamed at her. Hunching over, it stepped forward. Luminescent gills flared up from its neck. A guttural gnarl escaped the lipless mouth of the seabed spirit.

Nika stepped back. She couldn't look away. A malicious spirit was here, at the highest point of the island, moving in the rain as if there were no storm at all. "Heren!" Had Yara eaten the food, breaking the bond her people had with *Ma'ha'lenti*? Were the spirits here, rampaging, devouring the islanders? "Heren! Help!"

"I'm sorry, Nika." Heren appeared at Nika's back.

She spun to face him. "There's a seabed—"

"I know." Heren struck Nika's throat with his hand.

Air fled from her. She clasped her throat, choking on nothing. Another blow hit her stomach, making her double over. Heren's leg swept Nika off her good foot. Her bad ankle failed to support her, sending her falling to the ground.

"You shouldn't have been late, Nika." Heren walked out of sight.

The rain fell on her face and into her eyes as Nika laid on her back. The seabed monster towered over her. Its arm reached down and pushed against her chest, pinning her with so much force she felt she would shatter under its weight.

"I'm sorry, Nika." Heren leaned over Nika's face, shielding her from the rain. "This will all feel like a dream soon enough." He clasped her cheeks and poured a bitter powder into her mouth.

Coughing and spitting, Nika tried not to taste whatever Heren was giving her. She could hardly move or even breathe, but she fought the monster's grip with everything she could. More powder fell into her mouth, on her lips, and around her nose. The scent swarmed her. Her muscles weakened, fatigued. The world blurred.

"Good girl. Go to sleep."

Nika blinked, but could barely muster the strength to open her eyes. Something tasted strange, bitter and sweet—but familiar. She'd tasted this concoction once before. Her head spun. *Remember this!* she screamed at herself. *You have to remember.*

DAY 8

Yara

The door to the rainbringer hut latched closed. The scent of freshly cooked chicken permeated the room. Yara rubbed her eyes. After writing back and forth with Rajani for half the night, she still hadn't settled down to sleep. Shaking her arms, the rainbringer dress loosened, sliding down her body. One week into starvation and the dress already didn't fit. There was still more cushion on her bones, but as the days went by, it vanished. Her body was sand in an hourglass, counting down to her death.

She rifled through her blankets, extracting the journal and turning to the last entry. Reading it over and over, none of the information Rajani gave her seemed to incriminate himself. She yawned, catching a whiff of the spices in the air. It seized her, making her forget her inability to eat for the smallest moment.

The food. Rajani said it glowed, which meant it tasted exceptional. Yara grunted. She couldn't disprove any of that information, which made it entirely useless to her. The thought to approach the tables, to smell the food and touch it, crept into her mind. If the food had become divine and she, herself, more capable of experiencing it, perhaps her other senses could clue her in on whether Rajani's claim was true. She shook her head. No. If the food were especially appealing, it was probably due to her extreme hunger – not some sort of spiritual consecration.

Yara reread the journal entry. What other information could she test? Rajani didn't know what he looked like. She hummed to herself. If she could press him on this issue, force him to describe himself in any capacity, that might show her his nature. Hopefully, he would give her something to compare him to.

Other than not knowing how he looked or where he came from or what he is, Rajani seemed to only know that he didn't have a name. And that there were only three names he was aware of – Yara's, Nika's, and *Ma'ha'lenti's*. Her eyes widened. How? How did he know those names? The journal – Rajani said so himself.

She reread the passage to make sure, only to confirm what she remembered. Rajani had read through the journal. He knew everything Yara had written. But that also meant that the unseen hand had physically taken the journal in the night, flipped through its pages, and put it back. Suspicious, considering the night before when Rajani woke Yara up and prompted her to pull out the journal – as if Rajani wasn't capable of doing so. Why not pull out the journal and present it to Yara? Why go through the extra step? For show?

She clasped her hands together. This was what she was looking for. An inconsistency. A lie, maybe. Rajani might have already made a mistake and better yet, wasn't aware of the fact. This was how she could press him to reveal himself – his true self. She could test his actions against the information in the journal. She would need to contrive situations—conversations—that forced Rajani into a corner.

Exhaustion tugged at her. Sleep. She needed to sleep, but her heart raced in anticipation. She flipped the journal to the opening page and started reading. Then she could rest. And tonight, she'd start playing mind games with Rajani. With any luck, he would start to trust her.

Yara's Journal

Rajani, I don't know if you'll be reading this, but I've decided to keep writing in this journal as if it were still merely a journal. So if you don't mind, please ignore this section and only read the pages where we converse. I'm not sure if this request is even necessary, but just in case, let's pretend that these sections are my actual journal and the other sections are for you. Thank you.

I have contacted a spirit residing in this hut and named him Rajani. I'm not sure what he is and neither is he. My guess is that he is temptation incarnate. He seems to have no idea what's going on and was born when the storm started. For now, I really don't have a reason to doubt him. I am curious though. I want to learn more.

My only trouble is how. How do I learn about a spirit I can't see, can barely hear, and can only communicate with during the night? It is a predicament. I'm already so tired and so hungry, it makes it hard to think. I don't think I've ever felt weaker in my life. There was once I got sick and couldn't eat for a couple days, but now it has been eight. Eight whole days. And it has gotten to me. I can barely look at the tables covered in food. Sometimes they draw my eyes and I find myself staring. Rajani told me to eat. That thought keeps swirling around in my head.

I'm not sure what is killing the rainbringers. It is either Rajani – which I have serious doubts about – or something I have yet to discover. And maybe it's the hunger talking, but I do wonder if I was wrong this whole time. Maybe there isn't anything. Maybe the stories are true. Maybe I really did sign myself up to be a martyr. The truth has never felt further from me and my mind is getting foggier by the day. Was I a fool to even start this?

I suppose time will tell. And the best thing I can do is learn more about the only company I have. That is, if there is anything more to learn.

Good evening, Yara.

Good evening, Rajani. Has anything changed for you today? Is the world just as blurry?

> *No. Each night when I open my eyes, the world becomes clearer. You become brighter. And the hunger hurts more.*

I'm wondering, since you don't know what you look like, do you have a stomach? How do you feel hunger?

> *I can feel a grinding. A burning. No, a stinging. It's like there is a tear inside me that is slowly ripping apart.*

When you look down on yourself, what do you see?

> *Nothing.*

And hands? Do you have hands?

> *I cannot see hands, but I do have them. I feel them.*

What do they feel like?

> *Heavy. But still frail.*

And you have a voice. I've heard it. Why write when we could talk?

It hurts to talk.

Then I'll talk.

*I cannot hear you clearly. Most everything sounds
dampened.*

Like you're underwater?

*I don't know what that sounds like. You have a lot of
questions tonight.*

You're the only person I can talk to right now.

I'm not a person.

Sorry. I know. That's why I'm trying to figure out what you are.

Is it my turn to ask you a question?

Sure.

Do you love Nika? Your friend. The next rainbringer.

Of course.

Do you intend for her to starve to death, like you?

No.

*Then what do you intend to do? All the rainbringers have
died of hunger. They listened to the shamans. They
obeyed. They perished.*
*If you want a different outcome, you must take different
actions.*

Not all of them starved. The rainbringer two years ago ate something before he died. And it didn't kill everyone.

All the more reason to eat now.

I can't be sure.

What more proof do you need?

I don't know.

I enjoy that.

Enjoy what?

You being the one writing 'I don't know'.

I'm falling asleep.

Until tomorrow then.

Nika

The crackling of firewood reached Nika's ears. Her head throbbed. It was warm and dark. The weight of a heavy blanket soothed her, but awakened a soreness in her muscles. Her head spun, dizzy, even with her eyes closed. She scrunched her face and squinted, peeking at the warm light of the fire.

"You're awake." Heren knelt at her feet, wrapping her ankle with a bandage.

"What are you doing?" Nika lifted herself onto her elbows.

"I've just reapplied a poultice." He stood.

"How did I get inside?" She put herself back down, settling her head onto a pillow.

Heren picked a book off the ground and tucked it under his arm. It read *Herbology*. "I found you asleep outside and couldn't wake you. Thought you must have blacked out."

"Blacked out?"

Heren returned the book to its proper place on the shelves. "It's not unheard of for rainbringers to lose themselves in their initiatory prayers to *Ma'ha'lenti*. A few have told me they experience something of a vision."

Nika frowned. "I don't remember a vision."

"And yet you seem to have escaped yourself for some period of time. But you're well now and back inside the hut." Heren stepped over Nika to stand next to the hearth. He hunched over, looking into a small cauldron. The light of the flames added a soft orange to his gray hair. "Hungry?"

Herbology. The word nagged at Nika, but she couldn't reason why. Something felt wrong—threatening even.

"Are you hungry?" Heren filled a bowl with what smelled like stew. "I can't say I'm much of a cook, but I try."

Nika sat up and took the bowl from Heren's outstretched hand. The warmth of the bowl somehow made her hungrier. She spooned a small sip, blew on it, then tasted it. The vegetable brew was no feast, but a welcome flavor all the same. She swallowed, igniting a soreness in her throat.

"Everything all right?" Heren tilted his head.

"Yes." Nika cleared her throat. "It's just...." Her thoughts drifted away as they tried to piece together why her throat would be hurting.

"Hot?" Heren served himself a bowl.

Nika nodded. "Yes. Just a little."

Stepping over Nika again, Heren placed himself at his table, which was now pushed against the wall. "I think by this time tomorrow, you'll be well enough to trek back down to the village. I'm sure everyone is eager to see you." He took a mouthful of stew. "Especially considering your tardiness."

You shouldn't have been late, Nika. The words echoed in her mind. They sounded like someone else. No. They sounded like Nika. She couldn't tell, but the words were right. She should have been on time.

DAY 9

Nika

"I have a couple things for you." Heren smiled and took his straw hat off the table. He extended it toward Nika.

"Your hat?" Nika paused, but took it. It was well built, woven tightly and dry on the underside. She extended it back toward Heren. "I can't. You'll need it."

"You need it more." Heren pushed the hat back to Nika. "You've got two days out in the rain before reaching the beach. And I can fashion a new one." His tone took on an unusual friendly nature.

Nika placed the hat on her head. "Thank you." She eyed him up and down. The sight of him no longer made her nervous. Had he lived in the village, they could have grown up near each other and been friends. A sadness bit her. Their time together had been strange, but pleasant. Heren had an inviting aura about him, even if at first glance he seemed more academic than tactful.

"One more thing." Heren whisked himself to the door, his pace hastened by something his forced smiles kept hidden. Stepping outside, he reached out of sight and pulled out a tall tree branch.

"A walking stick?" Nika tilted her head. Another gift? This wave of generosity tugged at her neck as if her body was telling her to retreat.

"We left your stick behind when I found you and put you on my back." He gave the stick over. "I'm sure your ankle will appreciate it."

"*I* appreciate it." She took the stick. The thoughtfulness made her want to smile, but Heren's warmth gave her chills. Something felt off. She looked into his eyes, searching for his true intentions but finding nothing more than a gleam. Her back stiffened. An urge told her to run.

"Everything all right?" Heren stared back, scratching head.

"Yes." Nika nodded, quenching the unnamed fear in her gut. "Best be off then."

They made their way to the start of the trail. Nika turned to face Heren one last time. "Thank you, for everything." The empty road called to her, begging her to put distance between her and Heren.

"You're very welcome. It is an honor to serve the future rain-bringer."

"Sorry I was late." She leaned on the walking stick, testing it.

Heren bowed his head. "You shouldn't have been late." He looked off into the sky, then flashed a smile back at Nika. "But no need to apologize for something so harmless. It was a pleasure meeting you."

Nika's hand clenched the walking stick. Her gut sank. An angry urge welled up inside her. His words circled her mind.

You shouldn't have been late.

An image flashed in her mind—Heren, standing over her. The taste of something bitter—and familiar—on her tongue. Nika licked her lips. The scent of the memory-tampering powder filled her nose as if it were still there. Yara had once introduced her to the powder's effects. It seemed Heren too had something for Nika to forget.

She tightened her grip on the walking stick. "Goodbye, Heren."

The shaman waved and turned to leave.

Taking the stick into both hands, Nika raised it and swung at

Heren's head. The stick knocked him off his feet and into a muddy puddle. She struck him again.

"What are you doing?" Heren rolled over on the ground, his hands raised in defense.

"You drugged me, you heartless monster!" Nika beat him over and over, hitting his hands, stomach, and his head once more.

A stream of blood spilled out of Heren's nose and swirled in the puddle. "Please, you don't understand." He shielded his face with his arms.

"And whose fault is that?" She raised the stick, but the sight of a battered Heren kept her from swinging again. "I *do* understand. You hide up here in the mountains by yourself, outside the knowledge of the village. Why?" She lifted the stick above her head. "The same reason you drugged me. You don't want me to find out why you're up here, working in secret, doing who-knows-what." She stamped the butt of the stick into the ground next to Heren's head.

He flinched.

"Unfortunately for you, I know what it's like to be drugged. It really shouldn't come as much of a surprise if you knew anything about our current rainbringer."

"She drugged you?" Heren withdrew his defense, collapsing into the mud.

Clenching her jaw, Nika tried to calm her breathing. "Yeah. She drugged both of us. On accident. Well, she said it was an accident but I'm sure it wasn't. She really likes experimenting with things she doesn't understand."

Heren wrapped an arm around his torso and heaved.

"Can you move?" Nika adjusted her grip on the staff.

"I think my rib might be broken." He rolled onto his side and curled up.

Nika looked to the stone hut. "So is your nose. Do what I tell you and that's all that needs to break."

"What are you hoping to accomplish?" He looked up at Nika, squinting through the raindrops landing on his face.

"Do you have rope in the hut?"

He nodded. "Why?"

"We're going to tie you up. And then I'm going to figure out what you made me forget."

Yara's Journal

Rajani, are you there?

Are you bored already? It's earlier than last night. There's still a hint of sunlight in the sky.

It's not my fault there's nothing to do in this confounded hut. And it took you long enough to respond. I've been waiting for what feels like hours.

I've only just awoken.

How long did you sleep?

From sunrise to merely a moment ago. Would you consider that a long time?

That's half the day. Most people would say that's long, but it's pretty normal for me. Especially now.

So you've slept that long before?

Yes. When I've been deprived of sleep or ill. Or just lazy.

Perhaps I'm ill.

I'm not sure you can get ill. Do you feel ill?

What does ill feel like?

It's hard to describe. There's a weakness that takes over your body. It makes it harder to move and function. Usually it's hard to breathe and gross goo drips out of your nose. There can be a fogginess in your thoughts. Sometimes you can't control how hot or cold you feel. I guess it depends on what type of sickness you have.

I have some of those things. Weakness. Fogginess. An insatiable chill.

Perhaps you are ill after all. But it's impossible to know if you can't compare it to how you feel when you're healthy.

I have known nothing else. Can I be ill if I've never been healthy?

I suppose you can.

I want to feel healthy.

I want you to feel healthy too.

Then eat. Take away my pain.

You know I can't.

You seem convinced of something you're not sure of. You don't know you can't.

Sure, but one wrong move could be the death of me. And Nika. And all of Asa'hali. As much as I hate playing it safe, I have to. But let me ask you something. Yesterday you asked if I love Nika. How do you know what love is?

I don't know. How do you know what love is?

It's something that I Actually, I don't know either. I thought it was something my parents and friends taught me as I grew up, but maybe that's not true. Maybe there was something inside me even when I was born. And my life has taught me to find it, to access and use it. The feelings and affection I have for others come from within, but I don't know if something was planted in my heart or if it is my heart that sprouts love. You've given me something to think about.

Something for both of us to think about.

Do you love anything?

No.

I think that's sad.

I only know sad.

So far at least.

You still there, Rajani?

Yara

Clasping the journal shut, Yara tucked it into her bedding. Her foot knocked over the bottle of ink. In a flurry, she dropped to her knees and tilted the bottle upright. Nothing spilled, the inkwell nearly empty.

She took a candle and marched over to the westward table. The aroma of meats and fruits assaulted her nose and climbed onto her tongue. Yara cleared her throat in a failed attempt to clear her head. She knelt, placing the candle on the ground and bending over to reach the underside of the table. A bamboo latch protruded from the corner. She unlocked it, revealing two more bottles of ink. Taking one, she snapped the latch back into place.

Yara plopped onto her bed. The soothing sound of rain reached her ears. The night's conversation with Rajani replayed in her mind. *What did I learn?* She thought through the conversation again, wondering if her questions were discerning enough to be fruitful.

Rajani sleeps. Or so he claims. Perhaps he's sleeping now. Yara twisted her finger in her hair, twirling it over and over. *He makes himself out to be so weak and frail and naïve. But he knows things. He understands love, but can't fathom health.*

She tsked. *Day nine down. Maybe fifty to go.* The urgency of the situation found her, making her tense up. *I have to test this information. I need to learn faster, ask more questions.* She rubbed her eyes. *But Rajani disappeared. The length of the conversation is limited. No more small talk.*

She took herself to the window and blankly peered into the night. *I need to know if I have any time in here when Rajani isn't watching.*

Red flickers of light sparkled from the beach. The seabed spirits waded through the tides, aimlessly wandering under the pressure of the storm. The moonlight glistened on their translucent skin, highlighting the frills on their necks and the muscles on their hunched backs.

A clunk sounded from beneath Yara.

She fell back and clenched her chest. "Rajani?"

Silence.

Another clunk sounded, this time from under the floor by the waste room.

"Rajani, is that you?" She stepped away from whatever was making the noise, wishing the missing dagger were in her hand.

A third clunk hit.

Yara closed her eyes and took a deep breath. She stepped toward the waste room and waited for more clunking. Nothing. She stepped closer.

Clunk.

She reminded her lungs to keep breathing. Sliding the waste room door open, she scanned the room.

Clunk.

A small blur of movement caught her eye. The hole she kicked into the wall revealed the bobbing of a creature. Yara squinted.

Clunk. The creature moved. A flash of red found her. The seabed spirit locked its gaze on her. Its jagged teeth jutted out of its lipless mouth.

Yara dashed away, landing at the entrance of the rainbringer hut. "Rajani, give me back the dagger."

No reply.

"Rajani!" She pounded her fist on the wall as if knocking. "Wake up Rajani. I need the dagger."

Nothing.

She scanned the room for anything that might aid her. The table, her bed, the food – nothing – *the boar!* She flew to the table and examined the full body of a roasted boar. The savory scent wrapped itself around her.

Yara reached for the leg and held the body in place. Jerking the leg back and forth, she dislodged the joint. The weakness in her muscles made her arms feel limp. Yara's fingers tore through the meat, greasing her hands and pulling out the femur. She placed one end of the bone at the edge of the table and pounded it with a fist, snapping the end off. Its bone was shorter, but now sharp on one side.

Stomping back to the waste room, Yara clenched her new weapon. She gazed into the hole to the outside world, but the spirit was gone. She waited. Her breathing steadied. The clunking stopped.

The sound of rain filled the air. The world returned to calm. Whatever the seabed spirit was doing, it stopped. Yara turned to face the tables. Now she had a mess to hide before morning. The shamans wouldn't be too pleased to see what she had done.

DAY 10

Nika

"What do you think you're going to find?" Heren shifted on the floor. Lifting his bound hands, he wiped his arm across his nose, smearing his wet sleeve with blood.

Nika took her eyes off the pages of a book on shamanic history. "I don't know yet." Flipping through the pages, nothing caught her eye. She was already well-versed in the history of the islands and the shamans who ran them. This book taught her nothing.

Heren cleared his throat. "Just ask. I'm, as you might say, an open book."

Nika slammed the history book shut and dropped it on the floor. Her wooden chair scraped the stone floor as she stood and reached for the next shelf of books she hadn't browsed. She flipped through books on mammals, birds, plants, recipes, weather patterns, and almost anything else she could think of – *almost*.

"Go ahead. Ask me a question." Heren leaned his head against the wall.

"Why did you drug me?" She glared.

"I didn't."

Nika dropped another book onto the floor. "What good is asking you questions if you're only going to lie?"

"I found you, injured on the road, days late to your appointment. I carried you on my back. I nursed you to health." He coughed. "I cooked for you. I gave you my cup, my hat, and my respect. And when you communed with the divine, your mind was enlightened. It wasn't me who got inside your head. Nor am I lying to you now."

Smiling, Nika sat down. "You called me a liar the moment we met. Looking back, you clearly had deception on your mind. How paranoid you must have been about whatever you're hiding."

"I'm not hiding anything." Heren's face blanked—either an intentional move to hide his emotions or an unintentional one that revealed them. His time spent alone did little to equip him with the nuance of social interaction.

"Oh really?" Nika stood and waved a hand at the pile of books on the floor. "Then answer this one question."

"Happily." He arched an eyebrow—the one with the scar that Nika no longer found charming.

"There are books here on everything imaginable. There are many volumes on the history of the shamans and the islanders. There are studies on every plant and animal alive. There are books filled with chants and hymns and praises to Ma'ha'lenti. Every detail of everything one could imagine has been jotted down in as much detail as humanly possible."

Heren nodded. "Yes. That is the job of the record keeper."

"Tell me then..." Nika walked to Heren and crouched down, eye-to-eye. "Where are the books on the rainbringers?"

Heren's eyes locked with Nika's. He clenched his jaw and turned his head, landing his gaze on the latch leading to his bedroom. "Down there."

"A bit of truth for a change." Nika patted Heren's head like she would a child's. "I hope." Marching to the latch, she pulled it open, revealing a staircase leading into darkness.

"Take a candle." Heren squirmed on the floor. Rope knots bound him to the legs of the table, keeping him from sitting comfortably.

With a light in one hand, Nika descended. The staircase was short, ending with just enough space for Nika to stand without hitting her head. A hammock hung from two poles on one side of the room. She held the candle out, illuminating each corner. Half the room was empty, but a nearly full bookcase stood in the corner.

The spines of the books were ordered by number, save the first two on the top shelf. She took one and sat down, flipping it open to the first page.

Record of the The Rainbringers
  1. *Udo Ba'ali – 72 – Male – 46 days – failure*
  2. *Imene Mi'ha – 72 – Female – 51 days – failure*
  3. *Sha'ri Cu'o – 40 – Female – 53 days – failure*
  4. *A'ha'i Duna – 36 – Female – 51 days – failure*
  5. *Bana Si – 36 – Male – 63 days – failure*
  6. *Ka'ri'a Na'li – 34 – Male – 26 days – failure*
  7. *Rana Si – 36 – Male – 49 days – failure*

Nika scrunched her eyes closed, not realizing how dry they were from staring at the list. Failure? What did that mean? She scanned through the rest of the names and flipped the page to look for Yara.

104. Yara Ondur – 16 – Female

One hundred and four? She shook her head. That was an error. Yara was the seventy-eighth rainbringer. There couldn't have been twenty-six rainbringers that she didn't know about. And the first name on the list, *Udo Ba'ali*, was correct. He was the first rainbringer – the one who pleaded with *Ma'ha'lenti* to save the island.

Nika turned to the books. They too were numbered to 104. She grabbed the last one and flipped it open. The only thing written inside was Yara's name. She grabbed the preceding year and flipped the pages to the last piece of writing.

Cause of death: starvation

She grabbed the 102nd and flipped to the end.

Manada Rii's body was found collapsed on the floor at dawn. Hands greased—smelled of pork spices. A section of boar meat had been eaten. Corpse delivered to mortician and her assistant after the hands had been cleaned. Dried blood was found under a fingernail.

Cause of death: unclear.

Nika reached for more books and read their final lines.

Cause of death: starvation
Cause of death: starvation
Cause of death: starvation

Nika rubbed her forehead. Starvation should have meant success, but the catalog marked them as failures. It also listed too many rainbringers and wasn't sure what killed Manada Rii two years ago. Heren was indeed hiding something, but she still didn't understand what.

A thought struck her. The wall! Heren had shown her a list of rainbringer names outside. The list there looked accurate to her and could show her which names in the book weren't written there. She hopped to her feet and shouted upstairs, "Heren! I have more questions for you."

The light of the gloomy day hit her as she reached the top of the stairs. She looked to where Heren sat on the floor, but the space was vacant. "Heren?"

The hut was empty.

———

Yara's Journal

Where were you last night? I needed the dagger.

Asleep. Why did you need the dagger?

One of the seabed spirits was loafing around under the hut. It saw me.

Did it attack you?

No. I didn't give it the chance. I yelled for you. Could you not hear me?

No. What happened?

I made a shiv out of bone from one of the cooked boar.

Clever.

I guess. I did my best to hide the torn-up meat for when the shamans came in this morning.

Did they notice the boar had been tampered with?

I honestly couldn't tell. I was so nervous about drawing attention to it that I just kept my head bowed and waited for them to leave.

How unlike you.

What is?

The subservience.

That's true. I hope that didn't raise any concerns.

Hide the journal. NOW.

Yara

The latch to the rainbringer hut clinked.

Yara blew out the candle, corked the ink bottle, and threw everything into bed. She tried to calm her breathing, but her heart raced.

The entrance doors swung open with a creak. Footsteps tapped the floor. One set drew near. "Yara. Wake up."

She rolled over and rubbed her eyes. "What?"

"No talking," said an older man. "Put this on."

A pile of clothes landed on top of her. Candles flickered around the room. A dozen or so shamans scattered about, shuffling uncomfortably.

Yara stood and unfurled the new clothes—shamanic robes. She turned to the elder and furrowed her brow.

"Just put them on."

Yara slipped on the robes with every eye in the room on her. She fiddled with the clothes with her sweaty palms, hoping not to look suspicious of anything.

"Follow me." The elder headed for the door.

Yara followed. The shamans flanked her.

At the porch, they stopped. The elder turned to the man at his side. "Search everything."

Air escaped her. They'd certainly find her journal and her whole experiment would be ruined. Any semblance of privacy would be gone and with it, her ability to investigate Rajani. Then the only outcome of being the rainbringer would be certain death. Her mind blanked.

"Nervous?" The elder met Yara's gaze.

Yara shook her head.

"You can talk now."

She looked at her feet. "Just confused."

"As am I." The elder picked up his walk. "So let's provide each other some clarity. Come along."

The door to the hut latched closed behind Yara. She dared not look back.

DAY 11

Yara

Yara rolled a pearl across the ground inside a shamanic hut no bigger than her bedroom at home. The pearl sped toward the rim of a tipped cup and bounced off the side. "Hmm." Stretching out her legs, she put her belly on the ground and looked directly across from the cup. Pulling another pearl from a stash at her side, she fiddled with it. "Come on, lucky number six." She rolled the pearl into the cup's mouth. "Hey hey! Getting better."

The door to the hut swung open. An elder shaman entered and rolled his eyes at Yara. "Please, Yara, have a seat." He took off his hat and placed it on the table between them.

Yara settled into a chair. "I thought when you said you wanted some clarity it didn't mean putting me in a different hut by myself for a whole day."

The shaman crossed his arms. "It took us some time to prepare for this meeting. We inspected the rainbringer hut."

"Inspected it for what?" Yara swallowed. Some of her things were hidden in spots she was sure they'd never find. The journal, however, should have been found in seconds. Why wait a whole day to talk to her if they found it from the get go?

"We saw that you had torn into the leg of a boar and extracted a bone. Why?" The shaman interlocked his fingers and rested his palms across the table.

Yara shifted in her seat. "There was a seabed spirit lurking around the hut. I got scared and wanted something to defend myself." It was the truth, which annoyed her. She wished she hadn't been so frightened.

"They can't hurt you, Yara. You know this." He bobbed his head.

She nodded. "I know. It was so close and I was by myself. I panicked."

The shaman hummed. "I see. And where is the bone now?"

"Well..." Yara's mind blanked. She had hidden the shiv in the compartment where she used to keep the knife, but she would never tell anyone about it. But there was something else bothering her about the question. Did they fail to find the hiding spot and were genuinely asking or did they find the shiv and were testing her to see if she'd lie? She bit her lip.

"Something wrong?"

"No." She looked down at her hands. They felt clammy. "I, again, panicked. I knew I shouldn't have done that and I didn't know what to do with the bone. So I dropped it down the hole in the waste room."

"Is that so?" The shaman's expression remained steadfast, unreadable.

Yara nodded. She refrained from blinking, thinking it would make her look believable.

"It is good to see some remorse considering your disregard for tradition." The shaman relaxed, settling into his chair and playing with his fingers.

The quip made Yara clench. "A disregard for tradition seems to be something we have in common, considering how you removed me from the rainbringer hut and are letting me talk."

The shaman smirked. "On the contrary. If a rainbringer displays behavior that could violate the pact between this island and *Ma'ha'-lenti*, then it is a shaman's duty to investigate. In extreme cases, that includes removal of the rainbringer and questioning from an elder."

Yara leaned forward. "You think I'm a danger to this island?"

The shaman leaned closer. "I think you are more unstable than you know. Many rainbringers struggle with the isolation."

"I used to eat when I was bored. Now I'm just bored." Yara huffed. "You'd go crazy too if you hadn't filled your stomach in eleven days."

The wrinkles on the shaman's face thickened as his eyes squinted into a half-smile. "Before my appointment as an elder, I had to fast for thirty-six days."

"You did that?" Yara stiffened.

The shaman lifted an eyebrow. "Without going mad."

Leaning back into her chair, Yara tilted her head and mirrored his expression. "You'd have to already be insane to volunteer for such torture."

A soft chuckle escaped the shaman's lips. "Perhaps."

"So we do have something in common." Yara folded her arms. "Is that all you wanted to ask me?"

"No." The shaman sighed. "We found what you did to the sacred rainbringer hut."

Yara's heart thumped like a drum. They must have found the journal, the shiv, everything.

"Tell me what you were doing with a bottle of ink." The shaman withdrew a half-empty bottle from his robes and placed it on the table.

She couldn't admit she snuck it into the hut. That would lead to more searching and the shamans finding everything she didn't want them to find, if they hadn't already. Could she say she found it hidden? Would that also lead to more searching?

A dash of hope struck her. They hadn't found the journal. If they had it, they would know what the ink was for. Rajani must have taken it, like the dagger.

The shaman put the bottle back into a pocket. "You seem to be at a loss for words."

"I snuck it in." She looked straight into his eyes. "It's sentimental. A token from home."

A disapproving stare met Yara's gaze. "I'm sorry, but I have no choice but to keep it." The shaman stood. "However, you may take the pearls back with you. It'll give you something to do when you're bored." He put on his hat and reached for the door. "But might I also suggest trying some meditation. It keeps the mind sharp."

"I'll make sure to give it a try." Yara stood. "Back to the hut then?"

"Not until morning. The others need more time replacing the walls of the waste room, seeing as how they had some crude and violent drawings inexplicably appear on them—not to mention a hole." He left with a wink.

Yara frowned. She liked tracing her drawings with a finger while she sat on the latrine. Now she'd have to picture them in her head. She clenched up, suddenly realizing that the drawings had been scratched—not inked. Was this a detail the shamans missed? They must have assumed that the scratchings were done by the bone shard. But it would have made more sense to use the ink. Her story didn't make as much sense as it needed to, but it was too late to change. Now, on top of everything else, she had to worry about them realizing this.

<hr />

Nika

Nika jotted down the last names onto an empty page of one of Heren's books. It took her hours to venture outside, memorize a few names and return indoors to write them down. She had to move a bookshelf in front of the door each time, just in case Heren returned and tried to get to her. She hadn't seen him in almost a full day. His only trace was muddy footprints that vanished into the jungle terrain.

The books were too valuable to leave. Something was here that she needed to learn—something that Heren didn't want her to know. And now she had transcribed the list of rainbringer names from outside, she could cross-reference it with the names Heren kept in the basement.

She flipped open the book from the basement and put it next to her freshly penned pages containing the list from outside. The first name matched, but the second didn't. Nor did the third through the twenty-seventh. Her eyes widened at the next name—*Udo Ba'ali*. The twenty-eighth rainbringer had the exact same name as the first. Then the lists lined up, save the numbers marking their order. Twenty-six names had been inserted into the list from outside. No. She held her hand over her mouth. Twenty-six names had been removed from the list records downstairs. But why?

Nika looked over to the door and the bookcase pressed against it. The back of her mind nagged at her to check it over and over, paranoid that Heren was seconds away from trying to break through her blockade. He would certainly be unhappy with the state of his home. The table was lodged against the window. Books from downstairs were scattered on the floor. She pulled her attention back to the texts in front of her.

Was it a coincidence that the first rainbringer and the twenty-eighth had the same name? That left a gap of twenty-six names, the exact number of extra rainbringers. She knew the story of the first rainbringer, *Udo Ba'ali*.

She put a finger on his name on the book with the shortened list.

1. Udo Ba'ali – 72 – Male – 46 days - Failure

She placed a finger on the complete list over the supposed 28th rainbringer's name.

28. Udo Ba'ali – 68 – Male – 45 days – Failure

. . .

The abridged list looked as if history was confusing the two men. The shamans taught that the rainbringer tradition started 78 years ago with *Udo Ba'ali*. But the lists suggested that the tradition started with another man, also named *Udo Ba'ali*, 104 years ago.

Small details, she thought. The information seemed to be pointing at something—a lie of sorts—but what that meant eluded her.

Nothing made sense. Not only were the lists contradictory, but every rainbringer had succeeded in their duty—not failed. They passed the test of temptation and hunger. They conjured the storm and died with it. The only reason the island had survived for this long was because of their success. What about them failed?

Nika laid on the floor and stared at the ceiling. She took in a deep breath. This puzzle gave her a headache. Who were these other rainbringers? Why did no one know about them? What had they failed to do?

She rolled onto her side and scanned the lists again. "*Udo Ba'ali*. Seventy-two. Male. Forty-six days. Failure." She sighed. "*Imene Mi'ha*. Seventy-two?" Nika paused. They first two rainbringers were the same age. Rainbringers are chosen through the guidance of the shaman's and their divination. It could be an adult of any age. The odds of them being the same age felt questionable—just like Yara and Nika's consecutive appointments were too unlikely to be believed as mere chance.

She stared again. The second rainbringer lasted five days longer than the first. The third lasted two days longer than the second and was thirty-two years younger. But they were both female. The fourth was also female, younger, and lasted two days fewer. Then the list switched back to a man. He lasted longer than the previous and the following rainbringer was also male. Nika's eyes widened. Each time a rainbringer lasted longer than their predecessor, they kept the same gender and lowered the age the following year. But each time a rainbringer didn't last longer than the previous, they switched genders.

For the first six rainbringers, there was only one variable from year to year. Nika threw a hand over her mouth. This was an experiment. "They were trying to figure something out."

She read over the whole list again. Number seven didn't fit her theory, but the rest of the secret rainbringers did.

Her gut clenched. Something was wrong with pattern. Rainbringers were chosen before their predecessor died. They couldn't have been selecting people based on their predecessor's longevity. Unless the choosing ceremony was different for them. Did something happen twenty-six years into the tradition? Something big?

Nika returned to the basement and pulled more books off the shelf. Opening the first numbered book, she squinted at the text. It was nothing more than nonsense—a language she had never seen— one composed of crude scratching. She flipped through pages, all of them full and all of them nonsense. One by one, she examined each numbered book and one by one she discovered that they were all unreadable—save the last page, offering only a brief summary of how their bodies were found.

Now six days late for her return and with nothing more to read, Nika knew she needed to go back to the beach. She tsked, not wanting to leave the two lists she found, but knowing she couldn't transport the paper through two days of rain. The knot in her stomach tightened. There was only one option—memorize them.

DAY 12

Yara

The wind tossed Yara's hair as she marched back toward the rainbringer hut. The morning sun hid behind gray clouds, offering light, but too weak to make shadows. She breathed, tasting a hint of salt in the air. Twelve days ago she entered this hut, potentially leaving the world behind forever. Yet here she was, returning to it.

One by one, the procession of twelve shamans walked through the door. Pausing, the shaman in front of her turned around. "Your hat and shaman robes, please."

Another shaman handed her the rainbringer dress and turned away to afford her some privacy.

Yara shed her outer layer of clothing and kicked it toward the shamans. She hastily threw the dress over her undergarments and tapped a shaman on the shoulder. Nodding, she nudged them out the door.

The procession left, closed the door, and the hinge clinked shut.

Yara threw off the dress and rushed to the bed. Her hands sifted through the blankets, finding nothing. "Rajani. You there?" She tromped to the waste room and peeked inside. The walls were new and lacking her drawings. The hole she kicked in was no longer there. "Talk to me, please!"

She examined the window sill, lifted a bamboo shaft, and plunged her arm into a hole. The shape of a broken boar bone greeted her fingers, making her relax. Marching to the tables, she ducked underneath and found her stash of ink bottles untouched. Her eyes turned to the waste room. Her last hidden compartment should be the one most difficult to find. She flinched, almost to get up and check if that compartment was as hidden as she thought. *No. Rajani might see.* Her gut hadn't decided to trust him yet.

A scratching noise slid across the floor toward her. The journal drifted into her knee. "Bless you, you beautiful ghost-creature." Uncorking a bottle of ink and extracting the plume from the journal pages, Yara leaned against the table to write.

Yara's Journal

Thank you! You've saved me a great deal of trouble by hiding the journal.

> *You're very welcome. I didn't want them finding out about your misbehaving. I do not trust them.*

Did you listen to them while they inspected the hut?

> *I did. And I watched them, though they were harder to see. You shine much brighter than they do.*

What did they say?

*They are concerned. Paranoid even. They talk about you
failing as the rainbringer. They think you are ill-
tempered, hard-headed, and flippant. One was sure you
had eaten the boar meat. The other was unconvinced.*

One of them thought I had eaten even though the rain kept
going?

That is what he said. It's as I said—paranoid.

Maybe. What else did they say?

*Both enjoyed the drawings you left in the waste room—
except the one with the shamans' heads exploding. And
neither was happy to tear them out and do the work of
replacing those panels. One of them mentioned that
next year's rainbringer has yet to return from the
shrine.*

That's Nika! If she hasn't returned, something must be wrong. Did
they say anything more?

*Only that they've sent a shaman to the shrine to check in on
her. Her parents and the elders are worried.*

Now I am too.

But there is nothing you can do.

Yeah. Thanks. I know that.

Does the truth offend you?

I'm not offended.

So you are annoyed? So quickly after you were singing my praises.

Sorry.

No need to apologize. I'm not offended either. Just annoyed.

Is that a joke?

My first one. Was it funny?

No.

I'll try to do better then. Perhaps I'll dream up something funnier.

You have dreams?

I do.

About what?

I'll tell you when I wake up.

Good night then. Or good morning, since that's when you sleep.

And Rajani. Your handwriting is getting better.

Nika

Leaning on her stick, Nika walked down the stone path back to the beach. She was still about a day out and her ankle started to protest the trek. The wet stones threatened to make her slip, forcing her to move slower than she wanted. But she kept a steady pace, singing to herself as she marched. "*Udo Ba'ali.* Seventy-two. Male. Forty-six days." She bobbed her head to the tune she created. "*Imene Mi'ha.* Seventy-two. Female. Fifty-one days."

On and on she sang, trying to keep the rainbringer information alive in her head. Every dozen or so names, she'd stop, panic at the thought of forgetting how many days someone lasted or how old they were. But the song sparked the memory of the list and the hours she spent memorizing it. In the back of her head nagged the thought of misremembering and changing the list permanently. Little by little, her faulty memory could lead to a completely wrong set of information. But she sang on, ignoring her fears and reminding herself of what she did know.

Hours passed and hours she sang the same tune to herself, unintentionally walking to the beat of the song. "Oh! *Udo Ba'ali.* Seventy-two. Male. Forty-six days."

"Hello?" A voice shouted from the distance.

A jolt of panic surged through Nika's body. Was it Heren? Or another shaman? No one was supposed to walk this trail save those destined to be a rainbringer.

"Nika? Is that you?" The voice grew louder.

She gripped her stick. "Hello? Who's there?"

A shaman's hat poked through the brush. A pudgy middle-aged man appeared, panting. "Oh good." He clenched his chest. "It's you."

"Uh, yes. Is everything okay?" Nika tried to relax, but her shoulders stayed stiff.

"That's what I wanted to ask you. You were meant to be back almost a week ago. We hadn't heard anything from you." He braced himself against a tree, heaving until his breath caught up to him. "Or Heren."

Heren's name made Nika's stomach squirm. At least they hadn't heard from him. Wherever that weasel disappeared to was still a mystery.

Nika stretched out her foot to expose her ankle. "I sprained my ankle on my way up the mountain. It took much longer to hike. But Heren took good care of me and sent me off no sooner than I was ready."

The shaman nodded. "Ah yes. He is a good one. Bright young boy." He stood himself back up. "I suppose I should go check on him too, in case the delay has put him behind on work."

"Actually." Nika stepped in front of the shaman. "I was worried about the same thing—that my extended presence was a problem. He assured me that I had not impeded his work in the slightest." She smiled.

The shaman put his hands on his hips and squinted. "I should probably check on him either way."

"Before that!" Nika threw up a hand. "Would you mind escorting me back to the village? I'm afraid my ankle is still giving me a bit of trouble and my walking stick just isn't bracing me as steadily as I would like."

"Of course." The shaman's eyes lit up. "It would be an honor to help out both a fine, young woman and the future rainbringer."

"Thank you." Nika dropped the stick and looped her arm into the shaman's. "That's very kind." At least her plea would buy her time. If she were lucky, she'd be able to distract the shaman from the thoughts of seeing Heren. Even if she failed, this man was clearly out of shape and would need plenty of time to take her down the mountain and then hike up to the peak. Perhaps his inability to climb would help persuade him from making the trek.

"What is that you're humming?" The shaman patted the hand Nika rested on his forearm.

"Oh." Nika paused. "I didn't realize I was humming. Must be the tune I can't seem to get out of my head. I hope my humming doesn't bother you."

"Not at all."

The list of rainbringers repeated in her mind as she hummed at the shaman's side.

DAY 13

Yara

Yara combed her fingers through her hair, unweaving the braids she had barely finished. As soon as the pattern untangled, her hands went to work separating her hair into pieces and braiding them together for the dozenth time. She blinked, only just noticing how dry they'd become from staring blankly at nothing in particular.

Nika had yet to return. She'd been gone for a week and a half. The trip to the shrine should have only taken six days. What was she doing? Was she in trouble? How would Yara ever figure out what was going on? A small rumble in her stomach begged for attention, but her thoughts were stuck on Nika.

Yara's eyes dried again and she forced them to blink. Her fingers fiddled with her hair, mindlessly weaving strands together until running out of length.

Why didn't the elder shaman mention Nika? Probably not to stress her. Or to keep himself from having an unnecessary and emotional conversation. As far as the shamans were concerned, Yara didn't need to know about the goings-on of the island. She was practically dead already. No need to bother her with matters of the future. Monsters, the lot of them—worse than the ones lurking outside, aching to bite into the villagers.

She blinked. Her hands reached the end of the braid and combed through it to start over.

This was the worst part of being the rainbringer—the silence. All day long she had nothing to do but listen to the rain. Hours and hours with no one to see, no one to touch, no one to talk to. At least Rajani was around at night. He might be evil, but at least he was company. No, the silence was the thing that threatened her most. It made her feel insane and the insanity made things less silent. Only then could she hear the quiet, panicked voices in the back of her mind.

Yara blinked—waking from a daze. She looked around as if seeing the room for the first time in hours. Uncrossing her legs, she stood. A tingling ran through them. She tried to think of how long she was sitting like that, but had no way to know. "So much for meditating."

Tapping her feet on the floor, blood returned to them and she stood upright. The cup of pearls sat at the edge of the eastward table, next to a plate of fruit and a charred chicken. The smell of seasoned meat met her nose as she scooped up the cup. She grimaced.

Placing the cup in the corner of the room, she walked ten paces from it, pearls in hand, and sat. She held the pearls up to her eyes. "Okay you little clam poops. It's time to do my bidding. Fourteen out of fourteen, let's go." She rolled the first pearl across the floor. It bounced off the rim and steered into the wall. "Ugh. Monkey butts."

Nika

The end of the trail came into view at the bottom of the hill. Nika couldn't see through the jungle as the light of the sun faded behind the horizon. She and the shaman walked out, exhausted of conversation.

"Almost there." The shaman cleared his throat.

"Yes. Thank you." Nika turned her head away to roll her eyes. Adults were boring—especially this one. She pulled her arm out of his. "I think I can manage the rest of the way. Thanks."

He bowed his head. "Very good."

As Nika descended the hill, two dark figures appeared at the end of the trail. She clenched her fists. Were they shamans? Were they angry?

"Nika?" shouted a voice—one Nika knew better than any other— her mother's.

"Mom?" Nika shouted back.

The figures ran toward her, taking the shape of her parents.

"We've been so worried." Her father wrapped his arms around her. "Are you alright?"

Nika wasn't sure if they were asking about her election as rainbringer or her week of being missing. Their relieved faces and familial voices eased her nerves, letting her relax for the first time since the choosing ceremony. "I'm fine." Nika peeled herself out of her father's grip. "I was just slowed down by a sprained ankle."

"Let me take a look." Her mother took her hand off her chest and reached for Nika's foot.

"No no." Nika pulled back. "It's fine now. I'm fine. I just want to go home and get dry." She eyed the shaman, hoping he'd dismiss himself and she could rush home to unload the names circling her brain.

"Let's get you home then. I'm sure you're famished." Nika's dad put his hand on her shoulder and gently pushed her to go. Something about him felt urgent. Nika suspected it was their inevitable conversation about being a rainbringer. They'd been waiting to have it for almost two weeks.

"Nika." Her mother's voice broke through the rainfall. "Don't forget to thank this kind man for going all that way to retrieve you."

"Thank you." She flashed a smile at the shaman.

He bowed. "My pleasure. I suppose I best be off to put everyone's minds at ease about our future rainbringer. Then your year of luxury starts tomorrow." With a tilt of a head, he scuttled away.

Her mom winced at the word 'luxury'.

Nika held back a grumble. As if a year of the shamans drowning her with attention and gifts was what she wanted right now—or ever.

"He seems nice." Nika's mother hugged herself.

"Yep." Nika picked up her feet and headed toward the beach.

The palm trees cleared away, exposing the open beach and the sight of dozens of seabed spirits loafing about on the shores. The red gleam of their eyes shot sparks through Nika's mind. A bitter taste, sprinkled with hints of sweet and sour coated her tongue. Her throat hurt. Her lungs shrunk. The sight of one of the spirits pushing her down took over. She could see Heren standing over her, pouring something on her lips—the same flashes of memories that swarmed her when she attacked Heren. But now the memory was clearer, a spirit was working with the shamans. A surge shot through her body like lightning in her veins, filling her with fear.

You shouldn't have been late, Nika. The words echoed in her mind over and over.

"Are you alright?" Nika's father took her hand.

She shook her head. "What?"

Her parents looked at each other.

"You stopped walking and were staring at the ocean." He stepped closer, looking over Nika with worried eyes.

"I'm fine. I just... it's them." She jutted her chin at the seabed spirits sloshing in the shallows. "I just haven't seen them in a while."

Her mother nodded. "I know they can be shocking." She wiped her daughter's cheek with her thumb.

"Well there's no need to get close to them. Let's get you home." Her father nudged her along the tree line, as far from the spirits as possible.

Nika pressed on, watching the creatures out of the corner of her eye. "Mom? When we get home, could you find me some paper and ink?"

"Of course. What for?" Her mother took Nika's hand.

"Just want to write some thoughts down before I forget."

Yara's Journal

So what do you dream about?

Many things, but mostly food. It smells incredible. The boar. The chicken. Even the fruit when I get up close. But I want to know what it tastes like.
I have dreams of you and me eating it together, feeding on the same passion fruit—probably because that's your favorite. We're always so happy. And the food, it tastes like it smells.

You're not too far off. Food kinda tastes like it smells.

How miraculous. I hope to know one day.

I thought you said you hunger for me to eat, not actual food. And now you dream of eating it yourself.

*Yes. It doesn't make the most sense. Most of my dreams
don't. Is that strange?*

No, actually. Most dreams don't make sense. I once dreamed that I transformed into a giant crab and rampaged across the whole island of Asa'hali. I snipped down the trees with my pincers and ate all the people. Then my parents forbade me from being a crab and I had to be a rat. So I bit their feet while they slept.

That doesn't make sense at all. You must be insane.

If dreams mean people are crazy, then we're all insane.

What do dreams mean?

I don't know. Maybe it's our way of entertaining ourselves while our bodies rest. Maybe it's a way of recording a day's events, but it gets all confused because there are so many thoughts and actions and feelings that get meshed together. Or maybe we're insane.

I wish I could dream your dreams with you.

I have had that thought before too. Nika always has weird dreams.

Weirder than the crab one?

Yeah. She had a dream that the ocean disappeared and was replaced by a really fat old lady. Then she had to go explore the old lady's mouth to find pearls.

What are pearls?

Funny you should ask. I happen to have some. When I was gone, the shamans gave me a cup of them so I could entertain myself. The cup is on the eastward table. The small, round objects are pearls. You find them inside clams.

They're beautiful.

They are. But now they're just toys. When you're not here to talk to, I get really bored. So now I roll the pearls into the cup to see how many I can get in.

I get bored when you're asleep too.

You can play with the pearls if you want. It's better than nothing. And it's a lot better than meditating.

What's meditating?

Meditating is trying to clear your mind and relax. It's supposed to be a way to stop thinking, but I am no good at it.

Sounds boring. I'd rather dream.

Me too.

DAY 14

Yara

Yara woke with the tap of the journal plopping onto her stomach. She squinted her eyes and cleared her throat. Her hands reached for the journal.

> *Thanks for letting me play with the pearls. I lost a few in a*
> *hole in the floor.*
> *Let me apologize with a gift. I left it in the wall where the*
> *bone shard is.*

She clapped the book shut and tucked it into her blanket. So Rajani had seen her hiding spots. Good thing she left the one in the waste room alone after she returned from her interrogation.

Peeling herself out of bed, Yara dropped to the floor and lazily threw the rainbringer dress on. She brought her cup to the window, filled it with rainwater, and sipped at it. Swishing water in her mouth, she peeked outside. None of the seabed spirits lurked close enough to spit on, so she spat without a target.

With a yawn, she shuffled to her spot on the floor and knelt. Bowing her head far down enough to rest it on the floor, she closed her eyes. Sleep found her again.

The clunk of the door latching shut shook her awake. The shamans must have come, placed more food, and left. She wondered if they had noticed she was asleep, but decided she didn't care either way. This routine had become boring.

Free of the dress, Yara dug into her hiding spot at the window in search of Rajani's present. Her fingers danced around in the space inside the wall. A cold metal greeted them. Fishing the object out of the hole, a smile stretched across her face. The dagger was back in her possession—at last.

She would have happily traded any number of the pearls to have the dagger back. But why now? Rajani was demonstrating some trust. Although he had wondered from the beginning if the dagger would have any effect on him. For all she knew, this gesture meant nothing. Tucking the sheath into her waistband, she walked to the corner of the room where the cup of pearls sat on the floor.

Pouring them into her hand, she counted ten. So much for her attempt to score a perfect fourteen out of fourteen. A small hole in the bamboo floor caught her eye. She dug a finger into it, trying to feel for the pearls in hopes of rescuing the lost ones. Her pinky had the most success touching any of them, which meant they were not too out of reach and still salvageable. Scoring ten out of ten would never be completely satisfying knowing more pearls were under the floorboards and rescuing them would give her something to do.

She withdrew the dagger and wedged it between two slats. Moving it side-to-side, the corner slat loosened, leaving space for her to reach underneath. Just barely out of her grasp, the pearls rolled away from her hand. She lifted the slat with a touch more force. A loud pop sounded, freeing the slat from the floor. Beneath it sat four pearls and something she hadn't expected—a folded piece of paper.

Yara furrowed her brow and took the paper in her hands.

To any future rainbringer,

Do not trust the ghost of the hut. He will lure you into a state of comfort and betray you. Do not fall for his tricks. The island depends on it. I have undoubtedly given my life to relay this message. No one else knows this ghost exists nor how dangerous he is. It is your duty to outsmart him. The day will be your respite from him. Use it wisely.

Signed in blood,

Sharii Na'a – 41

These words of Sharii Na'a are true. I will add my voice to their validity.

O'ani Umena—49

Tala Si—50

Sha'ari Nabatu—56

O'a Nihili—58

Su'Ono Na'di—61

Ba'adu—67

Nor'ii Ehu—73

Yara swallowed hard. She finally had confirmation of Rajani's ill intent, but a discomfort settled into her, not relief. Rajani wanted Yara to trust him. Was that why he gave back the dagger? Was it a trap? Goosebumps spread over her arms. She saw no reason the note couldn't be trusted, but something about it felt wrong. Perhaps it was the message, proof that who she hoped was a friend actually wasn't. Was it denial aching in her bones? Fear?

She folded the note. The dark-red letters imprinted onto her brain, dried blood from thirty-seven years ago. Did it stand to reason that a piece of paper could have survived this long in such a humid place? It was the hut after all—the only place she knew where things happened that couldn't be explained. The shamans would not have left the note here. Anything out of place made their brains fall apart. Rajani wouldn't have left it—it incriminated him. He also had little memory and to his own admittance long before she found this note, he only knew three names. Not eight and definitely not names that Yara should know.

She bit her lip. She should know the names of the rainbringers. That would have confirmed its validity, but Yara was never one for memorizing rote information. Nika was the one for books and history and trivia. *Udo Ba'ali* was the first rainbringer. Everyone knew that. Yara knew the names of the rainbringers from the past few years, but only because she actually knew them.

But Nika could find this information for her. Yara would have to preserve the note—keep it in a place no one, especially Rajani, would find it. Her hiding spots were all compromised, save the last one, which even now she dared not touch. She gripped the dagger, thinking of stuffing the note inside the sheath. But Rajani had taken it once. And she had been taken out of the hut before, making her person an unreliable place to store it.

The food. She turned to it. Two weeks of deliveries had started adding up. The shamans never moved the plates to make room for the next. They only added, meaning most of the food would be left untouched for long periods of time—if not indefinitely.

She stood and eyed the tables, searching them for a hiding spot. A small plate stood out to her for reasons she didn't understand. Her gut knew something—that that was the best place for the note. Lifting a ripe passion fruit, her stomach churned. Most days the hunger rested idly at the back of her mind. But the touch of the fruit ignited her memory, reminding her of her favorite sour taste.

Whisking herself away to the waste room, she took the dagger to the shell of the passion fruit and cut a small hole. The aroma swarmed her, making her mouth water. She poked a finger through the hole and a little by little, scraped the contents out. The hole in the fruit widened as she worked, making her worry that it had become noticeable. The slimy interior of the fruit clung to her nail. She flicked the last of it down the hole of the waste room and brought the fruit to the rainbringer dress.

Wrapping a corner of the dress around her finger, she dabbed the inside of the fruit until it felt dry. Taking it to her mouth, she blew inside, hoping that any last liquid would not damage the old note. Finally satisfied with her work, she rolled the note and stuffed it inside. With the fruit back on the plate, she washed her hands and the rainbringer dress with the rain from the window.

Now to find a way to contact Nika.

Nika

Thirty-one blank spaces. That's how many there were on Nika's list of rainbringers. She couldn't remember some of their names, how long they lived, or how old they were. No matter how many times she sang her song, the blank spaces were always there. She'd forgotten.

A knock on her bedroom door interrupted her thoughts. "Nika?" Her mom's voice sounded lighter than it had the night before—when Nika could hear her parents crying on the other side of the wall. Bamboo did little to dampen the sounds between rooms in their hut.

"Yes?" Nika tucked the list of names into her journal.

"A couple shamans are here to see you."

Nika swung open her door to see her mother force a smile. "Thank you."

They walked to the front room where her dad was serving tea to the shamans. He turned to his family. "Care for a drink?"

"Let me help." Her mother waved Nika toward a chair as she fetched a teapot.

"Hello, Nika. How are you doing?" An elder shaman put down his cup.

"Very well, thank you." Nika sat and clasped her hands together.

"This is Onaru." The elder tilted his head toward his much younger companion.

"Hello." The young shaman looked nearly the same age as Nika.

"He has been assigned as your liaison. Anything you need, you tell him and he'll arrange it. That includes meals, although things will be much easier when this storm is over." The elder turned his gaze to a window.

"Is the storm a hassle to you?" Nika made no effort to hide her annoyance. Yara's suffering was heroic and tragic, not a nuisance.

The elder turned back to Nika, his expression stoic. "I only meant to say that our resources will be greater when they can focus on you."

Nika clenched her jaw, staring down the elder.

"Here you are." Her mother handed her a steaming cup of tea.

"We best be off." The elder stood, followed by Nika's father.

"Are you leaving?" Her mother frowned at her husband.

"Yes." Nika's father gathered his shoes. "There was a small mudslide uphill from some crops. A few of us are going to reinforce the barricades."

"I'm gonna go too." Nika stood. "Just on a walk."

Onaru stood. "I'll join you."

Nika held out her hand. "No. Thank you. I'd rather walk alone."

Onaru looked at the elder shaman who gave him a short nod. "Alright."

Nika slipped on her sandals by the door. "I'll be back by dinner."

"What would you like the shamans to prepare?" Onaru stepped toward her.

"Surprise me." Nika took a hat off the wall and slipped outside.

The wind greeted her, sending rain into her face. The storm had steadily grown stronger over the course of two weeks, but had not reached its peak. She wondered how long it would take before the wind shook the houses and not just the leaves. The wet sand squished underneath her feet as she marched toward the rainbringer hut. The beach was vacant, save the collection of seabed spirits that slowly came into view. They waded through the water around the hut, looking like glowing, lost monstrosities.

An eerie chill ran Nika's back. She looked over her shoulder. In the distance, the silhouette of a man stopped in his tracks—Onaru. She tsked. Of course, the shamans would have her tailed. But she needed to see Yara and let her know what she learned at Heren's hut.

Nika paused in her tracks. She shouldn't go farther, nor could she turn back—not yet. Digging up the ladder she made and placing it under the hut was the last thing she wanted Onaru to see. But if she turned back the moment she saw him, he would know his following her was getting in her way—of something. And any suspicion was unwanted. But it seemed the shamans already didn't trust Nika after her extended absence in the mountain.

She sat and crossed her legs. Removing the hat, she placed it in her lap, closed her eyes and tilted her chin up. Rainwater washed her face, dripping down from her forehead and into her clothes. She breathed deeply, trying to relax and think. Getting to Yara was now her priority. But first she'd have to escape her chaperone.

———

Yara's Journal

I need a favor.

What kind of favor?

I want you to deliver a note to Nika. Are you able to leave the hut?

*Yes, but not very far. The first few nights here left me bored,
so I tried to explore. At first, I could barely get off the
porch before my strength failed me. Everything dimmed
and I felt weak, so I didn't try to go farther.*

Go see how far you can go now.

What do you need Nika for?

Please just go. I'll explain once we figure out if you're able to get very far.

Fine...

You there?

Forty paces past the porch—so not far.

Is that where things get dim and you feel weak?

Yes.

Go farther.

No.

Just try it. Maybe you can go farther than you think.

I was just now on the brink of losing consciousness. If I pass out, who will save me?

Fine. But you can see farther than you can walk?

Of course. What is the point of all this? Nika has yet to return from the mountain and no one knows where she is. How am I supposed to deliver a note to her?

You've seen her though. When she came to visit after only a couple nights here. Do you remember what she looks like? Could you pick her out of a crowd?

Yes. I have seen two girls in my lifetime and my vision is no longer blurry. I think I can pick her out of a crowd.

Will you watch for her?

Why?

I need to talk to her.

Yes, but why?

If you find her, deliver the note, and if she comes here... then I'll know I can trust you.

You don't trust me?

I don't know if I can. You *do* keep telling me to eat. But if you bring Nika to me, then I'll know your intentions are innocent.

If that's what it takes, then I will do it.

Take this note I've torn off the corner of the page.

It just says, "Come talk to me." How will she know it's from you?

She'll know my handwriting. Besides, if anyone else were to find it, I don't want them tracing it back to me. Got it?

Rajani, you there?

She's outside. Sitting on the beach.

She's back? Are you sure it's her?

Yes. She's shining—like you.

Give her the note.

She's too far. Does this mean you won't trust me?

Go wait outside. Maybe she'll come closer.

Rajani? You still outside? Did you get Nika the note?

Sorry, no. She never got closer and then left.

DAY 15

Nika

Nika rolled over in bed and fixed the pillow under her head. After a day of failing to shake Onaru and reach Yara, sleep somehow evaded her. The rain sounded on the roof, seemingly louder at night than during the day. She sighed, wondering if the rain only seemed louder now because there was nothing else to keep her mind busy. Pat, pat, pat, pat, pat–like a hundred little feet barraging the bamboo without pause. At any other time, the pattering would lull her to sleep. Now it only reminded her of Yara's doom. She imagined Yara off in the rainbringer hut, listening to the same tapping sounds.

A soft pressure pushed against her mouth—a hand, muffling a yelp.

Twisting around, Nika flung around to face whoever silenced her.

"Hi," whispered Yara.

Nika's nerves instantly calmed. The two embraced—dampening Nika's clothes.

"What are you doing here?" Nika pulled back to try and get a look at Yara. The darkness obscured her, but the faintest of moonlight outlined her face. It felt like ages since Yara had visited Nika's home.

"I need your help." Yara combed her fingers through her long, wet hair. "Can you get a list of all the rainbringers?"

"Well this is insane timing." Nika smirked. "I've been trying to get to you since I came back, but the shamans assigned me a babysitter and I haven't been able to escape him."

"Oh. Is that who that guy sleeping on your porch is?" Yara pointed a thumb.

Nika nodded. "Yep. And I have a list for you. Two, actually. While I was up in the mountains, I found out there are twenty-six secret rainbringers. There have actually been one hundred and four. Plus, the records say that they were all failures."

"What? How does that make any sense?" Yara scratched her cheek. "How did you even see the records? I just went up to the name wall, snoozed for a day and then came back."

"That's not all. I saw one of the seabed spirits up there." Nika paused for Yara's inevitable shock, but the two sat in silence.

Yara froze. "Are you sure?"

"Yes!" Nika threw up her arms. "It was working with Heren. It pinned me down. Heren drugged me so I would forget. But I knew something was off so I beat him up, tied him down, and scoured the place. That's when I discovered the full list of rainbringer names."

"But you were drugged." Yara scowled.

Nika groaned. "I know. But you have to believe me. I am absolutely sure I saw what I saw. And to make things weirder, the spirit moved as if the rain had no effect on it."

The tapping of raindrops filled the air.

Yara bit her finger. "Assuming that's true—"

"It's true." Nika locked eyes with her friend. "You have to believe me."

Yara nodded. "Okay." She took in a deep breath and played with her jaw. "Did you bring the list of rainbringers with you? I need to confirm a few names."

"Yes and no." Nika sat back and crossed her legs.

Yara sighed.

"I memorized the list, but I've forgotten a few of the details." Nika shrugged. "So what names do you need confirmed?"

Yara shook her head. "I don't remember. I just found a note in the hut written by previous rainbringers. It said not to trust the ghost."

"Ghost?" Nika pouted.

"The voice—the breathing. Whatever it is. I've named him Rajani and we've been communicating through my journal." Yara cleared her throat.

Nika folded her arms. "He's literate?"

"Yeah." Yara rolled her eyes. "So I need you to come to the hut, look at the note, and tell me if the information is accurate. That way I'll know if the note actually came from the rainbringers or not."

"Why didn't you just bring it here?" Nika shrugged a shoulder.

"I can't risk leaving during the day and Rajani is awake at night. I'd rather he didn't know about the note." Yara bit her bottom lip. "So can you come to the rainbringer hut?"

"Yeah. I guess I can do that." Nika's chest warmed, her heart pounding. "I'll just have to wait until my chaperone falls asleep and sneak over real quick." The pressure to go to the rainbringer hut sunk in. She'd tried all day with no success, but didn't want Yara to think she couldn't do it.

"Uh." Yara cleared her throat. "About that. It has to be during the day."

"What? Why? How am I going to do that?" She threw out her hands. Everything felt suddenly hot.

Yara wobbled back and forth. "Like I said, Rajani can't see the note. Even him seeing you would raise questions."

Nika let out a long, quiet moan.

"But I know how you can get away from the boy out there." Yara pointed her thumb in the direction of the shaman again. "Just tell him you have to go take care of a girl problem and he'll give you all the space you could possibly want. Then you can venture off into the jungle without a tail."

"Why would I have to go into the jungle to take care of a girl problem?" Nika's whole body relaxed, the stress now turned to confusion.

Yara laughed. "I don't know. But neither does he and he *does not want* to know. Boys are idiots, but I guarantee you it will work." She put a hand on Nika's knee.

A knock on the door broke through the conversation. "Nika?" whispered a hushed voice, "You awake?"

Nika froze.

Yara shook her head and put a finger across her lips.

Nika shrugged.

They waited. Footsteps echoed away from them.

"I'm gonna go." Yara tip-toed to the window and opened it. "Oh, wait. Where did you put the ladder that you used to see me in the hut?"

Nika tilted her head. "You need it to get back in the hut?"

Yara nodded.

"You came here not knowing how you were going to get back in the hut?" Nika's jaw went slack.

"Yeah. So...?"

"It's underneath the hut, buried in some sand. Just dig around. You'll find it." Nika took in a deep breath. "Hey, Yara."

"Yeah?" Yara swung one leg out of the window.

"I've missed you."

Yara swung the other leg over the edge. She looked over her shoulder at Nika. "I've missed you too." With a short push, she fell from the window sill and vanished into the night.

Yara

The moon on the horizon illuminated the sky. The light pierced through the rain, catching on the bodies of the meandering sea spirits. Dozens of them wandered around the hut, all of them seeming to head in different directions. Their towering, muscular figures hunched over, bearing sharp teeth. Frills on their necks flared as they breathed.

Yara hunched over a bush, scanning the shore for any sign of human life. The coast clear, she darted toward the hut. The crowd of monsters turned in unison to face her, their eyes flashing red sparks as their attention converged. Even as their eyes locked on Yara, their movements kept a slothful speed, as if they were floating underwater.

Beneath the hut, the sand became dry. She weaved between the poles holding up the hut, scraping her feet along in search of the ladder. She crouched, plunging her hands in the sand and brushed them through every inch her arms could reach.

A knock sounded as her hand bumped something. She dug, retrieving the ladder. "Aha. Bless you, Nika, and all the useful things your soft, little hands can make. Though your crab traps could still use some work."

Pulling out the ladder took more navigating than she anticipated. Its length proved cumbersome when the many poles stood in her way. But with a thunk, the top of the ladder reached the hut's only window as she propped it up. She'd have to kick it down and hope no one found it before Nika arrived tomorrow. Until then, her only hope was that the rain and the spirits would scare anyone away from this particular spot.

The bottom rung creaked as she stepped on it, but held strong. Nika's handiwork was as reliable as ever. The eerie quiet of the hut met her ear as she approached the window, filling her with a dread she had become accustomed to.

A strangling force wrapped itself around Yara, pulling her from the ladder. She screamed without thinking, half-hoping someone would come to the rescue, half-hoping no one would catch her outside. She craned her neck to see the monstrous face of a spirit holding her in the air. The glint in its eyes cut through her body, paralyzing her until her wits returned. She writhed in its grip, barely moving at all.

The spirit swung its clenched claw in the air, blowing Yara's hair into her face and obscuring her view. Before she could catch her breath, it pushed her down, pressing her into the wet beach sand. Its strength was immense, but its hold somehow gentle. It kept her in place, keeping her wriggling free, but the pressure was still far from crushing.

Yara whipped her head, clearing the hair from her eyes. The monster towered over her, blocking the rain from falling in her face. Her heart raced. Her breath shortened. This couldn't be happening. The rain should be making the creature lethargic.

The monster sucked in a deep breath, paused, and exhaled. It looked into Yara's eyes and nodded. It breathed again.

A strange calm crept in. Yara swallowed and inhaled slowly, hoping she could forcefully ease her fears. With a few breaths, she relaxed. Whatever the seabed spirit was doing, it did not seem to be hurting her.

"What do you want?" Yara clenched her teeth.

The spirit took its other hand and placed it over its belly. It looked down at itself, then to Yara.

"You want food? To eat me?" She squinted. "Well, you are clearly in the position to do so."

The monster shook its head.

Yara's mind went fuzzy. It was communicating. It understood language. Maybe these creatures were not the carnal beasts she thought they were.

The spirit replaced the hand over Yara with a foot and stood up straight. Turning its body, the moonlight illuminated the muscles underneath the skin. Again, it placed a hand on its belly and looked down.

Yara stared at the creature. It moved its hand off its stomach, revealing a series of cuts she hadn't noticed without the light. Each of the cuts were small, probably shallow, but done in a confined area on the stomach—as if they were done systematically. This was not done in a fight.

The monster lifted its foot, freeing Yara. She stood and looked over the creature, not sure if she should take this chance to flee. Her gaze returned to the cuts. The moonlight glistened on them and their shape brought an air of familiarity. She stepped back, and tilted her head. A wave of terror washed over her. The cuts formed a word, one written backwards—stomach.

Her mind jumped to the autopsy of the rainbringer two years prior and the cuts he had made on his belly. It too spelled 'stomach', but not backwards. Were they linked—that rainbringer and this spirit?

Yara walked backwards, her eyes watering as they locked on the ferocious face of the spirit. It reached for her, but her feet fled before she knew what was happening. As fast as she could, she ran to the ladder and climbed its rungs. Her hands took hold of the window sill just as the grip of the spirit pinched her ankle. "No!"

She kicked her foot free and flopped into the hut.

A deep, unearthly bellow exploded outside like thunder.

Jumping up, she pushed the ladder off the window. It hit the spirit and dropped to the ground.

The spirit writhed on its back. Its muscles contorted and breath shortened, as if pain had taken control. Lurching upward, the spirit's mouth gaped open as if to scream, but no sound escaped its lipless face.

Yara slumped to the floor and tucked her knees to her chest. Whatever that spirit was, it wasn't like the others.

Yara's Journal

Are you alright? What happened?

I don't want to talk tonight.

That doesn't sound like you. And I've been sitting here for hours, waiting to have a conversation with the only person I know. Can't we just talk a little?

Not tonight.

Will you at least tell me what's going on? I heard that thing let out a fairly worrisome scream. Did it attack you?

Not tonight, Rajani.

Did you at least talk to Nika?

Yara?

Fine. But you owe me.

DAY 16

Yara

Manada Rii. That was the name of the rainbringer who carved the word 'stomach' onto his skin with his fingernail. He died at the age of about fifty, if Yara remembered correctly. But he lasted forty-seven days. That was a number she was sure of.

He was a handsome man. Married. Two children. Pet dog. Very normal—too normal, in fact, for Yara to find him at all interesting. Not that she found many adults interesting anyway.

The image of his sunken, shriveled face stuck in Yara's mind. That's how all the rainbringers looked when they died—depleted. Then she would help carry them away to an altar far from the village, but close to their burial grounds. She and the head mortician would wash the body, coat it with oils and salts meant for preservation, dress it in fresh clothes, wrap it in cloth and lay it in the ground next to where the other rainbringers were... abandoned. At least that's how Yara saw it. She had once made the mistake of calling the rainbringer burials an act of abandonment—a mistake she made only once after catching the hand of the head mortician. But there was no funeral. As far as tradition was concerned, the rainbringer wasn't dead, and instead lived on in the storms of *Ma'ha'lenti*.

Nonsense.

They were dead. Yara knew it. She was the one putting them in the ground. She was the only one who said goodbye to Manada Rii. The master mortician would lecture Yara every time she caught her talking to the deceased, but she still did, whenever she worked on them. It was more human that way.

Yara clutched the knife in her hand as she stared out the window. The sea spirit with Manada's backwards writing was nowhere to be seen. Neither was Nika, who was due at any moment. Now Yara had a new threat to worry about, one that was tied to Manada and one that might try to take hold of her and Nika. If only she hadn't told her best friend to come to the hut, then she wouldn't be in danger—at least not from this. A smile stretched across Yara's face as she remembered Nika telling her about beating up Heren.

A dash of movement from the tree line caught Yara's eyes. Nika ran to the side of the hut with the window, looping around the few seabed spirits in her way.

"The ladder's on the ground. Hurry up!" Yara waved a hand.

Nika lifted the ladder and climbed inside, Yara tugging at Nika's clothes to speed her along. Just as soon as Nika landed, Yara flung the ladder off the hut wall.

Nika panted. "I can't even tell you how annoying it was trying to get here."

"But you're here and that's what matters." Yara marched to the tables, pulled up a passion fruit, and dug out the note left by rainbringers past. "Can you verify these names and their numbers?" She held the note out to Nika.

"Give me a moment." Nika held her hands on her hips as her breath caught up to her.

Yara lifted the note to Nika's face.

"Give it here." Nika took the list and scanned it.

"Well?" Yara tapped her toes.

Closing her eyes, Nika mouthed a series of words Yara couldn't read.

"Well?"

"Give me a moment." Nika continued to mouth something as she bobbed her head. She peeked at the list, continued thinking, and then peeked again. "Yes. These are correct."

Yara's shoulders slumped. Rajani couldn't be trusted; her only company was something malicious. But at least now she was sure. "Thank you." Yara took the note and returned it to its hiding spot.

"What now?" Nika frowned.

"Well..." Yara looked out the window. "I need to go dig up a grave."

Nika went bug-eyed. "What are you talking about?"

"One of the seabed spirits has the word 'stomach' cut into its skin, just like the rainbringer from two years ago."

"Manada Rii." Nika nodded.

"Yes. I want to go dig up his grave to see if his body is still there." Yara pulled back her hair and tied it into a knot.

"You think his body *isn't* there?" Nika put a hand on her chest, still winded.

Yara shook her head. "I think it's been taken and... transformed."

"Why? That doesn't make any sense." Nika sat on the floor and crossed her arms.

"I know. But I think I need to find out." Yara clenched her hands into fists. "My gut's telling me that that's where I need to go."

"Have you thought this through? The graveyard is kind of far away. It'll take you more than a day to get there and back. The shamans are going to notice." Nika wiped her hands on her sides, clearing wet sand off them.

"About that." Yara forced an innocent smile and pointed a finger at Nika.

"You can't be serious." Nika shook her head. "What do you want *me* to do?"

"Just pretend to be me." Yara walked in between the tables.

"How?" Nika held her head.

"First thing in the morning, kneel here with your face practically on the floor." Yara demonstrated. "We have practically the same hair, they won't notice. And I'm not allowed to talk to them, so you don't have to worry about that."

"But...." Nika sighed. "But we have different sized bodies."

"Not a problem!" Yara rose and took herself to her bed. "Just put this on." She lifted the rainbringer dress. "It's entirely bulky and I've lost lots of weight since being here, so it doesn't fit me anymore anyway. It will completely hide your skinny frame."

"What about Onaru? I was barely able to get away from him to get here—" Nika slapped the rainbringer dress out of Yara's hands.

Yara arched an eyebrow. "Did you tell him you had a *girl problem*?" A mocking tone coated the last two words.

Nika rolled her eyes. "Yes."

"Told you it would work." Yara lightly punched Nika's shoulder.

Nika glared. "I hate when you're right."

"And we'll worry about him later. Just tell him you had another girl problem and if he pries, just start describing your period. He'll shut right up." Yara backed up to the window.

Nika stepped toward her. "What are you doing?"

"Going to dig up a grave." Yara swung a leg over the windowsill.

"Right now?!" Nika flung herself at Yara, her hands reaching in desperation.

"Yep. Bye." Yara jumped from the window and landed on the soft, wet sand.

Nika stuck her head out of the hut. "I did not agree to this!"

"Thank you." Yara stuck her tongue out at Nika and made a sluggish dash for the trees.

Nika

The weight of the rainbringer dress made Nika's shoulders slump. Wearing all five layers felt like being inside a dog's mouth—humid, sweaty, smelly. She sat cross-legged on the floor with her head in her hands. Yara hadn't left her much information about the invisible being inside the hut, but now they both knew not to trust it. She wanted to believe her friend wouldn't abandon her in a place where an evil ghost might harm her, but here she was—completely unsure if that's the exact reality she was living.

The shamans were a bigger concern, at least according to the pit in her stomach. If they caught her, they wouldn't leave Yara alone in the hut to do whatever she pleased. They'd put an end to hers and Nika's investigations, leaving them to die just like every other person who ever occupied the hut.

Her head slipped off her hand, jarring her awake. Any minute she knew her body would give in to sleep and the next thing she hoped would be waking up to the door opening, leaving her just enough time to flop over and hide her face. Then they would leave, Yara would return, and she could try and convince Onaru that she just needed some space. Finding out you only have a year to live should be enough reason to want some personal time. Although that's not how the shamans acted. They somehow always seem to try and talk away the pain of the rainbringer tradition. Idiots.

Nika chuckled. Yes, idiots. Yara was right about that at least.

A blur of motion dropped in front of her. A thwack on the ground sent a jolt through her body.

A book, flipped open, sat in front of her. Next to it, somehow, sat a plume and a bottle of ink. A warm light ignited at her other side, a candle inexplicably brought to life.

She rubbed her eyes and leaned forward to read the last message scribbled on the pages.

———————

Yara's Journal

You must be Nika. I'm Rajani, as Yara calls me. Go ahead and pick up the plume. This is how Yara and I communicate.

Rajani? As in, 'The Unseen Hand'?

That's correct.

So what are you, exactly? A person? An animal? A ghost?

Yara has been trying to figure that out since we first met. To be honest, I don't actually know. But what does it matter?

I suppose it doesn't. So what do you want?

To chat. That's all I really want. Well, that and for Yara to eat of the food here in the hut.

She can't. She's the rainbringer.

That I know. But I hunger as she does, not for food, but for relief. Her eating would erase my pain. And she's wearing thin. I'm sure you've noticed. If only she were to eat, then my hunger would be satisfied.

That doesn't sound like a thing a person would feel.

Nor an animal.

So you're a ghost then.

If you say so. You look hungry. Are you going to eat some of that delicious food?

Do you want me to?

I do not care. It is Yara, and Yara only, that can nourish me.

Either way, I will pass. Don't want the shamans to notice anything amiss.

They wouldn't. The plates are stacking up. The bounty overflowing. Those brainless workers couldn't spot a bird in its nest.

Still, I'm not hungry.

You're nervous.

What makes you say that?

Sweaty palms. Tense muscles. Insomnia.

Fair. I just want to make sure the shamans don't notice that I'm not Yara. And if I don't wake up before they arrive, they might.

I'll wake you before they get here. I am awake during the night and will watch for their approach. When the time comes, if you're asleep, I will prod your arm. Does that help?

Nika? Does that sound agreeable to you?

Yes. Thank you.

DAY 17

Nika

A poke to the cheek jerked Nika out of her sleep. A clink echoed through the room. Daylight broke through the crack in the door as it slid open, casting a spotlight on Nika. She lurched forward, catching herself with her hands and flipping her hair over her face. Still half asleep, Nika's heart raced as the muttering of shamans drew closer.

"Ah, Yara." Footsteps approached. "Glad to see you in full rain-bringer regalia. For once you seem to be following tradition."

Nika tilted her head slightly, just enough that she could see the toes of a shaman standing not two feet away.

The shaman stayed put.

Was he expecting Nika to react? She wasn't supposed to say anything, but the man in front of her seemed to be begging for a response. Was this a taunt? Nika clenched her teeth.

"You're not going to even look at me?" He gave her a soft kick. "What utter disrespect."

Nika faked a snore. The room fell into a hush. She snored louder.

"Hmm." The man walked away. "Just when I thought the girl was showing a shred of decency." His voice turned into a grumble as it disappeared.

More footsteps pattered around the room. The sounds of plates bumping and pieces of fruit rolling kept Nika on edge, until finally the buzz of the room seemed to settle.

"May *Ma'ha'lenti* watch over you," said the shaman. "That's it for the day. Let's go—ow!"

"What's wrong?" asked another shaman, his tone more subdued.

"Something cut me. Look, my hand, it's bleeding." The shaman stomped off.

The doors creaked shut and a clink marked its locking.

Nika took a deep breath and sat up.

"You alright?" a whisper of a voice called from her side.

She fell back and scanned the room, terrified that a shaman had stayed behind to catch her. Only empty walls greeted her.

"Rajani?" Nika looked around.

"Yes."

"You can talk?" Nika stood and began pulling away the extra layers of the dress.

"A little. I find it uncomfortable." Rajani's voice moved throughout the room with no semblance of a pattern.

"Well, I'm alright." She stepped out of the bulk of the dress and flung it toward the bed. "Do you know what cut that shaman?"

"Yes. I did. I do not like him."

Nika paused. The ghost had acted violently, but not against her. "Yeah, me neither. Oh. Thanks for waking me." A weight sunk into her gut. The ghost wasn't meant to be trusted, but here she was, thanking it for saving her in a time of need. She had verified that the rainbringer note had correct information on it, meaning Rajani was an enemy. But now it made no sense to her. Perhaps Rajani wasn't the ghost after all.

"Goodnight, Nika."

"You're sleeping now?" Nika looked around the room, thinking for a second she'd see Rajani somewhere in it.

"Yes." The word trailed off.

"Good night."

Yara

The bamboo spade in Yara's hands snapped in half. The unexpected break made her lose her footing, launching her into the mud. She groaned as she pushed herself up. "Stupid, little—!" The spade shard flew through the air.

Yara panted, catching her breath after hours of shoveling. Her muscles trembled from the burden of starvation. She'd dug several graves for rainbringers, including the one she was now revisiting. Never before had the labor been this taxing.

The path to the graveyard was completely empty. The grave was easy to spot, being the second to last in a series of seventy-seven. Even finding a tool to dig was a breeze since the morticians kept a small stash in a shed at the site. But the digging. The digging was exhausting, especially in the mud. As far as she knew, there was no body to find, and several feet into the ground there was no proof either way.

Mustering her strength, she returned to the shed, took another shovel and began digging anew. Scoop after scoop, clump after clump, the grave emptied. Mindlessly, Yara worked until the spade met a rock—no, the body.

She scraped the spade over the corpse, pushing mud off of it. Afraid of damaging what was left of the corpse, she tossed the spade aside and pulled the soil off with her hands. As she cleaned, her fingers found his chest, then his head. The memories of preparing this man for burial returned to her, the look of his sunken face etched in her mind.

She bent over, her back aching, and pulled apart the cloth covering his face. She had to be sure the body here belonged to *Manada Rii*. The cloth came loose with little effort. She ripped it apart, revealing his face.

Yara gasped. The face that greeted her was not of a worn down, old man. But it did belong to *Manada Rii*. His skin was smooth, his hair intact, his shape as healthy as a living man. Her mind jumped to his stomach. She turned around and pulled apart the wrappings and clothing over his belly. The word 'stomach' greeted her, but it was not a fresh wound. It had scarred. It had healed. And his matching abdomen looked as healthy as could be.

She sat down on his legs. Her theory that the seabed spirit at the hut was this body transformed no longer made sense. The body was still here, in the grave, and somehow looking better than when he was alive. This excursion to the graveyard was a dead end—and one that cost her precious time. But what did it mean? How was any of this possible?

"Manada Rii? Can you hear me?"

No response came, not that Yara expected one.

"I guess I should go back then." She stood, but an idea froze her in her tracks. Reaching for the spade, she held it over the stomach. "Sorry 'bout this." She scraped the tip of the spade through the word on his belly, scratching it out. "But if that monster is linked to you, then this should prove it."

Yara pulled herself out of the grave and walked away. Looking back, her eyes scrunched into a smile, knowing she'd never have to clean up the mess she just made.

Yara's Journal

Nika, you're still here.

Yep. Yara isn't back yet.

Are you worried?

Always. Yara acts before she thinks. She jumps into things head first, makes a mess, and only then tries to fix anything she's broken. She's never on time. Her plans always go wrong. But she always pulls through.

But you're still worried.

Of course. There's nothing to do in here but worry.

We could play the pearl game.

What's that?

I'll show you.

And Rajani? What food on the table do you think could disappear without anyone noticing?

Just about anything.

DAY 18

Yara

Crouched at the tree line, Yara scanned the shore around the rainbringer hut. The seabed spirits roamed around, the moonlight catching on their ruby eyes. A nervousness coursed through her body, reminding her that she no longer thought the spirits would leave her alone—at least not one of them. But from this distance, it was impossible to tell if the one linked to Manada Rii was among the ones at the hut. It didn't seem to be done with her, whatever it wanted.

She mustered all her strength and jogged for the steps leading up to the hut, making sure they were clear of any shamans before ducking underneath them. Crawling, she moved toward the water where the ladder was hidden and where she'd have more headroom to move about. Her hands dug through the sand, as she watched the monsters lurk.

One by one they noticed her, but remained standing in place.

Yara's search grew more frantic, her hands raking the sand as fast as possible. A pole in the sand caught her eye—the edge of the ladder sticking out of the ground. She hopped to it and jerked at the pole to free it. The ladder budged, but caught on something. She tugged at it, but could barely make it move. "Come on."

The ladder jolted away from her, sinking deeper into the sand. Still holding onto it, the jerk threw her forward, her face planting into the wet ground. She spat out the gravel and wiped her eyes clear.

A giant claw burst from underground, sending mud flying in every direction. A seabed spirit erupted from the sand below, stepping on the ladder and breaking it to pieces.

Yara clambered to get away, looking for refuge underneath the hut.

A monstrous hand took hold of her foot.

"Noo!" Yara dug her fingers into the sand as the spirit pulled her into the open air. Flipping onto her back, she kicked at the creature.

It pinned her to the ground, immobilizing her movements. The spirit took its free hand and pointed to its belly, dragging a finger across its stomach to highlight the word carved there. A fresh cut spread from either side, crossing out the word.

"Manada Rii?" Yara swallowed hard.

The spirit nodded.

"Is that really you? What happened? How did you become..." She motioned at his monstrous body.

Manada pointed at the hut, then took his hand off Yara, freeing her.

"I don't understand." She cleared sand off her face with her arm.

The spirit whipped his head around. Frills on his neck spread open. Dragging a finger through the sand, Manada drew an arrow to the hut. He nodded at Yara, then dashed for the water before disappearing underneath the waves.

"Nika!" yelled a distant voice.

Yara stopped breathing. She turned to face the voice, spotting a shaman, running at her from the trees. With no time to think, nor anywhere to escape, she froze.

"Nika?" The shaman, a young man, reached her. He tilted his hat up, revealing a familiar face—the boy that slept outside Nika's house two nights ago, Onaru. "Yara? What are you doing out here?"

A dozen thoughts flooded her mind, none of them helpful. "I..." Her eyes turned to the hut. "fell out the window."

Onaru furrowed his brow. "Are you injured?"

"Nope. Just stuck outside." Yara shrugged.

"How did you fall out of the window?" His tone turned skeptical.

"I was... trying to get a drink, with the cup they gave me." She motioned holding a cup out in front of her. "You know, holding it out so it would fill with water. It slipped and out of instinct, I lunged forward—a little too hard, obviously. And here I am."

The shaman paused, expressionless. "Okay. Let's get you back inside." He motioned towards the steps to the hut. "Where's the cup?"

Yara shook her head. "Couldn't find it in the dark. I think the waves may have swept it away."

Onaru nodded.

At the porch, Yara wrapped her arms around herself. "Thanks for your help!" she shouted, hoping Nika would hear and have time to hide.

Unlatching the door, Onaru pushed it open.

Yara stepped inside, happy to see that Nika was nowhere to be seen—probably tucked away in the waste room. "Thank you for your help."

"No talking in the walls of the hut." Onaru flashed an annoyed glance Yara's way. His eyes narrowed, looking past her. He walked inside, reaching the end of one of the tables. His back faced Yara, hiding whatever it was that caught his attention. Onaru spun around, a cup in hand. "Lost this, now did you?"

Yara could feel her face flush.

"Step outside and explain yourself." He scowled.

The world felt heavy, crashing down around Yara in an instant. She couldn't bring herself to move. Staying inside meant keeping silent, protecting her from whatever punishment was heading her way. But keeping silent made her look guilty. A myriad of aromas from the food hit her nose, reminding her that the pit in her stomach was emptier than ever.

Onaru stomped a foot. "Step outside."

The door of the waste room slid open, producing a stern Nika. "Stop!"

"Nika?" Onaru stood back. "How did you get—you two switched places." He clenched his jaw.

"Yes, we did." Nika walked to Yara and put a hand on her shoulder. "And we did it under your watch."

Onaru's anger washed away, leaving a look of embarrassment on his face.

Nika stepped toward him. "I've been here for two days while you were supposed to be keeping an eye on me. How do you think that's going to make you look?" She crossed her arms. "It's sad really, to see the end of your career as a shaman at such a young age. That is, unless no one knows."

Onaru took his eyes off the floor. "What are you saying?"

"Have you told anyone that you lost track of me?"

The shaman shook his head.

"Then Yara and I won't tell anyone either, if you don't tell anyone about us switching places." Nika folded her arms.

He licked his lips. "But what were you doing?"

Nika wagged a finger at him. "No. You don't get to know that. Because we are all going to act like the last couple days never happened. Got it?"

Onaru nodded.

"Good. Now let's go. We'll have to figure out what to tell my parents as you walk me back to my home." Nika headed for the door. She stopped by Yara and gave her a hug. "The information on the note is right, but I'm not sure it can be trusted. Rajani saved me yesterday," she whispered.

Yara looked Nika eye-to-eye and whispered, "Thank you." She wanted to tell her how impressed she was by how she handled Onaru, but merely hoped that Nika knew what Yara was thinking without any words. If anyone could, it would be her best friend.

Nika squeezed Yara's hand and left. Onaru followed. As the door to the hut closed, Nika looked to her friend. "Stay safe."

Yara mouthed the words 'you too' and held a hand to her heart.

Yara's Journal

Where have you been?

Nika said you saved her. How?

You're not going to answer my question?

Are you going to answer mine?

She wasn't going to wake up in time to fool the shamans. So I woke her.

Why did you do that?

It's your turn to answer a question.

I went to dig up a grave.

Is that a joke?

Your turn. Why did you help Nika?

She needed the help. I didn't want you two to get in trouble. All I want is what I've said since we began talking—for you to eat.

I'm starting to think that no amount of asking is going to get me anywhere.

And what happens if I eat?

I don't know. My only hope is that my pain goes away. I'm honestly surprised you're still listening to those idiots. One of them kicked Nika.

Well, they are idiots.

You're running out of time, Yara. Who knows how much longer you will last. Just look at yourself.
How much have you worn away?
Are you any closer to answering any of your questions?
Why did that one rainbringer eat something?
How did his eating not end in the island's ruin?
What is the rainbringer?
Do any of these questions even have answers?

Do you think you're helping?

I know one question that can be answered right now.

And what is that?

What will happen if you eat? Just taste something. Start small. Then you will be on the path of figuring this all out—just like the man two years ago. He ate, which means he knows more about all of this than you do.

I've started to think things didn't turn out well for him.

Because he died?

No. He didn't die. Something else happened to him.

How cryptic of you.

I'm going to bed, Rajani.

No more talking?

No. I need to think. And sleep.

And eat.

DAY 19

Yara

The thumping of footsteps and clinking of plates sounded from throughout the room as Yara knelt, her face to the floor. The morning sun barely woke her in time to toss on the rainbringer dress before the shamans arrived to place food. A day of digging up a grave had sent her into the deepest sleep she'd had in weeks. Most nights were spent talking with Rajani, followed by a battle of hunger-induced insomnia versus the fatigue of starvation.

Yara opened her eyes and stared at the floor. If only she could dig her way through the wood and spend time underneath the hut communing with the seabed version of Manada Rii. He'd drawn an arrow in the sand before running away, but she didn't know if it was meant to tell her to return to the hut or to meet him at the hut later. He seemed to want to talk more and the last place they met was under the hut. It was also the only place with dry sand—a place to write messages that wouldn't get washed out by the rain or the sea. Maybe that's what the arrow meant.

The sound of footsteps ceased. The door creaked shut. The latch clinked outside.

"Finally." Yara stretched her arms upward.

Two shamans stood on either side of the entrance.

"Uh..." Yara leaned back, furrowing her brow. "Are you not leaving?"

"No talking." One of the shamans crossed his arms and shot an annoyed look at his companion.

Gathering the weight of the dress in her arms, Yara picked herself up and planted herself on the bed. She slid an arm out of a sleeve.

"Keep it on." The angry shaman stepped forward.

Yara bit her lip. The shamans staying meant only one thing—Onaru snitched. She huffed. He probably only agreed to stay silent last night to get Yara and Nika back where they belonged. His career as a shaman was in danger, but as far as he knew, he'd fixed the problem. The biggest danger then was not telling his superiors. Nika's plan was stupid. It didn't work. Worse yet, Yara didn't even have a plan—making her more worthless than Nika.

This was exactly what she feared—guards keeping watch, not being able to write in the journal. Her mind jumped to the waste room. For the time being, it was her only solace. She gathered the dress and walked to the waste room, glancing over her shoulder to see the gaze of the guards following her.

The hefty dressed filled much of the room, making sitting down much more cramped, but also more comfortable. Yara cleared her throat. Tears watered her eyes. Her lip trembled, much to her own annoyance. Defeat. The weight of it bore down on her. She clenched her jaw, fighting back every emotion. Crying was stupid. It doesn't help anything. But that's all she could think to do.

Nika

A soft knock tapped Nika's bedroom door, undoubtedly made by her mother's hand. "Nika?"

"Yes?" Nika put down her list of rainbringer names. She'd try to remember the ones that she hadn't written down, but still couldn't produce them.

"An elder is here to see you." Her mother's voice trailed up.

Nika followed her mother to the front room.

An elder stood, cane in hand, smiling. "Hello, dear Nika. How are you today?"

"I'm well." Nika bowed her head. "How are you?"

The elder's hands trembled as it fiddled with the head of the cane. "Very well. Just feeling the need to stretch my legs for a bit—thought I'd go for a walk and wanted to ask if you would join me."

"Me?" Nika tensed. "Are you sure you're up to it? The storm is getting strong, the wind especially so."

The elder nodded. "I have weathered far worse." The old man chuckled. "Weathered."

Nika's mother gathered a hat. "Go on, dear." She handed it to Nika and leaned in. "Don't be rude."

"Alright." Nika flipped the hat onto her head.

"Splendid." The elder reached for Nika's arm. "Would you mind steadying an old frog like myself?"

Nika stuck out an elbow for the man to take hold of. "Not at all. But you are no frog." She tried to smile at him, but felt like her nerves were weighing it down. "Maybe more like an old prune."

"Nika." Her mother face-palmed.

"Sorry." Nika stiffened, hoping her joke landed better with the shaman than it did with her mother.

The old man laughed. "Old prune? I like it. I'll have to use that some time."

The pair left the house and waddled to the beach, keeping at the pace of the elder shaman. Nika tried to make small-talk, but the old man struggled to hear her over the sound of the rain in the trees. A nagging sense of dread sat at the back of her mind as they walked. What did the shaman really want?

"This way." The elder pointed to a man-made canopy at the tree line where paddle boats and oars were stored.

They sat on a boulder, side-by-side, and the shaman removed his hat. "There. Now I can hear you without the rain hitting my hat and keeping me deaf."

Nika nodded.

"Tell me, young Nika." The shaman put his hand on her arm. "Do you trust the shamans?"

The world silenced around her. This was a trap—she would have to say yes. How could she not? "Of course." She nodded. "Why do you ask?"

"It is very important that the rainbringer and the shamans work together. We are on the same side. The shamans appease *Ma'ha'lenti*, doing everything he asks to make the storm return and protect us from the seabed creatures that crawl out from the depths. And the rainbringer." The shaman took a deep breath. "A rainbringer is chosen because they are the strongest among us. They sacrifice themselves for the good of the island. They battle temptation and starvation. And the longer they last, the safer the island is in the year that follows." He shook his head. "It is no easy task." He gently squeezed Nika's arm. "But they do not do it alone. We, the shamans, are there to help the rainbringer with anything she needs. So it is helpful if we trust one another."

Nika bit her lip, not sure what to say.

The old man fiddled with his cane. "Why did you take Yara's place for two days?"

An electric current shot through Nika's body. "What?"

"And where is Heren?" The old man remained stoic, as if his question were purely academic.

Nika's mind blanked. She couldn't move. Her body felt like glass, ready to shatter at the slightest tap.

"I'm not angry." The shaman fingered his cane. "But I need to know what's going on."

"I assume Heren is still at his home on the mountain." She let in a breath, but it came like a stutter. Talking about Heren felt like the easier question to address. No one had asked about him in a week so she'd at least thought she'd gotten away with beating him, binding him, trashing his house, and then losing him. But they didn't know where he was. Heren hadn't talked to them since Nika saw him. They didn't know what happened. "Is something wrong with him?"

The shaman nodded. "He's vanished. His house went up in flames."

"It caught fire?" Nika's eyes wandered. Someone had been there since she left. Who would have burned down his house? And why? Was it to frame Nika? A stream of questions flooded her head, blocking her ability to focus.

"Had his house been made of anything but stone, there'd be nothing left." The cane slipped out of the shaman's hands and he bent over to reach it.

Nika beat him to it and handed the cane back.

"Then again, a stone house is practically a furnace. And there was plenty of kindling inside." The shaman held unusually still, like a predator on the verge of attack.

Had she left the hearth lit? Was this her fault? Nika shook her head. No. Someone else did this. Heren could have returned to his home and destroyed it before disappearing. Or another shaman wanted to cover up the secrets written inside. Or the seabed spirit returned and set the place aflame. None of these made sense.

"This is news to me." Nika hunched over, her mind occupied by her memories of Heren.

"Unfortunate. You were the last one to see him. If you don't know what happened to him, I'm afraid tragedy has struck."

"You think he's dead?" Nika turned to the old man. A forlorn look washed over his face.

"He was a pupil of mine—a good one. Faithful. Diligent. Talented." The shaman's nostrils flared. "Loyal. He would never abandon his post."

"I'm so sorry." Nika put a hand on his back.

"Hopefully when the storm has passed, we will find him." His head wobbled in a slight nod. "And what of yours and Yara's schemes?" His eyes met Nika's.

She looked at the ground. "I went to see her. She's my best friend and I wanted to see if I could talk to her. I managed to climb a tree trunk to get inside. She said she needed to leave, just for a day. But she sounded frantic—not like herself. She seemed unwell and I started to worry that the isolation was making her unstable. So I agreed to take her place, for one day, as long as she didn't eat anything. She agreed and left and then came back late." The lies felt like needles—a dread that pricked her as if she already knew her words would come back to bite her.

"Where did she go?" The shaman leaned closer.

"I don't know." Nika rubbed her forehead. Had they already confronted Yara about this? What had she told them? They hadn't planned on getting caught. More talking meant more information that could incriminate them both. She ached, sensing a springing trap.

"You didn't ask where she went?" The shaman squinted.

"I did. But she just said she went as far away as she could. It didn't make a lot of sense to me. But at least she came back." Nika wrapped her arms around herself.

The shaman nodded. "Oh Nika." He put a hand on her arm again. "I wish you had told me the truth."

A painful weight sank into Nika's stomach.

Two shamans walked up from behind, flanking her. She looked up to her left.

Onaru scowled.

She turned to her right. Her eyes widened at the sight of a face she thought she'd never see again—Heren's.

He frowned, seemingly holding back a pain behind his eyes.

The old man cleared his throat. "Now then, let us try to sort this all out."

A cloth gag flew over Nika's head and covered her mouth. Her hands shot up to remove it, but were stopped by Onaru. Another cloth appeared, covering her eyes. Hands pushed her to the ground and pinned her. More cloth tied her wrists and ankles. She wheezed a muffled scream.

Yara's Journal

I see we have company.

I need to get rid of them.

How?

I don't know. I was hoping we could talk outside of the waste room, but they yell at me if I'm in here too long. And they changed guards earlier, so I bet the ones here now will be awake all night.

Maybe. I'll keep an eye on them.

Yara? How many times do you think you can get away with going to the waste room in the night?

Yara?

This is going to be exceptionally boring.

DAY 20

Nika

Nika sat across from Heren and the elder shaman at a table. The interior of the small hut provided no clues as to where she was, nor did the shamans give any answers. A hearth at her back kept the room warm. She stared at the table, tired of ignoring her captors' questions.

The door creaked open. Onaru slipped inside, a plate of food in hand. He placed it in front of her.

The elder nodded. "Eat something."

Nika looked down at the plate, then back to the shamans. "Where am I?"

"Ah." The elder waved a hand. "At long last. You're in a hut we use for privacy—to have unpleasant conversations. Perhaps Yara told you about it. She was here not long ago."

The roasted chicken leg in front of her ignited the hunger in her stomach. She picked at it with her fingers, pulling strings of meat into her mouth. The spices tasted better than the ones her mother used.

"Why did you burn down Heren's home?" The elder arched a brow.

Nika shook her head. "I didn't."

"Lies." Heren glared, but his eyes hinted at something other than anger.

"I didn't." She dropped the chicken back onto the plate, her appetite gone.

Nodding, the elder clutched his hands together. "Then what *did* happen?"

Nika turned her head and jutted out her jaw.

"Nika?" The calm in the elder's voice surprised her. He hadn't shown the smallest trace of frustration, while Nika couldn't help but feel on fire.

"He drugged me." Nika pointed a finger in Heren's face.

Heren rolled his eyes.

"Tell us the truth." The elder smacked his lips. "Please."

Nika leaned in closer. "What's the point of talking if you don't believe a word I say?"

Nodding, the elder stood. "Perhaps a day or two in here will change your mind."

Onaru scooped up the plate.

Heading for the door, the elder looked over his shoulder. "We can help you, Nika. But if you don't want us, we won't stay. We won't feed you. And we won't free you."

"So we're skipping ahead to a year from now, are we?" Nika fell back into her chair and crossed her arms.

The glib comment put a frown on the elder's face. Onaru opened the door and followed the elder out.

She turned to Heren. "What are you still doing here?"

"I'm here to kidnap you." Heren's face sobered, his anger giving way to worry.

Nika shrugged. "You already did."

"No. Again." Heren leaned closer, his voice quieting. "If you'll come with me. I need your help."

Nika leaned back. Everything Heren had done didn't add up. She went to speak, but nothing came to mind.

"I know you don't trust me. And I won't force you to go with me. But give me a chance to explain." Heren bowed his head. "Please." A desperation filled the plea. His blue eyes looked up at her, softened by what felt like sincerity.

"You burned down your house, didn't you?" Nika covered her mouth with a hand.

Heren nodded. "You'd gotten into my books. My research was private—even from the others." He looked to the door, then back to Nika.

"Is that why some of your books were written in a strange language?"

"Yes. Only I can read it." A glimmer of light appeared in his expression. His scarred eyebrow twitched.

"But the list of rainbringer names wasn't in your secret language. Anyone could read it. Anyone like me." Nika chewed on her lip, not sure if she believed Heren's claims.

"Only anyone who knows about that book—which the shamans do. That's why I'm posted there. I record the names, ages, sexes, and number of days a rainbringer starves. I am also there to keep that information away from everyone else." His expression turned cold and his tone nothing more than a whisper. "They think that information is the secret to killing *Ma'ha'lenti*."

"*Killing* him?" Nika tilted her head. "You mean *appease* him."

Heren shook his head.

Nika swallowed hard. She sat back, losing every shred of posturing she'd tried to maintain. "But he is the great spirit that protects us."

Heren shook his head again.

The door opened, sending a panic through Nika. She took a deep breath and sat up in her chair.

Onaru stepped inside.

Heren turned to him, instantly as stern as he was before the elder left. "Ah, Onaru. We're just about wrapped up here." He looked to

Nika. "I was just reiterating that she'll starve unless she decides to help us out. So what shall it be?"

Licking her teeth, Nika could feel her eyes glaze over. Heren was really asking if she'd help him out, not the shamans, but she hadn't had a chance to ask what that meant. Her mind jumped to her parents, flooding her with guilt. She'd already put them through so much—not only being the rainbringer, but spending far too long up the mountain at Heren's, then disappearing for two days while hiding in the rainbringer hut, now this. Who knows how long she'd be away? She cleared her throat.

Heren didn't need to volunteer the information about his research and she saw no need for him to lie in private. Was this a ruse to trick her and get her in more trouble with the elders? Would he lie to her face and then turn his back on her, like Onaru? Not that she could talk—her life since her designation as next year's rainbringer was filled with lies.

But Heren knew more than she did and Yara was running out of time. She didn't trust Heren, but maybe she didn't have to—not completely.

"I'll take that as a no." Heren bowed his head. His gray curls fell over his face, hiding the fading bruises Nika had given him up the mountain. With his injuries obscured, the softness of his face showed how young he was—not much older than Nika. For the first time, he looked like a peer, a friend, an ally. He too could be working under the oppressive thumb of the shamans, defying them in ways he thought best. Like Nika. And Yara.

"Yes," Nika blurted out. "I will help you. If starving in a cage is the alternative, then I suppose I have no choice."

"Good." Heren sat back down. His hand twitched as if trying to contain a surge of relief.

Onaru stepped forward. "We'll have to continue the interrogation this evening. The elders are gathering everyone for a meeting."

Heren pulled a small book from his robes. "No problem. Nika is finally willing to tell the truth. She can write it down for us." He pushed the book across the table and produced a bottle of ink. "I want every detail, from our first meeting to when you left my house in flames."

He stood and pulled his hat off a hook on the wall. "I hope you think long and hard about what you've done."

Nika fought back a smile. Heren clearly wanted to give her time to think up a believable lie.

The shamans left. A clink outside the door told Nika she didn't need to check to see if it locked. The sound reminded her of the rainbringer hut—and Yara.

Yara's Journal

What happened last night?

No 'Hello, how are you?'

I don't have time for this Rajani. Did the guards fall asleep?

Yes. After a while. To be honest I wasn't watching as closely after a few hours. They just stood there, like statues, not even talking.
I have not been alive for long, but it was the worst night of my life.

Don't be dramatic. Were they asleep at the same time?

I think so.

You think so? That's not good enough.

Yara

A thunderous pounding shook the door to the waste room as if a giant were knocking on it.

Yara's hand shook as she wrote the last of her note in the journal —not that it was important to be snarky with Rajani.

"Hurry up!" The shaman hit the door again.

"Sorry, I—"

"No talking."

Yara shifted around in her seat, letting the heavy rainbringer dress brush the walls and floor to make it sound like she was busying herself. She tucked the journal into her waistband, leaving the plume in its pages, and the ink in her hand. Lifting her candle, she slid the door open to see one of the shamans looking both angry and sleepy. She wanted to make fun of how dumb he looked, but bit her tongue.

With a puff, she blew out her candle and dropped herself in bed. The guards yelled every time she tried to remove any part of the dress, so the ill-fitting contraption's best use was making her bed more soft and her skin more sweaty.

Time moved slowly. Sleep escaped her. The blissful distance between her and hunger was starting to fade, leaving a gnawing feeling in her gut. Hours seemed to pass as her mind raced, recounting everything that had happened since being locked up in this place. The note from past rainbringers sat inside a hollowed passion fruit—waiting to be signed by Yara. The seabed spirit version of Manada Rii could be outside, waiting for her, wanting to tell her something. Nika's lies about her disappearance could have failed, throwing her into trouble even Yara couldn't imagine. The whole island could be praying to *Ma'ha'lenti* that Yara wouldn't screw up this one job. She wanted to throw up. The water in her stomach didn't sit well by itself.

A snore cut into the room from the far wall.

Yara sat up, waiting to see if the snoring continued. Both guards were meant to be awake. If one was snoring and wasn't woken up, then his companion must be sleeping too.

Silence.

The pattering of rain.

Another snore.

Yara wiggled herself out of the dress, shedding the noisy fabric so she could creep around as stealthily as possible in her undergarments. She kept an ear focused on the front of the room where the guards now slept.

Tip-toeing, she took the unlit candle and tinder box to the waste room. The snoring continued. She nudged the door closed. It creaked, hitting her with fear that felt like lightning.

Another snore.

More silence.

The door closed, hopefully blocking out any noise she'd make and any light her candle would produce. Yara pulled the book from her waistband and turned it in the dark. She opened it to the back page and tore a corner off to use as kindling. With the flint, steel, and box, she started a fire and ignited the candle. The light filled the room with a comforting glow.

She looked down at the journal. A shadow of a crooked line on the inside seem caught her eye. She brushed the line with a finger. Torn paper. Pulling the book close to her eyes, she held the candle to it. Her first guess was right, a page had been torn out.

Thoughts swirled around her head, trying to recall when she had removed a page. No memory came. She hadn't. She was the one who bound the book. No one else even knew about it. Except Nika. And Rajani.

She gasped. The note from the rainbringers was written on a torn page. Was it a fake? Who would have forged it? Nika wouldn't have. Rajani then? When would he even have had the chance? It couldn't have been at night, when they wrote with each other. And he slept during the day, supposedly. Yara froze. She found the note after the shamans removed her from the hut. Rajani had had the journal and the opportunity to fabricate the message. The timeline made sense, but the names on the note were accurate. Nika confirmed them. Rajani couldn't have known them. Right?

Yara clenched her jaw, terror swelling up inside her. She should've known better. She should have examined the journal—looked in the back—the moment she returned. Had Rajani tricked her? He knew more than he admitted and that might include names. Did the note mean he didn't want Yara to trust him? That's what it said. *Don't trust the ghost.* And Rajani had always asked for one thing—for Yara to eat. But was that what Rajani really wanted? Did he intend for her to spend her time refusing him? For what purpose? To not eat?

She clapped the book shut. The fake note meant one thing—Rajani was the enemy. Only he could have forged it. Something in her gut knew this was true. And if the note was meant to keep her from eating, then that meant she needed to. And now was the time.

A pounding on the door interrupted her.

Yara dropped the book. "Coming."

Another thud hit the door. "No talking."

She slid the journal into her waistband and blew out the candle, hoping the darkness would conceal her secrets.

The shaman made no comment as he escorted her back to bed and took up his post.

Yara slipped the rainbringer dress back on, eager to put some food in her stomach. She just needed to find a moment away from both the guards and Rajani.

DAY 21

Yara's Journal

L ooks like there's nothing I can do anymore.

What do you mean?

The guards. They fall asleep, but they're never asleep for long. I can't even stay here in the waste room long enough to hold any meaningful conversation. There's no way I'll be able to get outside without being caught. For all I know, there are shamans standing guard there too.

There are. Two under the hut near the window. Another two just outside the entrance.

If there were ever a time I'd want some comfort food, it would be now.

I could sneak you some. They won't see me and I can deliver it.

Probably shouldn't.

What else are you going to do? Wait here, starving, until you die?

Yes.

Yara

Hours passed since her last message to Rajani. Yara laid in bed, her eyes closed, but her mind more awake than ever. She hungered. The decision to eat awakened something inside her—a mixture of excitement and dread. Her life was on the line, as was all of Asa'hali. But something about their traditions were wrong and all signs pointed to the rainbringer. Maybe she should have called Rajani's bluff when he offered to sneak her food. No, that made no sense. She didn't want him knowing she planned on eating.

Her stomach churned.

The wind kicked up, making the hut creak. The storm was growing stronger. Between the sound of rain on the roof and the wind hitting the walls, the guards shouldn't be able to hear her sneak out of bed and grab something to eat. But she also had to listen for snoring. She focused, telling her ears to ignore the rustling all around her and try to pinpoint the guards.

Rajani was probably watching too. He was most alert at night and had nothing better to do. He acted like he wanted Yara to eat, but tried to trick her into not eating. His games kept her fasting for weeks. Now it was time to see how he truly felt.

A snore broke through the noise of the storm.

Yara's eyes shot open. She waited for more snoring, hoping to confirm that the guards were not just dozing, but lost in a dream.

A snort sounded from the door.

Dressing down to her undergarments, Yara crawled out of bed and hurried to the tables—keeping light on her feet. She reached for nearest plate and plucked a grape from a vine.

"Yara," whispered a voice at her back.

She turned her head but saw no one.

Her fingers played with the grape. A lurking doubt made her pause, but she shook her head as if knocking it from her mind. She lifted her hand to her mouth.

Something took hold of her wrist, holding it back.

Yara fought against it, but couldn't get her arm to budge. "Rajani," she whispered.

"Drop the grape," whispered Rajani's harsh and labored voice.

She sliced the air with her free hand, hoping to connect with the rest of Rajani's body, but there was nothing there. "Let me go."

"I will not let you eat."

Yara grabbed the grape with her free hand.

A blow to her temple sent her falling. Her head hit the edge of the table before crashing to the floor. Pain erupted. Her vision blurred. She wanted to relish in the fact that she'd discovered Rajani's true intentions once and for all. But a thumping in her head cut short her thoughts.

"Yara!" Footsteps rushed to her side.

Before Yara could sort out her surroundings, someone lifted her up and leaned her against the leg of the table. The light of a candle made her squint.

"What happened?" A guard lightly took hold of her chin and turned her head.

"I don't know." The light moved to the side of her head where it had met the table. "She's bleeding."

Yara groaned. She could hardly think straight. Her foremost

concern was making sure they didn't know about the grape, wherever it had gone. "Sleepwalking."

A guard hushed her. "Go get one of the healers. I'll stay with her."

Footsteps moved away and knocked at the door. It unlatched. Muffled conversation turned into sounds of the door closing and locking shut.

Yara bowed her head. The guards may have not believed her when she said she was sleepwalking, but at least she had planted the idea. This also meant they were less likely to fall asleep at night, not that it mattered. They kept vigilant watch during the day. Between them and Rajani, she'd never get a chance at the food. She had one move left—pulling out the last hidden object stashed away under the waste room.

Nika

Nika jolted awake. A rhythmic thunder shook the walls of the interrogation hut. The booming grew louder and faster, shaking the ground.

A chilling roar exploded from every direction.

The shaman outside the door screamed before his panicked footsteps disappeared into the night.

Another roar erupted. Cracking and snapping cut into the night, the sounds of a monster rampaging through the jungle.

Nika ran to the door and pounded on it with a fist. "Let me out!"

The door unlocked. Heren stepped through. "Time to go."

Nika caught her breath. "What's going on out there?"

"A distraction." Heren grabbed Nika's arm and pulled her outside. He dashed into the jungle, holding her in tow until her pace caught up to his.

"Where are we going?" Nika reached out her arms, clearing plants from her path as she tried to follow Heren.

"I'll tell you when we get there." Heren stopped, causing Nika to nearly run into his back.

A seabed spirit tromped through the trees. Its giant frame towered above them as it came to a halt. Its eyes flashed red. Its skin shimmered, even in the darkness, casting a light on its jagged teeth and lipless mouth.

Nika stepped behind Heren. "Tell me that thing is with you."

"Indeed she is." Heren clasped his hands together and bowed to the spirit. "Thank you, my dear. As always, you've exceeded expectations. Please meet me at the cave."

"Cave?" Nika hugged herself. Her fear of the spirit shrunk, but was far from gone.

"Yes. Let's hurry. It will take about six hours to reach it, even if we can keep up our pace. Though I expect it will take longer in the dark." Heren reached into a bag and produced a rope. "Let's tie our wrists together. We can't afford getting separated."

"No." Nika shook her head. "You tie that to your wrist and I'll hold the other end."

"Ah." Heren looped the rope around his wrist. "You don't trust me yet."

"Are you surprised?" Nika took the free end of the rope.

"I suppose not." Heren turned to the spirit. "Don't forget to trash the hut." He pointed back to the interrogation hut with a thumb.

The spirit nodded and dashed away.

"Why destroy the hut?" Nika tugged the rope, checking to see if Heren's knot was sufficient.

"To buy us some time." Heren picked up his walk.

The two departed into the jungle. The crashing of monstrous claws toppling a hut boomed behind them.

DAY 22

Nika

"You know, when you said we'd be going to a cave, I imagined something bigger." Nika pouted at a hole inside the mountain wall. She eyed it up and down, wondering if she'd fit through it.

"It's a bit tight at first, but trust me, it's a lot bigger than it looks." Heren stuck a shoulder into the crack and began wiggling his way through.

Nika followed. "How is your friend going to get in here? She's a lot bigger than we are."

"There's another entrance through a pool of water. She'll swim over." Heren leaned under some protruding rock. "She's probably already there."

"And who is she exactly? Other than a titanic monster from my childhood nightmares?" Nika's shirt caught on something. She stepped back, adjusted, and pressed on.

"A friend. You've met before, at my home." Heren lurched forward, free from the crevasse.

"Oh yes. What fond memories." Nika stepped into the cavernous chamber. The light of day barely reached inside, but sounds echoed around the room as if the mountain were hollow.

Heren lit a torch and passed it to Nika before lighting a second. A dark hallway extended before them. "This way."

"So, Heren, are you going to explain to me what's going on?" Nika followed Heren's footsteps and waved her torch from side to side in case there was anything to see but stone.

"I took up the position of record keeper when I was fifteen—about six years ago."

"I meant explain the truth of the rainbringer tradition and why you need my help." A flash of movement overhead caught Nika's eyes. Bats?

"We'll get there." Heren turned a corner. "As you move up the ranks of being a shaman, you are trusted with more and more information. The record keeper has access to all of it—as do the elders. That's when I learned that there are twenty-six secret rainbringers."

"Yes, I saw that in your books. But why are they secret?"

"Because the rainbringer tradition was done in secret for those twenty-six years. The shamans were trying to handle the matter privately, without the island's knowledge."

The cavern walls grew wider, opening up into a chamber. The sudden space made Nika relax. "That doesn't make sense. The storm is here to keep the seabed spirits at bay. The islanders would have known this from the beginning."

"I thought that strange too. And in my exile as the record keeper, I researched everything. Past record keepers took meticulous notes and I spent my days devouring them. And yes, the records say that the rain keeps the spirits lethargic and unable to attack us. But that wasn't always the case. In fact, the spirits aren't mentioned in the first year of records. And then only one is mentioned, very briefly, in the second year."

"What did it say?"

"The shadow of a giant was seen standing on a sandbar." Heren sighed and shook his head.

"That's it?"

"That's it. Until the third year, the record says there were two sightings at two different locations. But it still doesn't describe them like the spirits we know today."

"When do the records reflect the story of today?" Nika spun around, chasing the sound of scrabbling critters.

Heren looked over his shoulder at Nika. "Take a guess. I'm sure you've figured that out."

She hummed to herself as she thought. "Ah." Nika snapped her fingers. "The twenty-sixth year."

"Correct." Heren nodded his head as he walked. "Which suggests to me that the spirits showed up on the shores, in plain view of the village. The shamans could no longer conduct the rainbringer tradition behind closed doors. Well..." Heren rubbed his head. "Well, I guess they still do—bad choice of words."

"I know what you mean." Nika rolled her eyes.

"So the next year they pretended to start the tradition. The story adapted, retroactively, to explain the seabed spirits."

"But where did they come from?"

Heren stopped. He turned to face Nika, his eyes somber. "The rainbringers don't stop the spirits. They create them."

Nika frowned. "Create them from what?"

Heren rested a hand on Nika's shoulder. "From themselves. Nika, the seabed spirits are the former rainbringers."

Everything began to swirl around her. She pressed her eyes closed. "I'm going to turn into one of those things?" A pang of guilt hit her. She'd thought of herself before she thought of Yara.

"Not if we can stop it. That's why we're here—to figure out how." Heren tried to force a smile. "The cave is just around the corner. Let's go."

Nika followed Heren into a chamber illuminated by what little sunlight made it through the storm clouds. A hole at the side of the roof cast light into the room from hundreds of feet above them. A pool of water filled the far end of the cave. Tables covered in books stretched out at Nika's side.

Heren pointed at them. "It took me a while, but I got them all here. Not that the elders know. They think they burnt up in that fire you somehow started."

"Right." Nika nodded through a daze.

The water from the pool splashed, disturbed by something underneath.

"Ah." Heren strutted to it. "Just in time."

The luminous skin of a seabed spirit lit up under the water's surface. Giant claws broke through the waves, pulling the creature out from the depths. It flopped onto the cavern floor. Dark blood spilled from various wounds.

Heren ran to the creature's side. "Ca'ari, are you okay?"

The creature moaned.

"There's a stash of medical supplies in that corner!" Heren pointed to Nika and then to a box. "Bring everything to me."

Nika rushed to the box and pulled everything into her arms. She hurried to Heren's side and placed everything in a pile on the ground.

Heren inspected the wounds with his hands. "Help me take care of her. Then we can worry about you."

Nika nodded.

Yara's Journal

So you didn't want me to eat after all?

Of course not.

Why pretend like you did?

Now why would I tell you that?

Because you've been aching for a conversation for days now. Or was that a lie too?

I suppose you're not just right, you're completely powerless.
Seems your trust is spent with the shamans. You're
nothing more than crab in a trap now.

You really know how to flatter a girl. So why did you pretend you wanted me to eat?

Because I knew you didn't trust me. I didn't want you to.
It's been fun—keeping you from knowing what to do—
making you doubt every action and afraid to make a
move. Siding with the shamans would never keep you
from eating.
You're too much of a rebel, so I gave you something to rebel
against.

You think you know me?

I know I know you.

So who are you? What are you?

I am Rajani, the unseen hand.

Don't play dumb. The game is up. And you lost. Even your antics couldn't keep me from listening to the shamans.

Yara, you fool. I haven't lost. You're here. You're trapped. I
will watch you at night. The shamans will watch you
in the day. There's no escape and there is no chance that
you will ever eat again.
You, yourself, have handed me my victory.

Is that what you've wanted this whole time? For me to be just another rainbringer?

You still don't see what's going on, do you? Yara—you are not the rainbringer. I am.

What do you mean?

It is not you who keeps the seabed spirits at bay. You have no power over the storm. It is all my doing.
Since the moment you were first locked in here, the moment of my birth, I have been the rainbringer. I command the storm. I control the spirits. I am Ma'ha'lenti, your great rain spirit.

I don't believe you.

It doesn't matter. You are nothing.

If I were nothing, you wouldn't be afraid of me.

Afraid? Of you? Your confidence is delusion.
I have no doubt your mind is hatching a plan as we speak. Perhaps you think the guards in the day might fall asleep or get distracted, or overlook some sleight of hand. I assure you they won't. There will not be two boys here, half-heartedly looking after you.
No. There will be many shamans. And you will be bound, unable to move, at the mercy of men who think you a monster.

You can't scare me. None of that is going to happen.

Isn't it odd how long we've been writing tonight? You'd

think one of your guards would have come knocking by now.

What did you do?

See for yourself.

Yara

The door to the waste room slid open. Yara stuck out a trembling hand, the candle's weak light barely reaching in front of her. She curved a hand around the flame, protecting it from the wind. "Hello?"

No response. Either the rain masked her whispers or the guards were asleep. She tip-toed closer to the entrance, squinting through the darkness.

Yara clenched her jaw. Her gut churned.

The light of the candle reached the wall where a guard should have been standing. She swung the candle closer to the other guard's post. Nothing. More wall. "Hello?"

A thud hit the floor behind her.

Yara swung around.

Choking breaths filled the air. One of the guards squirmed on the floor, holding his neck with bloodied hands.

Every ounce of strength in Yara's body disappeared. She collapsed to her knees. "Help!"

Another thud hit the floor next to the guard. A second shaman lay motionless at his companion's side.

"Help!" Yara pressed her hands against the dying shaman's neck, coating her fingers in blood. "Get in here! Now!" She bent over his face. Her voice trembled. "You're going to be okay. I'm here. I'll help you."

An invisible force struck her chest like a rockslide. Her body flung onto its back. She gasped for air.

The door swung open. Four guards rushed into the rooms, lighting it with torches. One rushed to the guards on the floor. "He's bleeding!"

"Go get the healer!"

Footsteps sped away as others stormed through the room.

Another knelt down next to the lifeless shaman. "He's dead."

One of the shamans looked down at Yara. "What did you do?"

Yara shook her head, still gasping for breath. She squeezed her hand, feeling something in her palm. Her stomach sank. She looked down over her chest and brought her hand into view. A wet, crimson bone-shard sat inside her grip.

"I win," whispered a hissing voice at Yara's ear.

DAY 23

Yara

The six guards in the room kept their gaze focused on Yara. One stood at the entrance, one at the window, one at the waste room, two by the food, and one at her side. She crossed her legs on the floor. Every guard fidgeted with her every movement, which almost put a smirk on her face. The blood-stained memories of last night hadn't even begun to fade from her mind, but watching the guards twitch made her feel in command. That faintest sense of superiority lifted her cheeks. She wasn't allowed to talk. Her wrists were tied. The guards kept her from pacing about the hut. But they were nervous and terrible at hiding it.

She reached for the cup sitting in front of her and tapped it on the floor for the tenth time that day. One of the shamans retrieved it, filled it at the window, and placed it in front of her. She drank. It had been twenty-three days since her last meal and her entire world had changed. She licked her lips. Had the rainbringer tradition forbidden drink as well as food, she'd be long gone.

The entrance doors swung open. None of the guards looked away from Yara.

Leaning on a cane, the island's chief healer hobbled into the room. A younger shaman followed, carrying a medical case. The healer handed his hat to a guard and waddled to Yara. "Good evening, dear. How are we feeling today?"

Yara shrugged.

The old healer dropped a knee and shaking, knelt down in front of her. "It's alright, Yara. You can talk to me."

She tilted her head.

He nodded.

"I thought I couldn't talk in the rainbringer hut." Yara rested her arms across her lap.

"Usually, no." The healer snapped a finger, signaling his attendant to put down the case. "We would normally remove you and talk in another hut—I'm told you've been there—but it is currently out of use." The healer laid his cane on the floor in front of him.

"Out of use? What happened?" Yara hoped the interrogation hut's sudden unavailability had something to do with Nika. The shamans were on Yara's nerves and the thought of Nika causing them trouble pleased her.

"It is simply undergoing some minor repairs." The healer dug around in his case.

Lies. Minor repairs would never happen during a storm, especially on a place as important as a secret interrogation room.

"How is your head feeling?" He dipped his fingers in a poultice and reached for Yara's head with his other hand.

Yara leaned in, unable to move her hair with her hands tied. "It's sore, but this sticky goop is helping."

The healer rubbed the poultice on her scalp, awakening a throbbing pain. "I'm surprised you're not concussed."

A stinging jolt shot down her neck. "Must be lucky."

"Must be." Wiping the remaining substance on a cloth, the healer packed up his things. "Is there anything else I can help you with, dear?" The attendant lifted the healer onto his feet and retrieved the cane.

Yara smiled up at him. "Just come back tomorrow."

Nodding, the healer turned for the door.

Yara eyed the guard at the waste room and stood up.

"Again?" The guard pouted, somehow unhappy that she needed to pee for the fifth time today.

Yara jerked her head at the cup on the floor.

The guard threw out his arms and slid the door to the waste room open.

Yara stepped inside and the door closed behind her.

Forty-seven seconds. That's how long her most recent break lasted before the guard started knocking. Her first trip to the waste room was about thirty seconds, as was the second. She needed to know how long she could be here without being disturbed. Her last hidden treasure was still sitting in a compartment reachable through the hole in the toilet. It would take a couple minutes to retrieve.

The guards were becoming more tolerant of her time in the waste room, not by much, but their initial uneasiness was wearing off. She just needed to find an excuse to be in here longer and her head injury gave her the perfect opportunity.

Yara sat down. She lifted both hands to her wound and scraped her nails into the poultice. The touching stung, but the pain did nothing to keep her from lifting the substance and plunging her fingers into her mouth. The poultice tasted bitter and grassy.

Her stomach churned. It was the first flavor she had tasted in weeks, but there was nothing pleasant about it. She swallowed and waited. Closing her eyes, she focused on the sound of rain around her, wondering if it would stop the moment the poultice reached her stomach. But the rainbringer trial involved two parts—starvation and temptation. She had once wondered if licking sweat off her hand counted as food, but decided it didn't fulfill the tempting part of the equation and was therefore safe. The poultice too was nothing of a temptation—at least according to her stomach. But if it did qualify, then she wouldn't have to dig around the hidden compartment underneath her.

The rain pattered the roof without the slightest break.

A heavy thud hit the door. "Hurry up."

"Almost done." Yara shook her head.

"No talking."

She relaxed, letting herself urinate in the hopes that the guard would somehow hear it over the rain and have no suspicions about her frequent trips to the waste room.

Her first plan seemed to have failed. Eating the poultice did nothing to disrupt the storm and Rajani's plans. Yara finished and knocked twice on the door. It slid open.

The back-up plan was now her best hope. She walked back to her spot on the floor and knelt down in front of the cup. If the poultice didn't count as food, it didn't matter. The small pot of honey under the waste room would. It was an emergency measure she had only thought of because of Manada Rii—the man who ate food and cut into his stomach so someone would know. If she too decided to eat in the hut, she should have had plenty of food to choose from. But if something went wrong, she'd need a backup. For once, her foresight would pay off.

For now, she needed to keep drinking water so she could keep returning to the waste room and eat medicine not meant for the stomach. It might take a few days, but it should make her sick, hopefully to the point of excessive vomiting. The guards would know she'd need to be in the waste room for long periods of time, allowing her time to retrieve the honey and eat something real.

She licked the grooves of her teeth, removing traces of the poultice, and swallowed. She wanted to smile, to see Rajani's face and laugh in it. If only the journal were still here and she could send him a message. Then she could tell him that this battle was far from won.

Nika

The battered seabed spirit rested against the wall of the cave. Heren had managed to bandage her wounds after treating them with ointments. Her breathing had steadied over the course of the day, a sign of improvement that slowly erased Heren's sullenness.

Heren patted the creature's leg, his eyes scanning her injuries once more. Most of the wounds were shallow cuts, but at least three plunged deep into her muscles—the mark of spears, a shaman's weapon. "I think she's finally resting."

"It seems the worst has passed." Nika clasped her hands together.

"I know we have work to do, but I could use some rest." He sat back, leaning against the wall.

Nika stretched her neck and bit her lip. "I'm not tired. What do you want me to do?"

Heren nodded, his baggy eyes making him look gaunt. "How fast can you read?"

"Faster than most." She stood up straight.

"Remember the books I kept in my basement written in code?" Heren pointed at the tables of books. "The originals, not written in code, are over there. I kept them here in case I never solved the mystery of the rainbringer and needed to pass on my research to a successor."

"Should I start at the beginning? With the first rainbringer?"

Heren shook his head. "No. Start with the rainbringer from last year. I am least familiar with her story and am most familiar with the earlier ones. Work your way backwards, chronologically. Then we can compare notes."

"Well..." Nika turned to the table, then back to Heren. "Is there anything I should know first? Since I'm skipping a hundred years of history."

"I should warn you." Heren coughed. "You are going to read some unsettling things about the shamans."

"I can't say I'm really sympathetic toward them anyway." She held out her hands and froze. "Except for you. I'm glad you're... well... different."

"We all have the same goal, Nika." Heren pushed himself upright. "You, me, the shamans. We want the same thing. And we're all failing. The shamans have tried to save this island from Ma'ha'lenti for a long time. They've done things, unsuccessful and admittedly horrible things, but they are on our side." A new life in his voice rose up. "Don't talk about them like they're villains."

"The rainbringer tradition is a failure and they're the ones in charge. And they're not the seventeen-year-old locked in a room starving to death." Nika put a hand on her hip. "They won't be tortured, killed, and turned into... this." She waved a hand at the sleeping spirit.

Heren tilted his head up, his glaring eyes meeting Nika's. He motioned to the sleeping spirit as Nika did. "They would be...this." The last word dripped with indignation. "If they could."

Nika stood back.

"The first rainbringer was *Udo Ba'ali*, an elder shaman. The second was his wife. The third, fourth, fifth, and sixth were their children. Every rainbringer until the fifty-fourth was either a shaman or a member of his family. This..." He motioned to the spirit. "...is *Ca'ari Una*, the last of her family, all of whom gave their lives in an effort to defeat *Ma'ha'lenti*." Heren sank back down to the ground.

Nika looked at her feet. "I didn't know."

"No you didn't. That's the point." Heren rubbed his head. "The shamans have done everything they can. The only reason shamans stopped being chosen as rainbringers is because *Ma'ha'lenti* forbade it." He stared up into the cave. "It wasn't working—the shamans, their families. They were, as he put it, unworthy."

Nika sat down next to him. "Who does *Ma'ha'lenti* think *is* worthy?"

A soft sigh escaped Heren's lips. "He doesn't know. Every time a rainbringer lasts longer than usual, he thinks he's getting closer to his goal—to a body. A physical and immortal form."

Nika rolled her head off the cavern wall. A glimmer of light reflected in his sunken eyes.

He sniffed. "This horrible tradition was designed by him to give him that body. The shamans have done everything they can to undermine him. They believe *Ma'ha'lenti* loses power as the storm passes. Every storm can only bring so much rain. Year by year, the rain falls. The longer a rainbringer survives, the more rain is depleted. One day, maybe, this storm will pass and with it... our doom."

The silence of the cave engulfed Nika. She shifted her feet, not wanting to look up. "After a hundred and two years, we might need a new strategy."

"That's why we're here." Heren pushed against the wall to bring himself to his feet. "But are we going to sit here and talk or are you going to go over there, read that book, and figure out how to save Yara's life?" Heren stomped past Nika.

Parting her hair, Nika looked up to see Heren place a torch on a stand at the table and start reading. "I thought you needed to rest."

"I do." He dropped himself into a chair. "But now I'm angry."

She picked up the torch left next to the sleeping spirit. A wave of admiration washed over her. Heren actually believed he could solve this problem—no, that wasn't quite right. He believed he and Nika could solve this problem—*the* problem. He believed whole-heartedly in someone else.

Her thoughts jumped to Yara. Something in the back of her mind told her that Yara would fail and Nika after that. They'd both be seabed spirits for however long it took for *Ma'ha'lenti* to succeed. It was time to stop listening to that thought. She and Yara would win this fight—and now they had an ally.

DAY 24

Yara

Yara hurled into the latrine of the waste room. Her stomach wrenched. Acid trailed her throat. She moaned out of nothing but instinct. Her plan was working. She'd spent the last hour hunched over the raised platform in the waste room that the shamans generously called a latrine. It was barely anything more than a hole in a seat. Her stomach clamped down as if being squeezed, sending more bile up her throat.

She wiped her arm across her brow, clearing the sweat that plastered strands of hair to her face.

"Normally, I'd give her a tea, but that's out of the question." The healer's soft voice floated to her ears. "Strange too. I was certain she wasn't concussed. Sadly, there's nothing I can do but keep an eye on her and make sure she's not getting worse." The waste room door was kept open, to her utmost annoyance, but made hearing the shamans easier. "This is usually the time when their bodies are weak and it's easy to contract disease. Are any of the men here sick?"

"No."

The healer hummed. "Odd though, that she'd fall ill so soon after the arrival of six guards in close quarters."

Yara spat into the hole. The grip on her stomach eased, but she doubted the relief would last long. She tried to take a deep breath, but found her lungs stuttering in their efforts.

"What do you want us to do?" The younger shaman sounded more fearful than caring, like he was in trouble.

"Replace the men here with others who we know have not been sick for at least a week. But keep tabs on the ones leaving. See if any of them develop symptoms in the next few days." He sighed. "And remove her hand ties. Is she not vulnerable enough?"

A jolt of excitement sparked in her. Her hands would be free. Now she just needed to get them to shut the door.

A shaman stepped up behind her. "Let me untie your restraints."

Nodding, Yara rolled onto her side and lifted her wrists.

The shaman tugged at the ends of the ropes until they loosened and fell into his hands.

Yara rubbed her wrists, soothing them from the burning the ropes had caused. Exhausting her strength, she pushed herself up onto the latrine and stared at the guard. "You're not going to want to see this."

The guard slid the door closed.

She plunged her arm into the hole, reaching an arm's length along the underside of the bamboo planks beneath her. Everything felt like how she left it, but a chilling fear that the honey was gone nagged her. This was the most important moment of her life and it would all be ruined if Rajani or anyone removed the honey. Her fingers found the wooden box she attached to the hut. The door was closed. She pushed her arm deeper into the latrine, giving her more room to pull out the pins of the box and reach inside.

"You okay in there?" Two raps sounded from the door.

"Yes." She forced a heave, hoping to sound pained. "Just pooping! Violently."

Her fingers found the last pin and pulled it. She reached for the box door, but her hand hit a wall. It had failed to open. She bit her tongue, choking back a scream. *Don't panic.* The latch felt stuck on one end, but part of it opened, leaving a space she could use to push the box clear. Nudging and tapping, the door to the box clicked open.

Yara looked up at the door, hoping it would keep shut. "Ugh." Her hand met the small pot and the world felt lighter. No one had found it. She pulled it up through the latrine and held it in her palm. Clicking the lid open, the sweet smell greeted her. Twenty-four days since she'd tasted something pleasant. Her stomach churned. She spun onto the floor and vomited into the hole.

The door slid open. "Everything all right?"

Yara pushed the pot of honey to her belly, hoping the bulk of the rainbringer dress hid its presence. She trembled as she nodded. "Yes." The acidic taste in her mouth filled her nose. With any luck, it also masked the scent of honey.

"Okay."

She focused on breathing. If she could catch her breath maybe her stomach would calm and she could eat.

"She's vomiting again." The shaman's voice was somber and all too easy to hear—a clear sign the idiot left the door ajar.

Yara looked over her shoulder and through the open door. Two guards were there. She was inches away from both the honey and the people bent on keeping her from it. Her stomach calmed once again—a temporary relief. She spat in the hole, failing to clear the taste of bile.

Hunched over and on her knees, she tried to relax, to let her stomach settle just enough to put some food inside it.

"You ready to come out? You can lay in bed."

Yara shook her head.

No response.

Her hand drifted toward the pot like a predator on the hunt, as if the smallest of movements would spoil her bounty. She dipped in two fingers. Ducking her head further, she choked back the vile remnants of vomit. Her heart raced.

"Are you sure you're all right?"

"Yes." Yara flinched. "Just catching my breath."

No response.

She lifted her fingers. The honey sagged, nearly dripping. With a flick of the wrist, she popped her honey-coated fingers into her mouth. The flavor blinded her—seizing every bit of her attention. Nothing had tasted so sweet, so pleasurable. It's as Rajani told her—the food inside the hut was the definition of divinity. Even the smallest drop of honey satisfied her entire being, as if she'd never spent weeks without food. Everything felt glorious. "I win."

A sharp pain cut through her abdomen as if someone were tearing her organs.

She screamed. Her body collapsed, falling to the side and dropping the honey.

"Yara?" The guard stood over her. His eyes darted back and forth. "What in the--?"

Burst of shocks rippled through her body like bolts of lightning.

Another voice screamed from the other room. His guttural yelps far louder than Yara's.

"Who is that?!" shouted one of the shamans.

"Go get the elders!" shouted another.

The world went silent. The wind vanished. The pattering of rain ceased.

Another scream cut through the hut.

Yara rolled herself over. The cracked door gave her a small view of the main room. A pale, emaciated man, cloaked in mist, writhed on the floor. Another wave of pains stung her whole body. She and the man screamed in unison.

The skeletal figure turned his head to Yara. Bearing his sharp teeth, he jutted out his jaw.

"What is he?" asked a shaman as he pressed himself against a wall.

A flurry of confused answers called back.

Yara looked out to him, meeting his glaring eyes with hers. "Rajani."

"Yara." The mist around him swirled, enveloping him in a cloud.

A deafening thunderclap exploded in the room and then the cloud and the man were gone.

The pattering of rain returned, bringing a hushing breeze with it.

A small weight fell on top of Yara. The object slid off her shoulder and landed in front of her face. The journal was back, but Rajani was gone.

———————

Nika

Nika dropped the 102nd rainbringer book on the table in front of Heren. "There. I finished last year's and now this one."

"You *are* a fast reader." Heren's eyes wandered up from his book.

"I can't say there was anything particularly insightful. We already knew Manada Rii had eaten something, but we still don't know why." Nika dragged a chair next to Heren and sank into it.

"Well, we have more information about the rainbringer tradition than anyone. If there is a solution to be found, we're the ones to find it." Heren turned a page.

"What if the answer isn't in these books?" Nika rubbed her eyes.

"What if it is?"

Nika scratched her head. Fatigue had finally caught up to her.

"You need to sleep," Heren said without looking up from his page.

"I need to help." Her arm propped her head up on the edge of the table.

"You'll be more helpful after you sleep."

Nika grunted in agreement. "Tell me something first. If the shamans were forbidden from being rainbringers, then they had to figure out how to choose them."

"And you're wondering how rainbringers are chosen."

"Yes." She leaned back in her chair. The memory of her appointment jumped to mind—the shamans tossing curved stones, reading their position and announcing her name. "Do random stones really reveal *Ma'ha'lenti's* will?"

Heren rested his book on the table. "No."

"I knew it."

"The foundation of the rainbringer tradition was invented by *Ma'ha'lenti*. When it became apparent it wasn't producing a habitable body for him, he blamed the shamans, forbid them from being rainbringers, and demanded they be the ones who choose."

"And what are the shamans' criteria?" Nika crossed her arms.

"The only goal the shamans ever had was to kill *Ma'ha'lenti*. They seemed to get better results with younger people, in the sense that they weakened him more. And he seemed pleased at the possibility of youth. But there have been many other factors over the years as they attempted to get different results—old, young, male, female, healthy, sick, everything. Sometimes a selection was made to eliminate people that might pose a threat to the tradition. Who would raise the most questions? Incite doubt? Interrupt their plans to save the island."

"Huh." Nika snorted out her nose and leaned forward. "I'm a threat?"

"Yes." Heren nodded.

"How?" She threw out her arms. "How am *I* a threat?"

"Yara." Heren picked up his book again. "She was the mortician's aide and asking questions the shamans did not want her to know the answers to. She was growing more and more problematic, unfortunately making her a prime candidate."

Nika clenched her fists. "And you think she compromised me."

"*I* do not think that." Heren paused. "But *they* did."

"And now they want me dead."

"Nobody wants you dead, Nika." Heren sniffled, his eyes looking puffy. "But if they don't choose someone, *Ma'ha'lenti* will drown this island and everyone on it. The shamans do not do this job happily. They know blood is on their hands. But they have saved this island for a hundred and three years."

Nika buried her head in her hands. Once again she wanted to

attack the shamans and their ways and once again Heren proved how wrong she was.

"Do you hear that?" Heren's book clapped shut.

Nika closed her eyes to listen. Nothing—and that was the problem. "The rain stopped." She looked up at the hole in the ceiling. "Yara. We should go."

Heren looked to the seabed spirit resting in the cavern. "I can't leave her. She's still hurting."

"Then you stay. I'm going." A surge of adrenaline fought back her fatigue.

"I don't think that's a good idea."

"I don't care." Nika grabbed the nearest torch and headed for the exit.

Yara's Journal

Rajani, are you here?

What's happening?

I want to talk. The guards have all left, if you couldn't tell. Maybe they figured out who you are and are tracking you down. If so, they're not here, and as far as I know, aren't coming back anytime soon.

Rajani?

DAY 25

Yara

Yara dug a fingernail into the grooves of her teeth, clearing shreds of chicken and spices. Everything tasted far more amazing than it ever had—savory, poignant, perfect. She'd spent the morning nibbling on the insides of a passion fruit, but her stomach didn't welcome anything. Her sickness had faded, but left her queasy. She hoped it would pass like any one of the times she had food poisoning, but even against her stomach's wishes, she still chewed on anything that smelled pleasant.

Tossing the empty plate across the room, she sank into bed. The sun rose hours ago, but the shamans hadn't returned after storming out when they saw she had eaten. No new food arrived, not that she didn't have plenty to choose from.

For the first time in ages, she couldn't think of what to do next. Now she was eating, she wasn't going to be dying. But last year's rain-bringer ate something and died all the same. Rajani's appearance was as shocking to the shamans as it was to her, which probably meant that nothing of the sort had ever happened before.

She curled up, her stomach churning in protest of the drumstick she'd picked clean. Maybe the shamans would return, remove the food, and let her die alone. Maybe they'd save time and just kill her themselves.

The guards were gone. Nika was gone. Rajani was gone—which had been more frightening than comforting. A night of clinging to her dagger did nothing to keep her from staying awake, flinching at every sound. But now the sun was up and she could rest her head. Her eyelids fluttered as she fought to stay alert, but it was a losing battle.

Nika

Peeking through the brush, Nika watched dozens of seabed spirits roam the shores at the rainbringer hut. One shaman stood guard at the entrance, but the path to the window was clear. Flashes of red sparkled as the spirits turned in their aimless tracks. Their colossal bodies shimmered in the light of the evening sun. Their monstrous frame and frightful visage gave her nightmares as a child. They once threatened to devour her, but now they scared her for another reason —they were her future.

She stepped onto the beach and dashed for the hut. One by one, the spirits faced her as she passed. Their crimson gazes threatened to paralyze her, locking her in fear. The rain was supposed to keep them at bay, but something was wrong with the rain and something was wrong with her long-held beliefs.

Ducking under the hut, she got down on all fours and searched the sand for the ladder. A sting met her hand. "Ow." Nika brushed the sand clear where something sharp lay hidden, revealing the broken end of a ladder. A lump hit her throat.

The shambling of heavy footsteps drummed toward her. One of the spirits approached at a snail's pace.

Nika leaned back, retreating between the bamboo stilts propping up the hut.

The spirit motioned to its belly, its claw swiping a collection of scars across its stomach.

Nika squinted.

The spirit's skin lit up, highlighting the scars in the shape of a word—stomach, but backwards and crossed-out.

Nika crept toward it. "Manada Rii?"

The spirit nodded.

"Can you help me?"

It nodded again.

She pulled herself out from under the hut and pointed to the window. "I need to get inside. Can you lift me?"

His fish-like nostrils flared as he reached out his monstrous claws.

Nika lifted her arms as the spirit gently picked her up and stretched toward the window. Even with the help of the spirit, she couldn't reach the sill. "Let me stand up."

Manada retracted his fingers, turning his palms into platforms.

Nika pushed against the hut's outer wall and stood up. Her fingers touched the window sill. She hopped, latching on and pulled herself up and through the window. Flopping onto the floor, she grunted.

"Nika?" Yara's familiar voice made Nika's eyes water.

"I'm here." Nika pushed her hair from her face and stood. "How are you?"

Yara sat up in bed. Dark circles clouded her eyes. Her slender, sullen face sent a chill through Nika. "I ate something."

Rushing to Yara's side, Nika sat down and wrapped her arms around her. "I thought so. I saw the rain stopped for a moment, but it came back. What's going on?"

Yara pulled back. "I don't know. Rajani faked the note. I knew I had to eat and I did. Then something happened. Something was pulled out of me—torn out of me."

Nika rubbed Yara's arm. "What does that mean?"

"Rajani. I saw him." Yara looked down. "He's not here. He has a body—a pale, weak body. But he disappeared. It was like he was..."

"Born." Nika slumped over. "He's alive."

Yara laid back in bed. "I think so. But why now? I wasn't the first rainbringer to eat inside this hut. I'm not even sure Manada Rii was. And now the shamans have abandoned me. I can't figure any of this out."

"I don't have answers either." Nika stood. "We need to leave. If Rajani is gone and the shamans aren't visiting, there's no reason for you to be here either."

"Where would I go?" Yara wheezed as she sat up and spun her feet out of bed.

"There's a cave about half a day away. Heren is there and he's helping us. If anyone can figure out what to do, it will be him. Where's your journal?"

Yara pointed to the waste room. "Who's Heren?"

"The shaman at the top of the mountain. The one you go to when you're appointed the next rainbringer." Nika collected the journal and pieces of the rainbringer dress on the floor.

"Oh, that guy. The young, but somehow gray-haired weirdo. I remember now." Yara reached out her arms as she stood, wobbling.

Nika wrapped the book in layers of cloth and hoped it would keep dry. If the key to defeating Rajani lay hidden inside the records—as Heren hoped—then the journal might be crucial. This time, she couldn't memorize the contents. They'd have to risk getting the journal wet. She put a hand on Yara's shoulder. "Are you okay?"

"Yeah." Yara took a deep breath through her nose. "Just a little light headed."

"Are you going to be able to travel? You look... weak."

"I'm good," Yara said, stumbling her way to the window.

Nika secured the wrapped journal in her waistband and made for the window. She stuck her head out, seeing Manada Rii staring up at her. "Hey, Manada, can you catch us?"

He nodded and lifted his claws.

"Okay, Yara, you first." Nika boosted Yara to the window sill and pushed her out. She stuck her head out to see Manada catch Yara and set her on the beach. "Glad that worked." Nika swung her legs out the window and dropped, landing in Manada's grip and then next to Yara.

"So you're friends with this guy?" Yara pointed to the spirit.

"Yeah." Nika turned to him. "Would you mind carrying her to a cave in the mountains?"

Manada nodded.

"Hey, I can walk."

Nika rolled her eyes. "No, she can't. Please just scoop her up and follow me."

"Agh!" Yara huffed as the spirit lifted her up and cradled her to his chest like an infant.

"Here." Nika lifted the journal up to Yara. "Try to keep this dry."

Yara took the book. "Are you going to explain any of this to me or do I just have to sit here smelling this fish-man and wonder what's going on?"

"We'll talk on the way." Nika set out along the shoreline.

DAY 26

Yara

"Well, he's never gonna fit inside." Yara looked up at Manada from the narrow passage of the cave's entrance.

Nika placed a hand on Manada's dangling arm. "Sorry. And thank you. I know there's another entrance that you could come through—a pool—but I don't know how to get to it." She shrugged. "It could be close, you could look for it if you want."

Manada nodded. His eyes shimmered.

"But please don't go too far." Nika stepped back toward the cave. "We might need you again."

The seabed spirit leaned up against the mountain wall and sank to the ground.

"Follow me." Nika nudged Yara to the side and stepped through the entrance. She lit a torch on the floor.

Yara held her journal to her chest. She'd managed to keep it mostly dry under the arched back of the seabed spirit on their walk to the cave. "Does it get any less cramped?"

"It will open up in a minute." Nika guided Yara through the mountain maze and turned a corner.

The cavern expanded into a giant room. A hole at the top welcomed a dim light. On the far end laid another seabed spirit next to a pool. On the other end sat a young man—a shaman—drowning in books. For someone with curly, gray hair, he looked somewhat handsome. The sight of him released a disgruntled annoyance inside her. Shamans—idiots. But at least this one was something she could enjoy looking at.

"Heren." Nika marched toward him.

He dropped his book on the table and stood. His eyes found Yara. "What's happening?"

"Actually..." Nika waved at Yara to join her and Heren at the table. "We were hoping you could help us figure that out."

Yara stepped closer to the Heren. "I ate inside the hut. The spirit there, who claims to be *Ma'ha'lenti*, appeared. He looked like a person—a man—pale, frail, and covered in mist. He was screaming in pain. I mean, so was I but I wasn't being a baby about it." Yara unwrapped the cloth covering her journal.

"Then it's over." Heren fell into his chair. "He's been born. He got exactly what he wanted."

"I'm not so sure about that." Yara handed Heren the journal.

"What's this?" He flipped through its pages.

"The journal I kept during my time in the rainbringer hut." Yara pushed some books to the side of the table and sat on the edge. "It's how Rajani and I communicated."

"Rajani?" Heren scanned the writing with a finger.

"That's what I named him." Yara leaned over the journal and turned its pages to Rajani's entry where he revealed himself to be the great rain spirit. "You know, before he told me he was *Ma'ha'lenti*. I didn't believe him, but I guess I was wrong."

"And what makes you think Rajani didn't get what he wanted?" Heren turned a page.

"He disappeared. He ran away." Yara's eyes glazed over as she looked up into the cave.

"Which is it?" Heren cleared his throat. "Did he disappear or did he run away?"

"Uh." Yara pursed her lips and squinted.

"Think." Heren uncrossed his legs and leaned closer. "We're treading into unknown territory. We need to understand what's going on—exactly."

Yara licked her lips. "There was a thunderclap and then he was gone."

"So we don't know if he disappeared or ran away or if those two things are the same." Heren leaned back and turned another page.

"Is that really any more helpful?" Yara scooted herself off the table.

"Yes." Heren flashed a glare. "And the last thing he said to you was that a cave won't save you?"

"What?" A chilling wave washed over Yara. "No. He said my name before he disappeared. That's the last communication we had."

"Then what's this?" Heren turned the journal to face Yara.

A cave won't save you.

Yara covered her mouth with a hand. Her head spun. "I hadn't seen that."

Nika took the journal. A panic filled her voice. "He knows we're here."

"Did he follow you?" Heren rushed to a pile of supplies in the corner of the room and began rummaging.

"We didn't see him or anyone." Nika marched to Heren's side.

"Rajani isn't active in the day." Yara paced the cavern floor. "And he wasn't responding to me in the journal. He'd made no contact since his birth."

Turning to Yara, Nika frowned. "He was listening to us. I told you while we were in the hut that I was going to bring you to the cave. That's how he knows."

"At least he can't leave the hut." Yara hugged herself.

Heren pulled a rusted spear out of his belongings. "What do you mean?"

"About two weeks ago, after the shamans took me out of the hut to interrogate me, I was trying to figure out a way to communicate with Nika. Rajani said he could go outside, but not very far. He'd lose consciousness. So he must still be in the hut, right?" Yara rubbed her arms.

Heren swung the spear around in the air. "We don't know how true that was then. And we can't be certain about that now."

Nika stepped away from Heren. "You expecting a fight?"

"Don't know." Heren gripped the spear with both hands. "But the cave isn't safe. We should leave."

"And go where?" Nika picked the rainbringer dress fragment off the floor and wrapped the journal in it.

Waves in the pool at the far end of the cave splashed against the rocky wall. A seabed spirit reached its claws out of the water.

"Ah. Manada must have found the entrance." Nika tucked the journal into her waistband.

The spirit rose, showing off its jagged teeth as it roared. Its glowing stomach bore no signs of blemish.

"That's not Manada." Yara grabbed Nika's arm and sprinted for the exit. Manada had been friendly, but always acted different from the rest of the spirits. He *was* different. He ate in the hut. He tried to communicate with Yara—and Nika. If this unfamiliar spirit appeared on the heels of Rajani's threat, it *was* the threat.

Thunderous pounding echoed through the cave.

"Ca'ari, go!" Heren let out a war cry and charged the enemy spirit.

Yara dared not look back. She reached a hand out in front of her, wishing she'd grabbed a torch before sprinting into the dark, narrowing hallways of the mountain.

More thunderous pounding sounded behind them, punctuated with Heren's shouts.

The cave's path split in two.

"This way." Nika side-stepped Yara, took her hand and pulled her through the cave.

A piercing light met Yara's eyes as they turned a corner. The exit loomed close. She turned back, hoping to see Heren, but finding nothing.

Yara crashed into Nika, not realizing she'd come to a stop. The two stumbled, landing on the ground outside.

The howl of the wind and the downpour of rain washed out the jungle sounds around them.

"What do we do?" Nika scanned the bush.

The cracking of felling trees erupted in front of them. A seabed spirit broke through the brush, charging toward them.

"Go, go, go!" Yara crawled on the ground, scrambling to get back up.

The spirit leapt over them, blocking the cave's entrance. It lifted a fist and swung, straight toward Yara.

She threw her hands in front of her and closed her eyes. "No!"

Silence.

Yara opened her eyes.

The rain stopped mid-fall. The droplets floated in the air. The spirit froze. Its fist hovered in front of Yara's face. She leaned back and lowered her hands. The spirit's fist relaxed and fell to its side. The muscles in its face drooped, looking like a subdued creature on the brink of sleep.

Yara looked to Nika who met her with wide eyes.

The rain shook, vibrating as if it didn't know which direction was down. A pressure swelled up inside Yara. She crawled away from the spirit, fighting her body as if it weighed as much as a boulder.

Every raindrop sat suspended in the air, then fell a foot before floating once again. The spirit clenched its fist and pulled back to swing.

"No!" Yara stood her ground.

The spirit froze.

"What's happening?" Nika fled to Yara's side.

"I think I'm controlling it, but something's fighting me." Yara clenched her jaw, focusing her gaze on the spirit in front of her.

"Rajani?" Nika picked a rock off the ground and held it up as if to pitch it.

"That's my guess too." The feeling in Yara's hands faded, leaving a cool numbness behind.

"Now what?"

"Uh..." Yara stared down the spirit. "Go to sleep."

Its eyelids flickered.

"Go to sleep. Go to sleep. Go to sleep. Go to sleep." Yara stepped closer to it.

The spirit swayed. Its fist fell, guiding its body to the ground with a thud.

The rainfall returned to normal. The weight inside Yara lifted.

Nika tossed her rock and stood over the sleeping spirit. "Well that's new."

"Nika? Yara?" The words echoed from the cave. Heren dashed outside, panting and holding his ribs. Blood ran down his face.

Nika ran to him. "Are you okay?"

"Eh." He shrugged. "I'll be fine."

A crash tore through the trees, revealing another seabed spirit.

Yara held up her fists.

The spirit paused and stood back. It motioned to the scratches on its belly.

"Manada?" Yara relaxed.

He nodded.

"You're not going to attack us, yeah?"

He shook his head.

"Good." Yara turned to Heren. "Can you explain why some of them are nice and some of them are trying to eat me?"

Heren lowered himself to the ground. "I believe the good ones are the rainbringers who ate during their time in the hut. The rest are mindless creatures." He jutted his chin toward the sleeping spirit. "I don't know this spirit. Why is it—how is it asleep right now? Shouldn't it be one that *Ma'ha'lenti* sent to kill us?"

"Yeah." Yara scratched her cheek. "I don't know how I did it, but I made it fall asleep."

Nika tore a strip of cloth off the journal and held it to Heren's head. "We need to find a safe place to go."

"Well, my secret cave is compromised." Heren looked back into the passageway. "And my home has been nothing more than scorched stone walls at this point."

Nika cleared blood from a fresh cut on Heren's face. "It's not like we can go to my parents'."

"Or mine." Yara walked past the sleeping spirit, keeping an eye on it in case it awakened. "And the rainbringer hut seems like the last place we want to be."

Nika dropped the bloodied cloth and tore more off the journal's wrapping. "Heren's home is two days away. We need to find safety *now*. Who knows how many of these things are out there?" She waved a hand at the sleeping spirit, then looked to Manada. "No offense."

"There are one hundred and one." Heren winced. He took the cloth from Nika and held it to his head. "But four of them are friendly."

"Great." Nika combed her hands through her hair. "We're outnumbered twenty-five to one."

"You know we could get there a lot faster if these hefty friends of ours don't mind carrying us." Yara turned to Manada and forced a smile.

He nodded.

Yara pointed to the cave. "Is your other friend... okay? Can she help?"

Heren nodded. "Ca'ari Una. And yes, she can help. We managed to knock out the spirit that attacked us in the cave. She'll be waiting for me at the pool's entrance."

"You didn't kill it?" Yara put her hands on her hips.

"No." Heren stood.

Yara couldn't help but scowl. She hadn't killed the one that attacked her either, but she didn't have a spear.

A fire lit in Heren's eyes. "They're people, Yara."

"Do they look like people to you?!" She threw her arms toward Manada, then over to the slumbering spirit.

Heren looked up into Manada's red eyes. "It doesn't matter what they *look* like."

Guilt sunk in. Yara looked over her shoulder at Manada and whispered an apology. "Well, let's get going then."

DAY 27

Nika

"We're close." Heren reappeared out of the jungle, carrying an armful of mangos.

Nika looked up from the rock she rested her head against. Hours of rhythmic stomping in the arms of a seabed spirit didn't afford her as much sleep as she'd hoped. She didn't want to complain—the former rainbringers looked far more exhausted hunched over on the ground. Ca'ari in particular looked spent as she favored her uninjured leg. As unrested as Nika felt, at least she'd put some sleep in her bones for the first time in over a day.

"Thank you." Yara plucked a mango out of Heren's arms.

He tossed one to Nika. "We shouldn't rest much longer."

She pulled back the mango skin and bit into it. Its juices seeped from the corners of her mouth. "I have a question for you, Heren."

"Hm?" He tucked his fruit into the pocket of his robes.

"You said there were four rainbringers who ate in the hut and they are more in control of themselves as seabed spirits, yeah?" The sweet taste erased her grogginess.

"Yes. Yara is the fifth."

Yara tossed her empty mango skin. "I would have thought there were more."

Heren shrugged a shoulder.

Resting back against the rock, Nika set down her mango. "Where are the other two?"

"Probably at the beach." Heren walked up to Ca'ari Una, inspecting her bandages. "I've met them. They both tried to help me at one point, but have since given up. Over time, they seemed to become more and more... like the others."

"That's stupid." Yara sat down cross-legged.

"Yara." Nika frowned. "I'm sure it's not easy after all they've been through."

"Giving up isn't going to help." Yara scrunched her face. The rain slowed, floating down to the ground as if something were working against it. "Ah ha!" She threw a hand in the air. "I just did that."

"So you can control it?" Heren put his hand on Ca'ari's cheek and looked into her eyes. He smiled and turned away.

"A little bit. It's hard." Yara scrunched her face again, but the rain-fall kept steady.

"Finally, some good news. Maybe this will be the key to killing Rajani." Nika bit into the last of her mango.

Heren crouched next to Manada. He ran his fingers along the spirit's belly, tracing the scars. "We're lucky Manada ate two years ago. They seem to behave more human-like when they haven't been in a spirit body for as long. Although, they tend to wander around, trying to catch glimpses of the families they left behind."

Nika clutched her chest. "That's so sad."

"I can't imagine how hard it must be." Heren looked Manada in his eyes and gave a nod. "They see their families once a year. Their kids are one year older and they think the spirits are monsters. I would probably lose hope too."

Nika shook her head. "No, you wouldn't."

Heren froze for a second. The hint of a smile crossed his face.

The rain picked up, falling heavier.

"Blast it." Yara grunted. "I've lost control."

Stomping sounded in the jungle underbrush from every direction.

"Something's coming." Nika ran to Manada.

"We got to go." Heren grabbed Yara and ran to Ca'ari.

A seabed spirit burst through the trees, landing in front of them. It snarled like thunder.

Manada leapt onto it, wrestling it to the ground.

"I can help." Yara broke free of Heren's grip and dashed to the spirits. She threw her hands in front of her. "Sleep."

The violent spirit went limp. Manada picked up Yara and jumped to Nika.

Another wave of booming footsteps rattled the ground. Four more spirits tore through the trees. Rays of red glinted from all sides.

Manada picked up Nika and held her to his chest.

"Sleep." Yara reached an arm out to the closest spirit. "Sleep."

It paced back and forth.

"This isn't working." Nika looked up at Manada. "We need to make a run for it."

Heren's voice broke through the sound of the downpour. "Follow us."

Manada fled.

The world blurred. Trees and rocks whirred past as the spirit charged through the jungle. Rain splattered Nika's face, making it near impossible to see the chaos around her. The wind howled. Manada's grip tightened, feeling like it would crush Nika any second.

Shrill bellows and volcanic footsteps shook the air.

Nika's heart drummed. Her nerves kept her still. She blocked the rain with her arm. The pathway zoomed past underfoot, but finally looked familiar.

An unseen strike knocked them off course. Nika flew through the air, free of Manada's protection. The ground sped toward her. She spun, landing on her side. Her shoulder cracked. She rolled through a small clearing. Whipping her head around, she looked up and wiped mud from her eyes. They'd arrived at the scorched remains of Heren's home.

"Sleep!" Yara screamed at a spirit wobbling in its tracks as if deciding whether or not to obey.

A warm claw took hold of Nika's leg. The spirit wore no bandages, nor had scars—an enemy. She screamed.

It dragged her along the ground.

She reached for something near—a rock, a branch, anything. "Yara!" Her hand met a loose stick. She flung her body to it, nearly missing as she slid through the brush. Nika swatted the spirit's claw.

It pressed on without a flinch.

She swung her body up, reaching forward and stabbed the spirit's hand.

The branch cut through its skin, forcing a pained bellow from its maw. It released her and reached to remove the stick.

Nika scrambled to her feet and ran.

"Get inside!" Heren limped to his home.

Yara ran up to him.

Manada and Ca'ari stood back to back, staring down a circle of enemy spirits.

One by one, they took their place in a ring of monstrous bodies surrounding the clearing. Each stilled, no longer shrieking.

Jolts of pain shot up from Nika's leg. Her shoulder ached. She dashed to Heren and looked around. "They stopped."

He nodded.

Yara scanned the spirits. "But why?"

More monsters took their place in the circle of enemies around the hut. They stood, shoulder to shoulder, unwavering.

Nika opened what was left of the burnt door. "Why do I get the feeling we are exactly where Rajani wants us to be?"

Heren ducked inside. Yara followed.

"Manada, Ca'ari," Nika called. "You just yell if things out here get messy."

Manada nodded.

She walked inside, closing the door behind her. Piles of ashes filled the room. Only the kettle on the hearth remained intact. "What now?"

DAY 28

Yara

The afternoon sun peeked out from the clouds on the horizon. Yara sat at the center of the clearing in front of Heren's stone hut. Rain poured over her like a waterfall. She exhaled. The rain relented. She inhaled. It drenched her.

The spirits shifted in their circle around her and the hut. Their heads tilted as a rumbling growl escaped their tongues. They hunched over, digging their claws in the ground, looking like angry animals behind a fence.

She reached an arm out. "Sleep."

The closest spirit punched the ground.

Her shoulders slumped, fighting a new weight in her muscles. It wasn't Yara keeping the spirits at bay. Hours of commanding the rain to ebb and flow started to feel more intuitive, but did nothing to control the spirits. Rajani wouldn't let her.

"You're a butt." She rested her hands in her lap. The extra weight dissipated. "A pale, misty, stupid, dirty monkey butt." She stood and pointed a finger to the sky. "You hear me?!"

Nika swung open the door to the hut. "Everything all right?"

"Yeah." Yara stomped inside.

"Any progress?" Heren stared out the window.

"No." Yara bent over and wrung out her hair. "The rain will listen to me, but the spirits won't. Not right now. I don't know what I'm doing wrong."

Heren turned around and offered her his dry robe. "I think we should go to the shamans for help."

"No." Nika beat Yara to saying it. "I don't trust them."

"Neither do I." Yara dismissed the robe with a scowl and a wave. "They've failed to kill Rajani for a hundred years. When was the last time they even made any progress toward that goal? And why would they even listen to us?"

"And how would we even get to them?" Nika pointed outside.

"Yeah." Yara pointed too. "We're a little trapped, if you haven't noticed."

"I hear your concerns." Heren picked up Yara's swaddled journal. "But if you can't move the spirits and we can't stay here, then we need to make a deal." He unwrapped the journal and handed it to Yara.

"You want me to ask Rajani for help?" She snatched the journal from him and rifled through the pages.

"Do you have any better ideas?" Heren looked back and forth between the girls.

"This is insane. He is the enemy. The last thing he is going to do is help us." Yara clapped the book shut and tucked it into her armpit. "He probably can't even write in it. We've only ever written each other while in the rainbringer hut."

Nika took Heren's dry robe and pulled the journal from Yara. "But if he is the one controlling the spirits and keeping them from attacking us, then he knows we're here." She wiped down the journal. "Maybe they're outside, because Rajani wants us in here to talk."

"So we're just going to give him exactly what he wants?" Yara jerked the robe from Nika's hands and patted her face.

"Let's at least find out what he wants. It's only to our advantage to have as much information as possible." Heren grabbed a glass ink bottle from the window sill. "Then we can figure out how best to move forward. Talking to Ma'ha'lenti isn't giving up, Yara. This is only the next move."

"How do you have ink?" Nika took the bottle.

"Before I burnt down the place, I buried some supplies for when I returned." He pulled a plume from the window sill.

"You're the one who burnt down this place?" Yara took the plume from Heren. "I thought this was your home."

"I did it to cover my tracks." Heren nodded, expressionless.

"That I can respect." Yara lightly punched his shoulder.

Nika handed the ink to Yara. "He also framed me in the process."

Yara shrugged. "Still...."

Nika glared. "But we still don't know if Rajani can respond when we're not in the rainbringer hut."

"Then perhaps we're in luck." Heren took his wet robe and draped it over the window sill.

"How's that?" Yara sat on the floor.

Heren pointed around the room. "This is the original rainbringer hut, the one the shamans used when the tradition was done in secret."

Nika nodded, looking around the room as if seeing it for the first time.

Yara uncorked the bottle and dipped the plume. "Well, let's see what our friend has to say. Although I should warn you that he might not respond until after sunset."

Yara's Journal

Hey there, Monkey Butt! You still alive, pale, and ugly as sin?

Go back to the rainbringer hut.

Finally! I've been waiting for hours. So are you in the room or somehow doing this from somewhere else? Your whole nature is a little confusing to me. Probably because you've lied to me so much.

Go back. Now.

In case you didn't know, I'm actually in a rainbringer hut already. It's the original. So, we can do whatever you want while I'm here. No need to travel all the way down to the beach just to say hello and make amends.

I see you've decided to be annoying.

Not annoying. Just genuine. This is who I am when I'm not hungry and irritable. I guess you've never really seen this side of me.

You're tiresome and I'm growing impatient.

Tell me, Rajani, what exactly do you want from me? I'm not going to starve to death anymore. So I'm not just going to sit inside a hut and wait for my demise. The storm can keep going forever for all I care.

My name is Ma'ha'lenti. And do you really think it's a good idea for a storm to last forever?

Isn't that your goal? To live forever? To be the spirit of a storm living inside a weird-looking man's body? Because that's the impression you're giving me. If you want something else, you might need to change some things—starting with your personality.

You don't understand your past.

I've never been one for history. I'm more the type of person who likes to charge head-first into the future.

> *If you don't head back to the hut, the only future will be me raining down on this island until it sinks back into the ocean.*

If you can.

> *You doubt me? Such foolishness.*

If you destroyed the island, you would never get what you want.

> *If I destroy this island, like I have done others, then I will move on to the next.*
> *I am the grand tempest, the Ma'ha'lenti, the most powerful of all storms.*

But you still need the help of a 17-year-old girl.

> *Thirty-four of my seabed pets are standing outside that hut. On my command, they will tear down that house, stone by stone, and drag you back to the beach.*
> *If you fight them, I will kill that shaman and the two spirit traitors with him. If you defy me, I will send more to your village and squash the life out of your parents.*
> *Or you can go willingly.*

Tough choice. On one hand, my parents have had quite the life and could probably use the rest after parenting *me*—a literal nightmare. On the other hand, I am not really in the mood to be dragged down a mountain. It could mess up my hair.

> *So you agree?*

Fine. But only if you leave everyone else alone. Nika, Heren, and the two traitors (you have to know that you calling them traitors makes me like them more, right?) will get to go back to the village and live a happy life holding hands and singing songs.

Fine. Bring the journal.

DAY 29

Nika

The rain dispersed overhead as everyone set out down the mountain trail. Nika leaned on her walking stick, stepping on the moss between the stones on the pass so she wouldn't slip. Yara walked behind her, followed by Heren, Manada, Ca'ari and three dozen hostile seabed spirits.

"I'll try to keep us as dry as possible." Yara hopped down a step. "But I can't seem to erase the storm completely."

The downpour parted on either side as if they were walking in a bubble.

"Now that you've cleared the clouds above us, I'd guess it's about midday." Heren joined Yara at her side. "Can we talk now?"

"Yeah. Rajani should be sleeping. Not that I'm sure he could hear us either way, but daytime is safest." Yara took the lead and turning around, stopped the procession. "I think I know how to kill Rajani."

"What?" Nika's eyes wandered. Yara's trademark confidence always made her at least a little nervous, if not entirely. "How?"

"How do I know or how do we kill him?" She flashed a smile.

Nika rolled her eyes. "Yes."

"He's a storm spirit, right?"

Heren nodded.

Yara pointed at him. "Then all we have to do is make the storm die out, right? Just like any other storm. That's what the shamans have been trying to do for decades after all."

Nika gave Heren an uncertain look. The logic sounded more poetic than factual. "True, but, I mean... It's a cute idea, in theory...."

"Cute...idea?" Yara crossed her arms. Her sudden grimace made Nika squirm.

Heren stroked his chin. "This time might be different. Past rainbriners haven't had any control over the storm." He turned to Yara. "You think you can take control and make it die out?"

"Yeah." Yara eyed Nika. "I do."

Nika rolled back her head. "You *just* said that you couldn't erase the storm completely."

"I'm getting better at it." Yara hit her palm with a fist. "Trust me. I can do this."

"You don't know that." Nika stared her down. "And we don't have much time for you to master this new power."

"Sure we do." Yara tapped her nose. "I'm not starving anymore. And we won't reach the rainbringer hut for about two days. I'll keep practicing."

Heren played with his jaw. "I agree with Nika."

The words put her at ease. "Thank you." She never had much success convincing Yara of anything on her own.

Yara glowered.

"It's too risky. We don't know how to do it or if it would even work." He crossed his arms. "We need a better plan."

"We have a great plan." Yara looked Heren over.

"And if you're wrong and it fails?" Nika straightened her stance, bolstered by Heren's support. "If you can't take control of the storm? If draining all the rain from the clouds doesn't kill him, what then?"

Yara tucked in her chin. Her eyes flitted back and forth.

"Rajani wins." Nika leaned toward Yara. "A tyrannical god claims our home for eternity. We've seen him kill before. He most certainly will kill you, me, Heren, and anyone else who dares oppose him."

Yara bit her lip. "I still have to go to the rainbringer hut. It's not like we have a lot of choice in that matter." Her countenance softened. "That will at least buy us some time. Then Heren will go to the shamans and convince them to fight Rajani and his horde of monsters."

Heren tilted his head. His eyes flinched as he scowled.

Yara threw out her hands. "I mean former rainbringer... monster things. Sorry, they're monsters. They're huge, fishy, muscle-monsters. I'm not saying it's a bad thing. I like it."

Yara and Heren locked eyes.

Nika poked Heren's shoulder. "I don't like you going to the shamans alone." She tapped Yara's leg with her walking stick. "And I don't like you going back into that hut alone either."

Yara put her hands on her hips. "I don't think Rajani is going to be happy if I bring company over. I think he was looking forward to a cozy night in."

"And if I call an all-hands meeting of the shamans, you won't be allowed to join us." Heren looked at the ground.

Nika refused to feel useless, but didn't know where to go. Yara returning to the hut would undoubtedly put her in the most danger. Nika's presence might help. But Yara was right—Rajani would not be happy about it and who knows how he'd respond? At least Yara thought she'd be fine—if not safe until Heren talked to the shamans and brought her an army... a small army.

"You don't call an all-hands shaman meeting then." Nika prodded Heren with her stick. "We call a meeting with everyone, shamans and non-shamans alike. We'll get the whole village together."

"Why?" Heren's face lit up.

Nika looked into his eyes, sensing a spark of curiosity. "It's time we stopped putting the responsibility of this island on the shamans' shoulders. We all live here. We all deserve to know what's going on and we should all have a say in what to do next."

"That sounds like chaos." Yara swiped a strand of hair out of her face.

"Maybe." Nika's mind jumped to the villagers and her election as the next rainbringer. They all looked so relieved when Nika was chosen and each and every one of them had escaped death. All she would need to do is convince them that acting now—fighting now— would let them escape such a terrible fate once and for all. "But I don't think it'll be chaos. They're scared. They don't know what to think. So we tell them what to think. We show them a better way."

Heren grabbed Nika's shoulder. "Well now I definitely want to make sure you're at this meeting, because I'm not sure I am the man for the job."

A warmth flushed Nika's face. She looked away and smiled.

"Don't you two get cute on me." Yara punched Nika's arm.

"Ow." Nika rubbed her arm where a bruise would soon appear. She felt like Heren—unfit for such a lofty job. But it needed to be done and there was no one else to do it.

"So we can all agree on the plan, then, right?" Yara leaned in. "Right?"

"Yes." Nika took in a deep breath.

Heren nodded.

"Good." Yara turned around and started down the trail. "Let's go find out how this all goes wrong."

DAY 31

Yara

Yara stood in front of the rainbringer hut and lifted an arm. She breathed out her nose, willing the storm to ease up over the hut. The rain complied. A sunbeam broke through the clouds, warming Yara's skin.

"Good luck." Nika embraced Yara.

"You too." Yara looked up from the hug at Heren. "You take care of my girl."

Heren gave a quick nod.

Nika pulled back. "We'll be back as soon as possible. Manada and Ca'ari will stay outside. Shout if you need something."

Yara nodded.

Nika and Heren took off along the beach, disappearing in the rain.

Yara pushed up the latch, unlocking the door and creaking it open. A strange sense of home filled her. She shook her head as if dispelling the idea that this hut was full of happy memories. No, it just felt familiar and everything was still in its place.

The two tables were still covered in food—cooked boar, chicken, plates of fruit, and bowls of rice. Her bed rested under a mosquito net at the far side. The waste room door was open, giving a peek into the small space. The outermost layers of the rainbringer dress lay in a clump on the floor. "Rajani? Did you miss me?" She picked up a passion fruit on her way to the window sill.

No response came—not that she expected one. Rajani almost never made contact in the day. Now that he had a body, she didn't know if anything had changed, but all signs pointed to no.

Yara tossed her journal on the floor and clicked open a panel on the window sill. She slid a bamboo slat into the wall and plunged her arm down into the hiding space. A wooden box met her fingers and she pulled it up. The dagger felt heavier than she remembered, but having it back in her hands filled her with glee. She'd finally get to use it, now that she knew who deserved a stab.

She pulled the hanging net down from the ceiling and threw it to the side. Plopping herself onto the bed, she cut open the passion fruit and sucked on its contents. The sour taste tickled her mouth. The sensation spread through her body, waking it from an achy torpor. If her gut was right, she'd have half a day to binge on food, strengthen her body, and practice controlling the storm. Then night would fall, Rajani would reveal himself, and if she were lucky, she'd get to put her dagger to good use.

Nika

The crowd under the canopy rumbled in confusion. Nika sat near the front of the arena, closest to the council of elders facing the rest of the villagers. More people spilled into the crowd, mumbling questions about why everyone was gathering. Her parents sat off to the side. She tried to prepare them for the meeting, but no amount of reassurance had eased their concerns.

One of the elders stood. His rise sent a hush over the crowd, giving way to the sounds of the wind against the trees. "I apologize for bringing you all here this evening without an explanation. But you see, I do not know myself and I am too growing rather impatient as we wait. So please, Heren, tell us why this gathering needed to be done so urgently."

Heren stood. "Actually, I am not the one who will be addressing the village this evening."

The elder hobbled toward him. "Then why were you the one who called upon us?"

"Because I knew you would listen to me." Heren bowed. "And I worried that Nika's pleas would fall on deaf ears."

The elder furrowed his brow.

The crowd broke into a restless hum.

Nika stepped in front of everyone. "I know you are all frustrated and a bit confused as to what's going on." She fidgeted, feeling self-conscious about how she stood. "But this is a matter of life and death —not just mine, but everyone's. It's an emergency. The rainbringer tradition has failed."

Annoyed moans and murmurs reached Nika's ears.

The elder turned to Heren. "What is she talking about, Heren?"

"Just listen to her, please." Heren bowed at the elder once more.

The elder pursed his lips and waved a hand, silencing the crowd.

Nika bowed to the elder. "Thank you." She took a step forward and calmed herself with a deep breath. Her guts felt twisted. She wiped her clammy palms on her skirt. "As I'm sure you all noticed, the rain stopped for a moment seven days ago."

People in the crowd exchanged knowing looks with each other, a mixture of concern and confusion apparent in their expressions. It was the exact reaction Nika wanted. They needed to understand that everything had changed. The evidence existed. They were witness to it, even if they didn't know.

"That happened because Yara..." Nika paused. She didn't want anyone jumping on the fact that Yara ate without knowing she was the first. The conversation could all too easily be steered in a direction she didn't want it to go. She needed to keep them from blaming Yara for any of this. If Nika were to succeed in swaying them to action, they needed to be on Yara's side. "The rain stopped at the moment Yara became the fifth rainbringer to eat inside the hut." The second after she said this felt like an hour. Her teeth jittered in anticipation of the village's response.

The crowd held still. They looked almost like a painting, if it hadn't been for the wind tousling their hair and clothes.

This was the moment she hoped for—a second to tell everyone what to think and how to feel before their fears set in and they tried to figure it out themselves. Nika cleared her throat. "Now we have a chance to end the rainbringer tradition forever."

"Why would we end something that protects us?" A disgruntled voice cut through the crowd.

Nika looked to Heren for encouragement.

He mouthed the words, 'Keep going'.

She fought back a lump in her throat and swallowed. "Because it is failing to protect us. The seabed spirits we were taught to fear are not the monsters we thought. They are the spirits of the former rainbringers."

Shouting and gasping erupted. Nika couldn't tell if their shock came from this new information or their utter dismay that she would say something so brazen.

"Lies!" called one of the shamans behind her.

"It's the truth!" Heren shouted back.

"Please, listen." Nika clasped her hands together.

The roar of the crowd continued before falling into an instant silence.

Nika turned back to see the eldest shaman, his hand lifted. He waved to her. "Please, continue. We're listening."

"Really?" The knot in Nika's stomach loosened.

"She speaks the truth." The elder bowed his head—another

signal that commanded silence from the people. "We, the shamans, know that things have changed this year. Permanently. They can't continue how they've been. We've failed you." He gestured toward the crowd, then turned to Nika. "Share what you know."

Nika's breathing stuttered. "Our great rain spirit, *Ma'ha'lenti*, is the one who threatens the island. He's tried to gain a human body for over a century in an effort to live forever. He forced the shamans to cooperate with his instructions, which led to the rainbringer tradition, but they've managed to keep him from being born into a human life. That is, until this year. He's here. He's alive. And we have one chance to stop him."

Inaudible rumblings of the crowd spread like fire.

"You lied to us!" A brooding man pointed a finger at the shamans.

The crowd hushed, seemingly unsure of how to act.

"Why should we trust you?" A woman pushed her way to the front.

Nika stepped between the man and the shamans. "Yes, they lied." She stared her down. "And I don't like it either."

The woman relaxed, but kept her jaw clenched.

Nika walked back to the center of the arena. "But they did it for the good of the island. You would have done the same thing if you were them. And we are on the same side. We need as much strength as we can muster—that means working together."

"What are we supposed to do?" A voice called out.

"Yara, our current rainbringer, is able to control the rainbringer storm." Nika's shoulders tensed.

"She's learning." Heren spoke up. His face looked apologetic, as if he knew his correction would weaken Nika's position. But his insistence on accurate information was ever present.

"That's impossible," said the voice from the midst of the buzzing crowd.

Nika looked down at her hands, realizing she'd been squeezing them into fists. "I know it sounds impossible, but I have seen her do it."

"As have I." Heren walked up behind Nika. "Everything she's said is true." His presence eased her worries, letting her stomach untangle itself.

She looked back into the crowd. "If Yara can take control of the storm and let it die out, then *Ma'ha'lenti* might die with it."

"Great. Then have her do it." The brooding man leaned on his knees.

"It's not that easy." Nika reminded herself to breathe. "*Ma'ha'lenti* will fight her. He can also control most of the seabed spirits."

"What do you want us to do? Fight them?" A woman stepped out from the crowd, an infant in her arms.

Nika closed her eyes.

Heren put a hand on her shoulder. His touch soothed her.

She opened her eyes and looked at the woman. "Only long enough to give Yara a chance to defeat *Ma'ha'lenti.*"

The sound of rainfall filled the air.

The woman shook her head. "You can't be serious." She cupped her child's head and rocked him in her arms.

"We have no choice." Nika found an empty stool and stood on top of it. The extra height gave her a better view of the crowd. She searched them, looking for any person who might be swayed to listen. "We cannot go back to the way things were. No matter what we choose to do, the tradition is dead. *Ma'ha'lenti* is here. He will kill any of you to get what he wants. That's what he's been doing for a hundred years—killing with no regard for a person's life, young or old."

A middle-aged man nodded along with her words. Nika locked eyes with him. If she could convince him to agree, the tide of the conversation might turn.

"You." She pointed at the man. "You would do anything to protect your family, right?"

He gave a quick nod. "Of course."

Nika spread out her arms, gesturing to people on both sides. "As I'm sure all of you would. Now is the time to test your resolve. A battle has reached our shores. Will we lay down our weapons and surrender to a tyrant or will you pick up your weapons and claim what is rightfully yours?" Nika's words surprised her as if she had convinced even herself. "Your home, your future, your *children's* future is in your hands. What are you going to do with it?"

More and more of the crowd nodded along. Determined looks spread like ink in water.

A wave of hope washed over Nika. The fear of battle greeted her, but her hands held steady. "It is time to fight."

"No." The voice of an elder shaman shattered the energy of the meeting.

Nika's jaw went slack. Her hands felt cold. A tenseness crawled over her back. With one word, everything seemed to slip out of her hands—the people, the future, and Yara's life.

"It would be a slaughter." An elder shaman walked in front of Nika. "One of the seabed spirits attacked a few days ago. We lost five good men. Four more were injured trying to keep one of them from destroying one of the shaman huts last week. There's no chance of us standing up to them. We are miserably outmuscled."

Nika clasped her hands together. "What else are we going to do? We have to do something."

The shaman shook his head. "The storm is too strong. *Ma'ha'lenti* has fully awakened. If this were the beginning of the storm, it would be a different story, but we're too late. The best we can hope for is that Yara dies and *Ma'ha'lenti* becomes dormant for another year."

"And then what?" A sharpness stung Nika's gut. "We can't just give up on Yara."

The shaman frowned. "There's nothing we can do. If we fight now, we lose. Then what was the point of all the rainbringers' sacrifices— including Yara's?" He swept his gaze away from Nika, ending the conversation in an instant.

"Let's just go. There's no point in being here," whispered one shaman to another.

"As if a girl would know anything about *Ma'ha'lenti*," whispered a third.

The crowd dissolved into pockets of conversations as people peeled off from the gathering.

"The shamans are right. We can't fight the spirits." A voice trailed off into the wind.

"They're too strong."

"What does this mean?"

"Our hands are tied."

The crowd shrunk until only Nika's parents remained. Her mother whispered to her father, frowning as she threw glances Nika's way.

Nika dropped from the stool and looked at Heren. "What do we do now?"

He bit his lip and shook his head. "I don't know.

Yara's Journal

I can't tell if you're not here or if you're just ignoring me.

You know, for someone who begged me to come back, you certainly like keeping a girl waiting. I know you missed my company. I'm delightful.

Rajani.

Rajani?

Ugh, fine, *Ma'ha'lenti*. Although I will say that Rajani is a much better name. You should change it, but I do want credit for it.

Seriously, where are you? I thought you'd be here rubbing my feet by now.

Are you dead?

Did I win?

Should I leave?

Stay.

At long last! How's my favorite, evil rain spirit doing?

*We are nearing the end, Yara. I suppose I must thank you. I
am not sure how you pulled it off, but you are the one
who succeeded and brought me into this world. And
your death will seal my fate.*

And then what? You disappear for another year? What exactly do
you do when you're not terrorizing the island? I mean, most of the
year you're just not here.

I wait. I rest. I lie dormant.

Boring.

It's almost sunrise. Enjoy your last day taking breath.

Yeah. I should throw a party or something. You're not invited
though. Nah. I take that back. You can come. But you have to be nice
to my other friends. I want them to like you.

DAY 32

Nika

"There has to be *something* we can do." Nika swung open the door to the rainbringer hut.

Yara sat up in bed. "That sounds like it's going to be bad news."

"Well, it's not good news." Heren closed the door behind him as he stepped inside.

"We met with the shamans and most of the village last night." Nika paced the floor. "They won't fight."

"We don't have the manpower." Heren knelt in front of the bed. "They are convinced any sort of fight would result in a slaughter." He shot Nika a sullen look. "And I agree."

"They want to try again next year." Nika threw a mango against the wall. Its juicy contents exploded in a satisfying squish.

Yara yawned. "Why do they think they'd be better off next year?"

Nika threw another mango. "Apparently, Rajani is weaker at the beginning of the storm. His memory seems to reset every year—not completely. He remembers things, but it takes time before he's fully awakened."

"My records corroborate the idea." Heren folded his hands in his lap. "But we're at a point where Rajani is at full strength. One of his seabed spirits can kill a dozen men before being taken down. We don't have the numbers. And who knows how much destruction Rajani can cause now that he's come into the physical world?"

Yara joined Nika at the food tables. She picked up a guava and hucked it. "So now what?"

Nika grabbed a chicken and broke off a leg. "We're still trying to come up with a plan." She threw the breast and bit into the leg. The chicken bumped the wall and flopped onto the floor.

Yara pointed at the leg. "Pretty good, right?"

Nika licked her lips. "I've had worse."

Heren spun around on the floor. "Can we keep talking or do you want more time throwing food against the wall?"

"Hold on." Yara grabbed the underside of the table and jerked upward. The table budged.

"Here." Nika took hold of it and the two toppled the table, sending fruit rolling on the floor.

"Do you feel better now?" Heren rubbed his temple.

"No." Nika kicked a passion fruit. "But I don't feel worse."

"I'm just here to party." Yara stepped onto a roasted boar, digging her heel into it.

Nika huffed. She grabbed a watermelon and held it over her head. "What happened in here last night? Any contact with Rajani?" The watermelon flew into the wall, sending bits of it in all directions.

"He wasn't very chatty last night, but we did talk." Yara paused. "There's not much to report back to you guys, sadly." A hint of dread informed her voice, slight enough to go unnoticed by anyone other than her best friend.

"What's wrong?" Nika's eyes narrowed as they locked on Yara.

Yara shook her head. "Nothing. Other than the lack of a plan." A forced smile failed to wipe away the sadness in her eyes. "What's our next move?"

Nika wiped her hands on her skirt. "Not sure. Heren wants to talk to just the elder shamans."

"You should do that." Yara perked up.

"I don't think it's gonna do any good." Nika sat in the mess and flicked a nearby grape across the room.

Heren stood. "They know things are different now. They may not want to fight, but they do want to help."

Nika glared up at Heren. "Yeah, help everyone but Yara."

The pattering of rain sat between them.

Nika picked up a bowl of rice and picked at it. "I'll stay here with Yara. We'll think of something."

"No." Yara nudged Nika with her foot. "Rajani wants me here alone. And seeing as how he's become more violent, it is safest for everyone if you don't stay. Plus, there's no one I'd rather have on the outside advocating for me."

An unsettling instinct told Nika to refuse. Something didn't feel right and it was tugging at her. She peered at Yara as if to see through whatever façade was plastered on her face, but she couldn't see past it. "Okay. If that's where you want me, that's where I'll be."

Yara offered a hand and pulled Nika to her feet. "Besides, I want to keep throwing food around. Although knowing how much of a disaster I tend to be, I might wind up flinging a bone into my eye and walking away with a really ugly scar across my face." She winked.

"Maybe more than one." Nika embraced Yara.

Heren headed for the exit. "We'll be back with good news—one way or the other. I promise."

"Thanks, weirdo." Yara looked at Nika face to face and whispered, "I guess I'll like him if you think he's cute."

Nika punched Yara in the arm and walked away. "Be safe."

"That's not really how I like to do things." Yara kicked a dragon-fruit at the door.

Nika dodged. "I love you."

"I love you too." Yara tapped her heart and pointed to Nika. She turned her attention to Heren. "Not you though. I barely know you."

Heren nodded and led Nika out the door.

Yara's Journal

My dear, sweet baby boy, Rajani,

It's me—your mother. I guess that's what I am. Although I am far too young to have kids. But let me be the first to say, I've kept my figure. In fact, I've really slimmed down over this past month. I do not recommend my lifestyle though. No eating for weeks? No thank you. And just because it worked for me, does not mean it is good for you. Learn from my mistakes.

Let me give you some advice, as your mother. Play nice with other kids, unless they're evil rain spirits bent on the destruction of everything you hold dear. In that case, beat them to a pulp and show them who's boss. Fight dirty if you have to. Kick 'em where it hurts.

That's what I'm going to do if I ever see myself pitted against a violent nature spirit. I will hurt them. I will kill them. I will not die without a fight. I will not lose without going to war. I will not give up even if my lungs stop breathing or my heart stops beating or my head stops thinking. I am a fighter and my enemies will learn to fear me.

Also, try to not be late to things. It's very inconsiderate of people's time.

See you tonight.

With love,
Mother Yara

Yara

One candle lit up the waste room. Another stood by the bed. The rest lay scattered around the hut, shining in the dark corners of the room. The last sat at Yara's side as she perched under the windowsill.

Yara held the unsheathed dagger in front of her. Candlelight flickered in its reflection. She swallowed hard and put the tip of the blade to her forehead. Holding her breath, she dragged the edge of the blade across her face, fighting the urge to wince. It stung, more pointedly than she expected, but she wasn't cutting deep—just enough to leave a scar. The blade cut across her brow, down the bridge of her nose, and onto her cheek. Blood followed.

"Let's do this." She stood. "Rajani, where are you?"

The last of the sunlight disappeared. A wave of thunder rattled the hut.

"Rajani, I told you it's rude to be late. Don't keep your mother waiting." She reaffirmed her grip on the dagger. "Don't tell me you're going to threaten my life and then not show. I raised you better than that. The least you could do is make good on your promises."

A creak from the corner of the room made Yara jump. She held the dagger in that direction. The rain outside grew heavier.

Yara looked down at the journal at her feet. She scanned the room, but saw no sign of anyone—let alone a boney, misty entity ready to attack.

"Come on. No point in making me wait. Either you can kill me easily or you just like making empty threats. Either way, let's get this over with."

The candles flickered in unison. The room remained silent.

"Fine." Yara picked up her journal and dropped it out the window. "We'll do this the hard way." She walked to the bed and kicked the candle over.

The flame met the rainbringer dress on the floor, igniting it. The room grew brighter, casting strong shadows on the walls.

Yara dragged the mosquito net to the far corner of the room and held it over a candle. The fire ate into the net and spread onto the wall. The bed mat lit up in flames. Yara set a candle at the leg of the table, then kicked over the one in the waste room before turning to the window.

"Now are you gonna come out, you miserable, little child?" Yara held the dagger out. She took in a deep breath. A cool numbness entered her fingers as the storm outside softened. Her back tightened as a heaviness plummeted from her throat into her stomach. "So you *are* here."

The smoke of the fire swirled at the center of the room. In its midst appeared a man—bald, pale, peaked, and angry. "Is this your plan? Take away the hut so I have no home?"

"So this is your home, then?" Yara released her hold on the storm.

"No." Rajani stepped forward. "This is my cradle." He crouched as if to pounce. His thin fingers sharpened into claws. "And your grave."

Yara ran toward him and swiped the dagger.

He scratched her arm as he dodged.

Her foot swung, connecting with his ribs and knocking him to the ground. "You clearly have never been in a fight." She thrust the dagger, but Rajani vanished in a cloud and a flash. She whipped around.

His grip met her throat.

She stabbed the dagger into his belly, but it met no resistance. Air escaped her. Her head dizzied. She swiped the dagger across Rajani's arm, but hit nothing. His hand puffed away, freeing her.

"You can't kill me." Rajani dropped and swung his leg over the floor, knocking Yara off her feet.

She landed on her back. The dagger fell out of her hand with a metallic clang. She reached for it, but Rajani stomped on her arm.

Yara tried to pull it free, but couldn't fight Rajani's strength. She closed her eyes—focusing on the storm. Every ounce of strength poured into her wish to disperse the rain, clear the clouds, and end

Rajani's life. Numbness flooded her, spreading from her fingertips, up her arms, and into her veins.

"Your efforts are pitiful." Rajani tensed his shoulders. He bent down, meeting her eyes with his crimson stare. "You're not strong enough to take the storm."

The weight of the storm sank into Yara's muscles, smashing her into the floor. She pushed against it, but the wave of Rajani's will overpowered her.

"Look at you. So sad. To think a starving, young girl would have the strength to kill me." Rajani bent over, his face inches from hers. Swirls of crimson danced in his eyes. "You'd have to be a lot stronger than that to be *my* equal."

"Thanks for the tip." Yara threw her head into Rajani's.

His foot slipped off her arm as he recoiled.

Yara rolled over, grabbing the dagger. "I have a question for you, son. Year after year, decade after decade, each rainbringer dies inside these walls. So how is it you never get what you want?" Yara brandished the dagger.

Rajani hunched over, ready to strike. "I'm getting exactly what I want."

Yara chuckled. "I used to think I would kill you and live the rest of my life as a hero."

"Well, you were never the brightest." Rajani flashed his jagged teeth.

"I may not be strong enough to best you, but I guess I can still die the hero and send you back to sleep for another year." Yara spun the dagger around in her palm and plunged it into her heart.

"No!" Rajani lunged forward. His body dissolved into a fog.

She slumped onto the ground. Warm flames encircled her. The faint sound of rain faded. Her chest felt like she was being ripped in two. The pain took over, extinguishing every other thought—only alleviated by the world getting darker.

DAY 33

Nika

The waves lapped up on shore under the morning sun, calm for the first time in a month. Nika sat in the sand, holding her knees, staring at the blackened remains of the rainbringer hut. Everything sounded silent. Her eyes dried. She reminded herself to blink.

Shamans dug through the rubble of the hut, tossing charred bamboo out of their way. They talked, but sounded muffled as if underwater.

Birds flew overhead, but Nika heard no squawk.

The world blurred as tears seeped into her vision. She cleared her eyes with a thumb.

A jumbled voice talked behind her.

She cleared her throat and ignored it. Yara was dead. That thought kept everything else out.

"Nika." Heren sat at her side. "Nika." His tone softened, no longer trying to catch her attention. He placed a hand on her shoulder. "We found the journal." He placed it at her feet.

She buried her head in her arms. "So?"

"You should read the last entry." He turned the pages to Yara's final words.

Nika peeked over her knees and read the pages. Yara's playful tone and not-so-subtle invitation to fight Rajani cut a new wound in Nika's heart. It was the last time she'd hear the words Yara used. This was the end.

"It seems there was more to this fire than we first thought." Heren closed the book and rested it at Nika's side. "We should review Yara's journal, see what we can learn."

Nika shook her head. "No." She pushed out her cheek with her tongue, trying to keep the tears from flowing. "I can't. We lost. Yara's gone." She sniffled. "And I'm next."

"We don't truly know what's happened or what lies ahead." Heren patted her back. "Rajani might be dead, but he might still be alive and..." He paused and made an audible gulp. "And residing in you right now." He rested his hand on her shoulder. "It's like Yara said, giving up doesn't help."

Nika pulled away from Heren's touch. "She's gone. The best I can hope for is to win this fight a year too late? Then what? Spend my life knowing I failed Yara and only saved myself."

"Yourself and everyone that would follow after you." Heren withdrew his hand.

"Just leave me alone." Nika ducked her face under her arms, blocking out all signs of the outside world.

"Nika, I understand you need some time, but you've overlooked something." Heren's voice turned stern.

"And what's that?" Nika turned her head and pursed her lips.

"You tell me." Heren pushed the journal toward her.

She looked at the cover of the book. Something spoke to her—a quiet voice telling her something was there, but she couldn't quite hear it. She put her hand on the journal. The voice spoke up. "This journal isn't burnt." She bit her lip.

"That's right. And what does that suggest to you?" Heren fought back the grin of a proud mentor.

"She saved it. She wanted to make sure it survived... which means she thought it would be useful to us." A hint of peace broke into the overwhelming flood of guilt and dread.

"I think so too." Heren bowed his head.

Chatter around the hut burst with excitement. A shaman on shore waved a hand at Heren. "Hey!" He cupped his hands over his mouth. "We found the body."

Nika sprang to her feet and dashed to the shore.

A couple shamans dragged a dark, limp figure to the dry sand and laid it out. Both of them brushed sand off their hands and stood over it, catching their breath.

The tattered clothes were singed, the skin dark red or entirely black. Nika slowed as Yara's face became visible. Her hair was charred and her face blistered, but her lifelessness was what made her shrink. Yara was never so muted. This was not her.

Nika held a hand over her mouth. She squinted, not sure if she should look away. A line across Yara's face caught her attention. The quiet voice in her head returned, whispering too softly to hear.

"Go on, take her to the graveyard," Heren said behind Nika as he caught up to her.

She buried her head in his shoulder. "I should have stayed with her. I could have helped."

Heren pulled Nika aside and wrapped his arms around her. "Don't do that to yourself. This isn't your fault."

She sniffed. A heavy dread settled inside her. Yara was gone. Her head was next on the chopping block and for the first time, she didn't care.

DAY 34

Yara

Bubbles. The swishing of moving water reached Yara. It sounded muffled as if she were pushing her palms against her ears. There was a faint stench in her nose and a saltiness on her tongue.

She rolled over, slower than intended. Her arms seemed to float. Her whole body seemed to float. It felt like a dream she once had of drifting up into the sky, but heavier. Something pushed down on every inch of her. Everything was dark—blacker than any night. She forced her eyes open. A coolness met them. She blinked, seeing nothing. A strange film covered her eyes like a second pair of eyelids. Yara looked back and forth, pushing her pupils against the film.

She squeezed her hand into a fist. Her fingers felt thicker than normal. And longer. She caressed her arm. Its muscles bulged. She couldn't wrap her hand around her bicep.

A flood of memories hit her—the rainbringer hut, Rajani, the fire.

She patted her chest, then her face. She looked up—or what she assumed was up.

It worked. She had turned herself into a seabed spirit. The rain-bringer ritual continued—probably. But if she were here, which she was—unless the afterlife was really just the bottom of the ocean—then that meant the rainbringer tradition *did* continue. Rajani hadn't won. She'd get the chance to have a real fight with him. If only she knew how long it had been since the fire.

A silver light grew in the distance. It took the shape of a seabed spirit. She hoped it was Manada Rii or the other one that was friends with Heren—whatever her name was. Otherwise it was an enemy.

"Yara." The voice cut through the deep as if coming from inside Yara's head.

"Who's there?" The words spilled out of her even though it didn't feel like her mouth was making them.

"It's Manada." The illuminated spirit hopped off the ocean floor and swam toward her. "The rainbringer ceremonies have started again. *Ma'ha'lenti*, she's awake."

"She?" Yara felt as if she were scrunching her brow, but wasn't sure her new face was capable of such a movement. "You mean *he*."

"In my time, she had the voice of a woman." His glowing body brightened as he approached. "But you always referred to Rajani as a man. I was confused at the time, but obviously couldn't say anything."

"Strange." Yara kicked off the ocean floor. "Rajani definitely sounded and looked like a man to me. He even told me he was male. But..." The rest of Manada's words finally registered. "He's awake? So he *did* go dormant?"

"I can only assume. When he wakes up, we wake up. And now we're awake."

Yara nodded, but wasn't sure if her thick neck gave her enough mobility to make that clear.

"We need to go." A flash of red shot out of Manada's eyes.

"Back to the island?" Yara spread her arms and pushed herself through the water. She moved so freely, it felt easier than walking.

"Yes." Manada reached Yara and kept himself in place with small kicks. "I think something's wrong. The other spirits are headed straight for the island. Last year they meandered for a while."

"Last year?" Yara let herself sink. It made sense. The seabed spirits returned once a year—they must go dormant, like Rajani, between seasons. "We've been down here a year?"

"Yes."

Her mind jumped to Nika, wondering what she had done with the time. But Yara's plan worked. She bought Nika and the others time while also making herself a much stronger adversary. Yara stretched out her legs, warming up the muscles. "Rajani must be gathering the spirits."

"We should hurry." Manada kicked off, headed in a seemingly random direction.

Yara swam after him. "How long does it take to get there?"

"Seven days if we're slow. Six if we hurry." He accelerated, leaving a trail of bubbles. "Try to keep up."

<hr>

Day 34
Year 2 – Day 1

Nika

The door to the new rainbringer hut latched closed. Nika walked to the small table at the far end of the room. A single piece of fruit sat on top—an apple, by her request.

A slight breeze kicked up, blowing through the open windows and tousling her hair. Memories of her days spent in the hut returned. But this time, there was no bed. There weren't giant tables decorated in food. Windows stretched around the entire room. The door didn't lock. A platoon of armed shamans stood outside, listening for the cue from Nika to storm the room and attack Rajani.

She leaned her spear against the wall. Her hands felt naked without it after spending months familiarizing herself with its movements like a newfound limb. She tapped the knives strapped to her arms, checking for the hundredth time that they were secure. The leather straps on her thigh chaffed her skin. The daggers there were heavier and required tighter bonds.

The sky dimmed under dark clouds. The prelude of a storm sent rain droplets to the roof like scattered notes.

She bit into the apple and swallowed. No sharp pain followed like she expected from Yara's recounting of eating the honey.

"Nika." A deep voice sang her name behind her.

She swept up the spear and pointed it at the pale man standing across the room. "Rajani." His skin shined like pearls. Soft muscles rippled over his body—a far cry from the starving image Yara saw a year ago.

"Is that any way to greet a guest?" Rajani folded his arms and lifted his legs into a sitting position as he floated in the air.

"Only an unwelcome guest." Nika changed her stance, freeing her to burst into a strike.

"Silly me. I was under the impression that the spear was meant for me—which is practically an invitation." He folded his hands in his lap like the shamans do when they meditate.

"I thought you didn't like to talk. You said it was... uncomfortable." Nika's eyes snuck a glance outside, hoping to see the shamans there. She reminded herself to focus on Rajani.

"Oh, I've grown so much since then. I really have you to thank for that." Wisps of gray mist floated around Rajani like clouds.

"And why's that?" Nika relaxed her shoulders, suddenly aware of how tense she'd become.

"Oh, you don't know?" Rajani smiled, flashing sharp teeth. "I would have thought you'd have figured it out by now."

Nika took a step toward the fifth window from the front. She glanced at an 'x' etched into the panel third up from the floor. "You'll have to explain it to me."

"Playing dumb, I see." A flash of light illuminated the small clouds around Rajani. "I know the shamans have no plans to appoint another rainbringer. Not this year, not ever." He twiddled his thumbs. "That makes you the last one. How historical."

"Well, we weren't much pleased with the way you've been treating the rainbringers. Inhabiting one until she died—or ate, then transporting yourself to the next appointed." Nika took another step closer to the 'x'. "So why appoint another? Might as well just end the line of succession."

"Bold, but pointless." His eyes flashed red.

"Yeah, we decided we're not interested in being controlled by a tyrannical ghost any longer." Nika kept her eyes on Rajani, looking for any sign that her movements might alert him.

"I'm sure your efforts to thwart me gave you hope." Another flash of light reflected off his skin. "But the truth is, you've done me favor."

"I'm sure you'll repay me, somehow." Nika stood in front of her mark.

"You still don't see it? You, a chosen rainbringer, ate inside the hut before today—but after you were chosen. I did not think it would matter at the time, you weren't the current rainbringer." He laughed to himself. "But in that moment, one year ago, you ended your appointment."

"Which is to say...?" Nika raised her spear.

"My being is transferred to the next rainbringer when they die... or when they eat—*if* they eat." A grin spread across his face, wider than a human's could.

Nika stiffened. Rajani's glee finally made sense. When Yara ate, Rajani should have transferred to the next rainbringer, Nika. But Nika had eaten inside the hut already, disqualifying her. With no rainbringer to follow Yara, that gave Rajani nowhere to go—except the physical world.

"Ah." He tapped his head. "So you've figured it out."

Nika clenched her jaw and tightened her grip on the spear.

Rajani drifted in the air. "If it weren't for you, I wouldn't have been born. Then Yara might still be alive."

Anger surged inside her. She kicked her heel into the 'x' on the wall.

A hatch door opened above Rajani. A pile of rocks dropped on top of him, sending him face-first into the floor. A pained cry escaped his lips.

Nika threw her spear into another marking across the room.

The floor below Rajani opened, swallowing him and the rocks.

Nika fetched her spear and rushed to the hole in the floor. Bamboo spikes shot up from the sand below. Rocks lay scattered about them, but no blood—nor Rajani.

A kick to the back sent Nika flying. "You must think you're clever."

Nika rolled onto her feet. She held up the spear. "I am clever —NOW!"

Footsteps pounded outside the doors. Shamans burst into the room, weapons in hand.

Nika charged.

Rajani dodged, moving through the air as if swimming through calm tides. He swatted away flying knives from the hands of the shamans. His fist met Nika's face.

Her head dizzied. Blackness erased her vision.

Sounds of guards yelling swarmed her.

She held her head as the blackness faded and the world stopped spinning.

Rajani kicked a guard into the open hole. A scream cried out below.

Nika unstrapped the knives on her legs and threw one at Rajani's chest.

He caught it mid-flight and threw it back.

It nicked her arm as she ducked. Grabbing her spear, she stuck it into the floor and launched herself into the air. Her foot slammed into Rajani. They tumbled to the ground.

He spun around. The gray clouds expanded into a shroud around his entire body.

Nika pulled a knife off her arm and threw it at a mark in the wall.

A puff of dust fell over him, dirtying the air.

He coughed and wheezed as he fell to the floor.

Nika covered her mouth and nose with a cloth wrapped around her neck. One breath of the dusty air would put her to sleep. She and Heren had perfected the concoction based on the drug he once used against her.

Pulling the last knife from her arm, she pitched it at Rajani's brow.

The knife passed through Rajani's head and lodged into a bamboo tile.

The gray clouds dissipated, taking Rajani with them.

Nika scanned the room, hunting for her prey. The rain tapped the roof. Pained grunts came from injured shamans. She reclaimed her spear and announced to the room, "He's gone."

She looked down the hole. A pair of shamans carried their bloodied friend off the sand. The wounded guard held his leg. "He all right?"

A shaman looked up and nodded. "He'll live."

Heren ran up the steps and into the room, his spear in hand. "What happened?"

Nika shook her head. "He got away."

Heren relaxed and swung his spear onto a strap on his back. "Well, there's no way I'm letting you stay in here alone."

"There's no point in me being in here." Nika looked around.

"What do you mean?" Heren helped a shaman up from the floor.

"I'm not the rainbringer." She wiped sweat from her brow. "And I already used my favorite traps."

Heren's face sobered. "It's as we feared, huh?"

She nodded. "My eating in here last year did exactly what we didn't want it to do."

"So you won't be able to control the storm?" Heren ducked under the arm of a shaman and held him upright.

"Nope." Nika walked outside. "We'll just have to wait for Yara and put up the best fight we can." She looked out onto the shores and the fortifications they'd built over the last year—trenches, pits, spiked barricades, and archery towers. "I just hope she gets here soon."

YEAR 2 - DAY 6

Yara

S ix straight days of swimming did nothing to tire Yara's new body. She swiped her arms to the side, speeding her along.

The sunlight scattered under the surface of the ocean. Manada kicked hard, moving in front of Yara. "We're almost there."

"Where are the others?" Yara looked back, expecting to see the rest of the seabed spirits racing to the shore.

"Don't know. Last I saw them was a few hours ago." Manada breached the surface.

The warm air greeted her face as she joined Manada. The island loomed in the distance, wreathed in thunderclouds. A longing for it burned within her. It had been a year since her death, but she only remembered the last six days. Still, she ached to be there.

"You sure Nika and the others won't attack us on sight?" Manada swam in place.

"Positive." She headed toward shore. "I left her enough clues to figure out what happened before I burnt down the hut. I'm sure she figured it out."

Miles passed like mere footsteps. Towers and barricades came into view. The sight confused her for a moment, before she realized just how much preparation Nika must have put into the impending battle. Yara kept reassuring Manada that she was confident in the clues she left behind, but her fears weren't extinguished until she saw Nika's defenses.

The water shallowed. Swimming turned to running, which was more difficult and far slower, but at long last, she was standing on dry ground.

Groups of shamans gathered on walkways suspended between the towers. A horn blew. Archers drew their arrows.

"Still sure they won't attack?" Manada crouched, half-turned toward the safety of the water.

"Just wait." Yara waved an arm, then dragged a finger across the scar on her face. Only then did she notice that it cut across her face in the wrong direction. It was like the word 'stomach' on Manada's belly —backwards. The memory of the dagger slicing her skin still stung, but it was the surest way she could think of to tell Nika she would return as a seabed spirit. *Although knowing how much of a disaster I tend to be... I might walk away with a really ugly scar across my face.*

Yara would have told Nika the plan had she not feared Nika's resistance. But with the shamans thwarting all effort to rally the people, she got desperate—and inspired. Her last journal entry wasn't just meant to threaten Rajani. It was for Nika. *I will not give up even if my lungs stop breathing or my heart stops beating or my head stops thinking.* The island needed time and muscle, so that's what Yara gave them.

A wall of spikes stood between Yara and the towers. The spikes stuck out of the sand diagonally, making them impossible to climb. A hole in the wall opened up like a secret door. A welcoming face revealed herself.

Nika stepped forward. A mixed look of concern and joy painted her face. "Yara?"

"It's me!" She threw up her giant claws.

Manada shook his head. "She can't understand you."

Nika took a deep breath. "Are you in control of yourself?"

Yara stopped to think of how to answer. She stuck a finger in her mouth, swirled it around, then plugged it in Manada's ear.

"Hey." He pulled back and slapped her hand.

"Stay right there." Nika ran along the wall, picking a seemingly random spot to cross from the barricade to the shoreline. She threw her arms around Yara's leg. "I'm so glad you're okay." She tilted her chin up and scrunched her face. "Well, at least alive—in some way or another."

Yara patted Nika's back.

Nika let go and wiped a tear from her cheek. She looked at Manada's belly, then up to his face. "Hello Manada."

He bowed his head.

"You two follow me." She headed back on the strange path she took to meet them. "There are pits here on the beach." She pointed at various spots. "They're deep enough for a seabed spirit to get trapped in one—hopefully."

Yara looked over the beach. No part of the sand looked any different from the rest. She wanted to tell Nika how impressed she was, but could do nothing more than make a mental note to tell her later—somehow.

A gateway opened up in the barricade, just large enough for Yara and Manada to squeeze through. On the other side, shamans and islanders busied themselves manning the defenses. Each of them carried weapons, either in hand or strapped to their backs.

Nika pointed at a line of palm fronds circling the towers. "This is a trench filled with kindling. Once Rajani arrives, we'll light it. Although it might not last long. He'll probably wash it out the moment it ignites." She huffed, then looked up at Yara. "I was hoping I could control the storm like you did. You know, keep the fires lit and disperse the storm." Her hand ran up and down her arm. "But I can't. I won't explain now, but I'm not the rainbringer. No one is."

Yara looked up into the clouds. The rain was still light, barely landing on her face. She wasn't sure if it would listen to her, but she told it to cease.

Raindrops stopped falling and hung in the air.

"Are you the one doing this?" Manada waved a hand, moving raindrops around like bubbles.

"Yara?" Nika tapped a raindrop. A smile crept onto her face.

Numbness sunk into Yara's fingers. She retreated into her mind and told the storm to dissipate. A crushing weight knocked her to the ground. Sand splashed into her eyes.

"Yara!" Nika crouched next to her.

Yara let go of her command and the rain continued to fall.

"It's Rajani, isn't it?" Nika placed her hand on Yara's.

Yara pushed herself off the ground. She snarled in an attempt to confirm Nika's suspicion. Rajani was fighting back and he felt stronger than when they skirmished last year. A latent fear awakened, making her feel like she was sinking into the sand. She thought if she returned with a stronger body, she'd have a better chance of defeating Rajani. Now she wasn't sure it would make any difference. Her death —her sacrifice—may have been pointless.

Nika tugged at Yara's hand. "Let's get you behind the towers and into your armor."

"Armor?" Manada looked at Yara.

"That's probably a bit confusing." Nika faked a laugh. "We'll be fighting a lot of seabed spirits and we don't want to get you mixed up with the others. Plus, it will help protect you."

Yara and Manada both nodded.

Nika waved at some guards to join them. "We don't know when Rajani and the seabed spirits will show up, but we have guards on alert at all times. They'll let us know when we're needed."

Yara stretched her neck and shoulders. She looked up at the sky, not sure if she wanted to try to control the storm again.

"We also have something to show you in the armory." Nika turned around. Her cheeks flushed. "I don't know how to say this without sounding a bit... uh, morbid." She scratched her neck. "Let me just show you."

Nika led the way to the canopy just through the tree line. The ground opened into a hallway, barely too short for Yara and Manada to stand upright. Torches lit the staircase that plunged deep into the earth.

The air cooled as they walked into the darkness. Yara's mind raced trying to imagine something Nika would consider morbid—but also something she'd *want* to show Yara. According to Nika, Yara was the morbid one because she worked as a mortician's assistant and had a strange fascination with death. But to Nika, 'morbid' could mean anything as insignificant as a dead fish.

The hallway opened into a large room. Yara stood back, trying to make sense of the scene in front of her. Motionless bodies lined either side of the room—dozens of them, maybe 80, maybe more. She couldn't tell. There were too many to count. She looked closer. Each was dressed in burial garments, but not one of them looked dead—until she stared long enough to see that they weren't breathing.

Nika clasped her hands behind her back. "These are the rain-bringers."

Manada stepped next to Yara. His face changed, struggling to express something through his monstrous features. "Why would they bring them here? And how are they all so... healthy-looking?"

"I dug up your grave last year. Your body was healthy then too." She pointed a finger at his belly. "That's when you got that new scratch across your stomach. I did that to your human body."

Nika walked up to Manada and pointed at the words written on his skin. "You seem to get the idea, I think." She craned her neck to look into Yara's eyes. "Thanks to your journal, we learned a few important things. Including the fact that rainbringer bodies don't decay. In fact, they seem to heal." She paced back and forth, a habit she fell into whenever she lectured. "And because of the scratch given to Manada by Yara, we learned that we can affect the spirit bodies through the human bodies. So..." Nika's voice trailed off as she marched to the corner of the room and picked up a large rock. "We're going to break their arms and legs."

Yara looked to Manada. "So that's what she meant by morbid."

"Well..." Nika shrugged a shoulder. "If we have to." She folded her arms and shifted her weight to her other foot. "I was hoping I could control the spirits like you did last year, maybe even get them to fight on our side." Her eyes met Yara's. "But now maybe you can. We'll have to see when they get here. And if it turns out we *can't* take control of the spirits, then—" She held her fists side-by-side and broke them apart as if snapping a twig. "Got it?"

Yara nodded. A mixture of pride and fear whirled inside her. Nika had done so much more preparation than Yara could have anticipated, but she still didn't know if it would be enough.

A group of shamans entered into the room, carrying bulky sheets of bamboo plating.

"Ah, your armor." Nika waved the shamans toward Yara. "Let's get you two ready."

The shamans spread the giant armor across the floor and went to work strapping it to Manada and Yara's legs and arms.

"I'm sure you're wondering where your bodies are." Nika took a rope from a shaman and looped it around Manada's shin. "They're somewhere else. We wanted to separate you from the spirits under Rajani's control. We're gonna try to save them, but if we can't, then we're gonna cave in this whole room."

YEAR 2 - DAY 7

Nika

The horns blew as the sun set. Shades of orange and violet painted the sky.

Nika ran up the stairs to the top of the nearest tower. Her heart thumped in her chest. Shamans and villagers sprinted to their posts.

The shores were empty. Lightning struck in the distance. Rain dripped out of the sky like the last drops from a bottle. On the horizon, a wall of water gushed out of the heavens and loomed closer with every second.

Heren sprang up from the stairs. "What do we got?"

"Quite the spectacle." Nika pointed out over the sea. "Looks like our old friend isn't holding back."

"That'll drown out the fires in seconds." Heren waved a hand at a bowl filled with dark liquid. "And I doubt the poisons will stay on the arrowheads with that much rain."

Nika squeezed the railing tight enough to hurt her hands. "I'm not sure they'll fly at all." She grabbed a dangling rope off the side of the tower. "I'll see if Yara can do anything about it."

Heren steadied the rope with one hand.

Wrapping her legs around it, Nika jumped off the ledge and slid to the ground. "Yara!?"

Three seabed spirits burst out of the tree line—each wearing bamboo breastplates, gauntlets, and greaves.

"Come here." Nika reached for the straps on Yara's gauntlets and tugged at them.

Yara huffed out her nose.

"We're gonna need you to try and temper the storm." Nika headed for the stand built into the backside of the barricade. "Rajani is bringing a downpour, but we want to keep the trenches lit." She climbed the stairs as Yara lifted herself onto the platform. "But more importantly, we don't want the water washing out the poisons on the tips of the arrows." She looked out to the approaching squall.

The wall of water neared the shore.

"Between the poisons and our plan to seize control of the spirits, we should be able to disable Rajani's army." Nika unclipped her spear from the strap on her back.

Yara tilted her head like a curious dog.

"I know it's a long shot and I wasn't going to say anything, but maybe they..." She looked up at Yara, a wave of remorse hitting her. "You.. all of you might have a second chance at life." Nika forced a smile. "Once Rajani is dead." She and Heren never figured out what would happen to the rainbringers after their fight. Would they die too? Would they live out their lives as monstrous creatures? There was no precedent for this. They tried to plan for any outcome. "If worse comes to worst, we'll have to fight to kill."

Yara nodded. The red glint in her eyes lit up, illuminating her face.

Thunder shook the sky. Lightning flashed in the distance. Rajani's storm reached the shoreline and halted.

"Here we go!" Nika shouted at the nearest tower, throwing up her hand for everyone to await her signal.

Red lights flickered through the rain. One by one, dozens of seabed spirits clawed out of the water. They marched to the edge of the downpour and waited.

Yara bowed her head. The rain around them slowed.

"Rajani!?" Nika shouted over the barricade into the tempest.

Out of the ranks of the spirits, Rajani emerged from the storm and stood in front of his army. "My dear, Nika. What a lovely gathering you've prepared. And here I am without so much as a hostess gift." He waved both hands at the spirits behind him. "I'll have to think of something."

She gripped her spear. "Turn back and leave forever."

"I see that you've still learned nothing about how to treat guests. Though I suppose I am a guest no longer. This island is mine." Rajani reached a hand out in front of him. "This, however, is *your* chance to surrender." His gaze drifted up to the towers. "Surrender Nika and I will spare the rest of you."

Nika shifted in place. Her nerves tangled themselves in her stomach. She could hear a thumping in her head as her pulse quickened.

Yara put her monstrous hand at Nika's back, in what she assumed was an attempt to comfort her—or protect her.

Nika put a hand to her chest. "You want *me*?"

"Yes. Just you—the last of the rainbringers and my last tether to mortality. With you dead, my transformation will be complete." Rajani lifted himself into the air, crossed his legs and folded his arms over his lap. "Nika is the only one that needs to die today. So either give her to me or you all die—Nika included."

The world muted itself. Nika's head spun. She could save everyone else and this would all be over. She swallowed hard and fought back a tingling in her eyes.

"No!" Heren shouted from atop a tower.

The word shook Nika out of her thoughts, filling her with both relief and fright. She wouldn't be sacrificed, but maybe she should be.

Heren lifted a bow and aimed it at Rajani. "Your thirst for blood will never be satisfied. We've given you too much already."

The villagers lifted their weapons and cheered.

The defiant shouts steadied Nika's hands. After a year of fighting to get everyone together, they finally were. No—not a year, it was a hundred years spent working in secret, hiding the truth in an effort to protect each other and failing all the same. They'd kept their backs turned on one another and hoped they'd walk in the same direction. But now, they were here as one.

Rajani scoffed. "To those of you who survive, when the rain has stopped and the sands are red, remember that I tried to settle this peacefully." Rajani cocked his head to the side.

The downpour advanced, rolling over the beach. The army of spirits roared.

Yara stared up at the sky.

The oncoming storm wavered in place as unsteady as Yara's trembling claws.

"You can do this." Nika rested her hand on Yara's arm. "You're stronger than he is."

The rainfall lightened.

Nika lifted two fingers above her head.

The trenches lit up in flames behind them.

The seabed spirits charged.

She dropped her hand.

A volley of arrows flew.

Yara

The weight of the storm bore down on Yara's shoulders, pinning her in place. She fought against it, her body shaking as if it were attempting to lift a mountain.

"You're weak." Rajani's voice echoed in her head.

Chaos erupted around her. The snarls and howls of seabed spirits spread out in front of the barricade. She wished she could redirect their frenzy toward Rajani, but the weight of the storm left her no strength to control them.

"No, Rajani. I've never been weak." Yara pushed herself up, standing as tall as her body would allow.

Rajani's army bounded for the fort. Spirits left and right fell into pits, disappearing into the sand. Others leapt to the front of the barricade, reaching to climb over the spiked wall, but falling prey to a barrage of arrows.

A drum-like pounding threatened to break through their defenses.

Trailed by heavy rainfall, Rajani flew over the wall, straight at Nika.

A wave of water fell over the beach as Yara shifted her focus from holding back the storm to Nika's safety. She tightened her fists, refocusing and pushing back against Rajani's downpour. Her gut told her to bound toward Rajani and throw her fists into his skull. She dismissed the urge. The most important thing she could do for Nika was hold back the storm and reach out to the spirits.

Nika rolled off the platform and planted her feet on the sand. Rajani spun around, landing in front of her, poised to strike.

The barricade burst open in an explosion of wood, spilling seabed spirits inside the defenses.

Yara reached out to them, commanding them to sleep.

Two stumbled, fighting to stay upright. But dozens more poured in behind them, sprinting along the burning trench, ignoring her orders.

Rajani pointed at Yara. "Weak."

The stumbling spirits shook free of Yara's control and joined their brothers in their rampage, spreading in every direction.

Nika thrust her spear at Rajani, missing his head as he dodged. She spun into a kick, connecting with his ribs.

The moment her foot met his side, the weight of the storm lifted from Yara's back. She reached for the spirits, sending them crashing to the ground as sleep overthrew them. All at once, they fell, disarmed—for now.

Rajani kicked Nika to the ground. An arrow shot into his arm.

A soothing sensation infiltrated Yara's forearm, weaving itself into her muscles and making them relax. She looked at Rajani, who pulled the arrow out at exactly the same spot Yara felt soothed—save on his opposite arm. *His pain,* she thought, *gives me strength?* Yara took a step before freezing, unsure if she should focus on the storm or crushing Rajani.

He snapped the arrow in two and sunk his teeth into the wound on his arm.

The calming balm beneath Yara's skin retreated as if Rajani were sucking it out.

He spat out a dark bile.

A tingling ran up Yara's spine. It crawled over her skin like sharp needles. The air crackled. A deafening clap erupted in a flash of blinding light.

The nearest tower went up in flames.

Yara fell back and rolled off the platform.

The rainfall surged, drowning the trenches and extinguishing the burning tower.

All at once, the seabed spirits twitched, writhing in the sand until rolling onto their feet. They looked to Rajani before running off at full speed.

Yara's head spun. Her vision blurred. She stretched out a hand, thinking to stop the spirits, but she couldn't put the world in focus.

Nika's yells broke through the sounds of the storm. She squared off against Rajani, failing to land a single blow.

Yara closed her eyes. She pushed back against the storm, but the pressure in her head sent her reeling. She screamed at the rain, hoping her anger would temper the squall. The pressure doubled on top of her. She gasped for air.

A burst of warmth cut into her shoulder. It spread down her arm, making it feel weightless and loose.

Nika screamed.

Yara's vision returned.

Nika held Rajani by the neck with one hand while the other

stabbed a knife into his shoulder—sending pain into his body and energy into Yara's.

A cascade of water dropped from the sky, washing Nika off Rajani.

Yara leapt over Nika, shielding her from the flood. She focused on her arm and the soothing feeling spreading through her muscles, channeling it into her control over the storm. *Stop!*

The rain obeyed. Amber tones of sunlight broke through the clouds. The downpour turned to drizzle.

Pained screams of monsters cut through the air. Seabed spirits toppled a tower. Shamans escaped on the ropes, but dropped to the ground too hard to land on their feet.

Manada and Ca'ari rushed to a group of people trapped by spirits. They pushed and kicked away the closest enemies, opening a path for people to escape.

Yara reached out with a hand, telling the hostile spirits to fall asleep.

"No." Rajani pulled the knife from his shoulder and threw it into Yara's stomach.

The cut stung. Her hide was thick, but the pain pulled the soothing feeling from her arms and replaced it with a biting sharpness.

"That's a handy trick you've learned, Yara." Rajani stuck his hand out toward Manada and Ca'ari. A river of rain poured over them. "Sleep."

The two armored spirits collapsed. The others piled on top of them, swiping with bloodied claws.

"No." Yara called out to the spirits, begging the rain to make them stop.

Their frenzy continued without the slightest pause.

A pained bellow sounded from across the beach, made by something far from human. A second screech cut through the air, followed by dozens more. The seabed spirits screamed through their lipless mouths, fumbling on the ground, their legs bending where they shouldn't. Not a moment too soon, someone had signaled the shamans to break the rainbringers' legs.

Rajani jumped into the air and surveyed the scene. A look of confusion washed over him.

The spirits hobbled about, nearly incapable of carrying themselves. Shattered bones protruded from their arms and legs.

Yara focused on Manada and Ca'ari. *Wake up!*

The two spirits pushed their mangled attackers off them and retreated into the jungle.

Yara leapt high into the air like a giant frog. She snatched a stunned Rajani in her claw and pushed him down to soften her landing. Their fall slowed, stalled by whatever power Rajani used to fly.

The two smacked into the ground. A surge of warmth spread over Yara's breast. Her body calmed—she'd hurt him. She pounded her fist, squashing him like a bug that refused to die. More and more light spread through her body—releasing it from all strains. Now more than ever, the storm was hers.

She held down Rajani with one hand, then lifted the other to the sky. The rain stopped in place, then reversed direction, returning to the clouds. Droplets lifted out of the sand, flying upwards. Her skin dried. Her mind jumped to the spirits. *Sleep.*

The seabed spirits tipped over in unison.

Yara heaved. The weight of the storm shrunk inside her. *Disperse,* she called to the clouds above.

"Futile." Rajani took hold of her thumb and pinky, twisting her wrist with a jolt.

It snapped in an explosion of pain. Yara swung with her good hand, but Rajani jumped into the air.

"Yara?" Nika looked herself over. Strands of her hair lifted themselves.

More stinging crawled up Yara's spine and spread over her skin. The air crackled. Lightning was coming—straight for Nika. Yara leapt to Rajani, swiping him out of the air. She threw him upward, launching him into the very clouds flashing white. *Strike him instead.* Light shot out above them.

Rajani plummeted.

A cloud of sand splashed as he hit the ground.

His body sizzled and smoked, motionless.

Yara looked to Nika who held out her spear.

Rain trickled from the sky.

"You're a fool, Yara." Rajani's voice echoed in her head. "You can't kill me."

She slammed her fist down on Rajani, meeting only sand.

A vapor whisked off the ground. It swirled in the air, reforming Rajani's burnt form. Raindrops dotted his skin, washing away the crisp blackness. His pale skin shone through charred remnants of his injuries as they fell away. He wagged his finger at Yara and Nika, tsking like a school teacher.

Yara held out her throbbing wrist. Rain met the pain, erasing it one drop at a time. She called out to the storm, telling it to die. Her head erupted in agony. The mountain of weight inside her knocked her to her knees. She pushed against the pressure. It made no sense —Rajani had been struck by lightning. His pain should have given her more power. She should be in control.

The sky darkened.

"You've still so much to learn." He wiped his tongue over his jagged teeth.

The storm started anew. The sleeping spirits twitched and flailed. Their limbs popped back into place. Red glints flashed as their eyes opened.

Yara froze. Her mind cleared. A jumble of thoughts sorted themselves in an instant. Their plan to take down Rajani was fatally flawed. His pain gave Yara strength. And Yara's pain gave Rajani strength, but she wasn't the only seabed spirit on the beach. A hundred and three others also fed into Rajani's power. With every broken leg, every shattered arm, the spirits may have been disabled—but Rajani's power heightened. They either had to fight an army of monsters or a god with the same might as that army.

Yara tucked her wrist into her chest. "Are you so afraid to die that you'll kill everything in your way?"

"I know what it is to fear death, but no. I have no need for that fear any longer." Rajani walked forward. "And yes, I will destroy *everything* that stands in my way."

Nika shot Yara a glance, clearly trying to piece together the conversation despite only hearing Rajani's half.

His eyes flickered red. "I have tasted that fear a hundred times. Each rainbringer, no matter how brave, shrivels at the thought of the next world. It is a feeling buried deep inside you creatures from birth. And as death nears, it crawls to the surface." He cracked his knuckles. "With Nika's death, I will never taste of fear again."

Yara straightened her stance. "I was not afraid to die."

Rajani scoffed. "You knew you'd become the monster in front of me."

"No, I didn't. You never really know anything until you do it." She clenched her jaw.

"Spoken like a child." Rajani took a fighting stance. "You were fun for a while, Yara, but you've started to bore me."

Yara braced herself for an attack. "I've been called many things, but boring—"

Rajani flew into Nika, nicking her off the ground, and pulling her off her feet. He sped away along the beach, picking up speed as he fled into the air, Nika in his grasp.

She darted after them.

Higher and higher, Rajani flew as he fought to hold an unwilling Nika. He glanced down at Yara far below, then cut sharply to the right, heading above the jungle.

Even on the open shores, Yara struggled to keep up. Her body wasn't meant for running. It belonged in the water. *If only I could fly.* An idea snapped into being. Mustering every ounce of strength, Yara called down a flood of rain. It hit her in an instant and on her command, stopped in place, creating a floating pool around her. She willed the water upward and kicked through it—moving the water with her as she swam in the air. It wasn't flying—but it was close.

Swimming over the jungle canopy, her eyes searched for Nika after losing her in the seconds it took to create the floating lake.

A faint scream cried out from above, pulling Yara's attention to a girl falling from the clouds. She raced to where Nika was headed. A wordless prayer filled her heart. Kicking and stroking as hard as she could, she knew she wouldn't reach Nika in time. Yara flung herself out of the pool, launching into the air and releasing the water under her command. She called out to the rain surrounding Nika, pulling it together into a sphere that caught Nika just as she reached the jungle canopy.

A flash of white surrounded Yara. Every inch of her burned as electricity cut through her body and locked up her muscles. Air whooshed past her ears as she fell. Her leg erupted in pain, smashing into what she assumed was a tree before her back thudded against the ground. Bones cracked as pain drowned her.

The world began to fade into darkness. Yara didn't know if she saved Nika or if she had fallen to her death. Nor did she know how to kill Rajani—or even hurt him. The seabed spirits would claim more and more lives the longer the battle lasted.

She was alone and worse, felt it. Once again, she was by herself like she was back in the hut. After all she learned, all she worked, all she sacrificed to save her people, she was no closer to victory. Her trial began with starvation and temptation. Here, it seemed, it would end in something far more miserable—isolation.

Isolation? Yara squirmed. The word tasted funny for some reason —like there was more to it than she could see. She had been isolated in the rainbringer hut, locked in, and forbidden to talk to the shamans—or anyone. Everyone knew the rainbringer's trial had two parts—starvation and temptation. But perhaps there was a third.

That was the real test. Being alone nearly drove her insane. But she had Nika and then Heren, Manada, and even the entire village at the end. Even from the beginning, she had Rajani. She had her journal—a tool no previous rainbringer ever had. *Maybe that's why they failed. They were alone... and I wasn't.*

Her lungs forced a deep breath. The slightest movement jabbed at her broken ribs. *Great.* With every sting came a sense of dread, knowing her pain made Rajani stronger. He was, as it turned out, like a reflection.

Reflection? Isolation?

An idea nagged at her—not fully formed and feeling out of reach. Rajani wanted to live. He wanted to be on this island, ruling over this people. He was alone—isolated. Yara's pain was his pleasure. Her starving gave him life. Her temptations, depriving herself of what she wanted, was his path to getting what he wanted. Her isolation was his way to destroy his own loneliness.

They were reflections of each other. Male and female. Day and Night. Pain and pleasure. Alone and not. By all appearances, the rainbringer trial reflected Rajani's existence—a way to counteract his misery.

The rain hit her skin, soothing the pain with every drop. The swelling in her muscles shrunk. Her bones cracked as they took their rightful shape. She pushed herself upright.

A swirling mist seeped through the treetops. It spun in the air, forming Rajani. "You've lost, Yara. Nika is dead."

The words hit Yara like a punch to the gut. But their sting didn't last. "You lie."

"Often, yes." Rajani paced in front of her. "But not now."

Thunder echoed overhead.

"You know, Rajani, I tried to keep the rain at bay because I thought that would weaken you."

Rajani swiped his tongue over his pointed teeth.

Yara stretched her claws. "But now that seems stupid. We share the power of the rainbringer and I want my half."

The sky gushed water. Rivers of rain drenched everything in sight, answering Yara's call to exhaust the skies.

Yara vaulted to Rajani. He met her in the storm, the two of them swimming in the downpour. His nails cut her face and pierced her neck. Her claw gripped his leg, squeezing it until it snapped. Pain and pleasure mixed.

Rajani flitted out of reach.

Yara chased after him.

The rain bent Rajani's leg back into shape as it rinsed clean her wounds.

Manada, are you there? She reached out her thoughts to anyone who might hear just like Manada had done when she woke up on the ocean floor. *Can you hear me?*

Yara? Manada's familiar voice echoed in her mind.

Knife-like nails cut across Yara's face as Rajani threw himself into her. She swiped back, pausing to let the rain wash away the blood and pain. *Where are you?*

I'm at the tunnel with the rainbringers. His voice sounded panicked. *Nika is here. She said we need to kill them.*

The news of Nika's safety sparked a fleeting relief inside her. *My thoughts exactly.*

Rajani dropped from the sky. He wrapped his hand around Yara's throat, his nails cutting into her skin. "You afraid to die now?"

Her vision blurred. A tension wrapped around her skull. She thrashed her claws, but Rajani kicked away her strikes.

She's right, Manada. It's the only way to weaken Rajani. Yara's claws caught Rajani. She squeezed him in her grip. *Do it now.*

Rajani heaved. His form loosened as it fought to turn to mist.

Yara reached her mind up into the heavens. A torrent of water cascaded down over them, threatening to knock them down. The rain pushed on Rajani.

He screamed. Like a clump of sand, his body broke inside her claw. His strength faded as if being chipped away. The seabed spirits were dying, one by one, and with them—his power. He was alone. *Isolation.*

Faces flashed in Yara's mind. Person after person appeared, sitting inside the rainbringer hut, dressed in the traditional garb. The rainbringers gave up their lives to save Asa'hali. They died once. Now they're dying again. From this day on, Rajani's temptation would have no power. *Temptation.*

Yara opened her maw and spread her mouth over Rajani's head. Her jagged teeth dug through his skin.

"Yara!" His wails dampened underwater and in her mouth.

Everything turned black. She watched as her eyes opened up inside a memory. Everything was dim. A hint of light shone in front of her. It grew, taking the shape of a person. Yara shook her head, trying to return to the real world, but the shining person remained inside the dim room. The light sat down, opened a book, and started writing. Yara tried to squint, the face of the light became clear. It was her—Yara—writing in her journal on the first night in the hut.

The images vanished in a snap. Fervent sensations pulsed through her veins.

She bit down, cutting through his neck and shoulder and swallowed his head. *Starvation.*

The rain ceased.

Everything was silent. There was no rain, no thunder, no shamans shouting orders or spirits growling in a frenzy.

Yara stumbled to her knees. Rajani slipped out of her claw. His headless corpse flopped onto the ground, gushing blood into a puddle.

Is it over? She looked at Rajani as if he would answer. Yara focused on her feelings—searching for the storm. An emptiness found her. *Rain.*

No clouds answered her call.

It's over. She nodded and looked down on herself, seeing the glowing skin of a seabed spirit.

Yara laid on her back. Her body ached. Her head throbbed. But at least she could finally rest. Sleep forced itself into her eyes and everything drifted into darkness.

YEAR 2 - DAY 8

Nika

A warm light hit Nika's face. She squinted and sluggishly lifted her sore head off the back of the chair she had curled up in. Had she fallen asleep? Maybe—for a minute or two.

Yara's human body laid across a table in the hut. Manada's laid on a table next to hers, with Ca'ari's on a third behind them.

"Tea?" Heren walked in the door, a steaming cup in one hand.

Nika reached for it, wincing at the aches all over her body. "I don't think they've moved at all." She rubbed her eyes.

Heren dropped himself into a chair next to her. "Hm." He took her hand. "Now that the sun is up, I've sent a search party to go find Yara. She can't have gotten too far."

The warm scent of lemon and honey met her nose. "I should go help. I know she was chasing after me when Rajani took me, but that was the last I saw her. I could retrace my footsteps." She blew on the tea, cooling it enough to bring it to her lips.

"I'm sure I couldn't stop you if I tried." He rubbed the back of her hand with his thumb. "But take a moment at least."

A knock on the door pushed it open. The torn-up face of a seabed spirit poked through.

Heren stood. "Ah. Manada, you're here."

The spirit crouched and sidled inside. His eyes scanned the room, landing on his human body.

Nika peeled herself off the chair and stood out of his way. "We're not sure what to do about you and the others." She walked up to the Manada on the table. His face remained lifeless, but healthful. She brushed stray hairs off his forehead.

The spirit reached out his claw and let it hover over his human body. As if afraid to make contact, he paused, fidgeted, and slowly rested it on his original form.

Heren joined them at the table. "Perhaps we could—"

The spirit toppled over, crashing into the wall. The bamboo panels splintered, nearly breaking in two. The entire hut shook at the impact. Dust dislodged from the ceiling.

"Manada!" Nika jumped to the spirit's side and crouched next to him. She held his scaly cheeks, but he had no reaction to her touch.

"Yes?" The Manada on the table pushed himself upright.

"Ah!" Nika threw herself into the broken wall and clutched her chest. Her head hit something blunt. "Ow."

Heren made quick work of supporting Manada in his struggle to hold himself up. He placed two fingers into Manada's neck, checking for a pulse that was certainly there—somehow. "How do you feel?"

"Alive." Manada held his head. "Dizzy. Tired." He smacked his gums. "Nauseous." He took a deep breath. "Where's my family?"

"Down at the beach, helping the injured." Nika picked herself up and brushed off her clothes.

"And Yara?" Manada rubbed the back of his neck.

Nika and Heren exchanged concerned looks. Nika swallowed hard. "We haven't seen her, yet."

"Might want to find her quickly. Ca'ari is down at the beach, but in terrible shape. Yara could be in the same condition." He spun his legs off the table. "Ooo." The motion made him wobble. "Dizzy."

"Take your time." Heren braced Manada. "And we'll take care of Ca'ari and Yara."

Yara

"Yara?!" A distant voice cut through the jungle—Nika's.

Took you long enough, Yara wanted to yell back, but she let out a monstrous shout instead.

"Yara?!" Nika drew near, shouting Yara's name as she followed her calls. "She's over here."

Flat on her back, Yara rested her claws on her stomach. Everything hurt and the sight of Nika, while pleasant, was not worth the pain of standing.

"Are you okay?" Nika's face popped up over Yara's, blocking the sun.

Yara gave a small nod and a huff.

"We have your human body. If you touch it, you'll be normal again." Nika's face disappeared. Footsteps slushed in the mud. "Well, as normal as you've ever been."

Yara rolled onto her side, agitating her ribs and neck. The thought of being human again sounded delightful—if only to escape the injuries still present in her spirit body. *Although*, she mused, *I kinda like being a giant fish monster.*

Heren stepped up beside her with Yara's limp, teenage body strapped to his back. Nika and Heren untied the straps and hoisted the body to the ground.

She leaned over and rested a claw on her defunct human form. The touch tired her—pulling out energy. A hint of color entered the corpse's cheeks. The connection sapped her strength. The world turned black.

Yara gasped for breath, suddenly trapped under the limp body of a seabed spirit. "Get this thing off of me!" Yara wiggled on the ground.

"You did it." Nika helped Heren push the spirit aside. She wrapped her arms around Yara, tears streaming.

Yara squirmed. "Get *this* thing off of me."

"Hey." Nika punched Yara's arm.

"Hey yourself." Yara sat up and punched Nika back. "Ugh. I am so tired."

"I thought I lost you." Nika wiped her eyes. "It's so good to hear your voice."

"Anus." Yara smiled, pleased with herself.

An annoyed frown sunk into Nika's face. "You ruined it."

Yara pulled Nika into a hug. "I love you." A fullness washed over Yara—something she had no words to describe. It was peace. It was happiness. It was gratitude—stronger and more perfect than she'd ever felt.

"I love you too." Nika patted Yara's back.

"Yes," whispered Yara. "But the real question is, do you love Heren?"

Nika squeezed Yara as if to strangle her. "Shut it."

Out of the corner of her eye, Yara could see a blushing Heren avert his gaze. She hadn't been as quiet as she intended, but enjoyed watching him squirm all the same. "How's the village? And my parents?"

"They're good. A little scratched up, but relatively unharmed." Nika stood and pulled Yara to her feet.

The movement made Yara's head spin. "Hold up."

"Dizzy?" Nika steadied her.

"Yeah." Yara inhaled as deeply as she could. The air cleared her head. She tapped the overturned body of the seabed spirit with her toe. "How long do you think it'll be before that decays?"

Nika shrugged.

Heren turned back at them, his cheeks no longer red. "A couple weeks, I imagine. Why?"

Yara crouched down next to it and put a hand on its shoulder. The scaly skin felt cold. "I want to keep the skull. You know, as a memento."

"You are so weird." Nika gathered the ropes they used to strap Yara's body to Heren's back.

"Sure, you say that now." Yara brushed the frills of the spirit with her finger. "But I was a fish-monster not five minutes ago."

"And what should we do with that?" Nika pointed at Rajani's headless corpse.

"I'll come back for his skull too." Yara poked the spirit's sharp teeth. Her finger bled at the slightest prick.

"And where might that be?" Nika grimaced.

Yara patted the spirit. "In here."

Nika's jaw went slack. "Frightening."

"Never cross me." Yara flashed a wide-eyed grin in an effort to be menacing.

"You two ready to go?" Heren rubbed his shoulder. "I'm sure they could use more hands at the beach."

"Yeah, yeah." Yara stood with a heave. "But can we stop for something to eat? This little lady..." She patted her belly. "Hasn't eaten in a year."

"I'm sure we can grab some passion fruit on the way back." Nika gave Yara a playful wink.

Hearing the word 'passion fruit' made Yara salivate. "You are a perfect, tropical, island goddess."

Nika bowed her head. "And you are a terrifying, giant fish-monster—at heart."

Yara bowed back. "That's why we're friends."

Yara's Journal

As it turns out, you actually could have turned to the end of these pages and found out how this all played out. Granted, I suppose this journal doesn't contain how I'm going to die either way. (Unless one of you wrote in it after me—which I strongly disapprove of!) But at least now I know that I won't die at the hands of an evil rain spirit or an army of freakish fish monsters. Too bad though, right? What a way to go.

Things on the island have settled into a new normal—a peaceful normal.

Nika won't leave me alone, which is annoying because she also comes with a shadow named Heren. Not that I would tell her this, but I do enjoy the company. Most days.

The rest of the time, I hide away far down the beach from the village. I've taken up meditation. It's stupid, but maybe not worthless. I mostly do it when it rains. Maybe it's the madness talking, but I could swear that sometimes the clouds still listen to me. Then again, maybe it's all in my imagination.

But Rajani is gone. The island is safe. And it all started with this silly journal.

Suffice to say, I am the most amazing person who has ever lived. And Nika is a close second.

THE END

COMING APRIL 30, 2021

The Broken Pantheon — Preorder now on Amazon

Eighteen-year-old Hagano witnesses the impossible—the death of his immortal god, Ecret. But in the wake of Ecret's demise, a series of clues leads Hagano on a path to fulfilling his god's dying wish.

ACKNOWLEDGMENTS

Part of the allure of writing my first novel was the idea that I could do it alone. Boy was that stupid.

I feel as if an army of family and friends have supported me through my creative journey. I wish I could thank everyone by name, but there are only so many trees in the Amazon. Instead, let me thank only a few as I retrace my steps that led to this book.

First, Charlie N. Holmberg. She was the first person "in the biz" to support my novel writing aspirations. She also directed me to the Storymakers Conference where I took her class on magical systems. That class is where Rainbringer was born.

Second, my left pointer finger. I spilled Coke on my keyboard at the beginning of the Covid pandemic and my 'F' key kept falling off. I couldn't get it fixed for months, which was a great time to write a novel. That finger put in a lot of extra work. Every time you see the letter 'F' in this book, I had to *earn* it.

Third, Clarissa Kae and Connie Williams. They are my first line of defense against my own bad writing. This book would not exist without them. I owe you both at least $5.

Fourth, my wonderful friends who read drafts and helped me shape it into the best version of itself I could—Dave Vance, Mike

Dalton, Tori Pence, Brenna Perry, Natalie Madsen, Matt Meese, James Perry, Stacey Harkey, Stephen Meek, Anthony Mills, Ashley Devereaux, Sarah Reynolds, and Loretta Porter. You guys are getting into heaven for sure.

Lastly, you, the reader. I'm sure it sounds cheesy, but I am truly humbled that anyone would give my story a chance. I know it's not perfect, but I hope this book makes your life just a little bit better, even for just a handful of hours. So thank you.

ABOUT THE AUTHOR

Adam Berg is a real human boy and not a figment of his dog's imagination. He started his career in sketch comedy, spent six years writing and acting for Studio C, and now works for JK Studios. Feed him cookies, please.

Find him online—
    Instagram: @heyadamberg
    Twitter: @theadamberg

Made in the USA
Coppell, TX
11 August 2021

60308354R00148